~Garden of Odin~

Written by: Daryl L Johnson

Foreword --   pg 3

Chapter 1 – Introduction   pg 4

Chapter 2 – The Valley and its Neighbors   pg 9

Chapter 3 – View through the Looking Glass   pg 22

Chapter 4 – Save the Sweetcorn   pg 31

Chapter 5 – Time to make Nectar   pg 39

Chapter 6 – The Onset of Winter   pg 54

Chapter 7 – Wild Hogs   pg 57

Chapter 8 – A New Twist   pg 77

Chapter 9 – The Plot Thickens   pg 88

Chapter 10 – Arrival of Guests   pg 92

Chapter 11 – Life is but a Dream   pg 100

Chapter 12 – After the Banquet   pg 123

Chapter 13 – An Epic Day of Hunting   pg 137

Chapter 14 – Putting SHEILA to the Test   pg 150

Chapter 15 – Last Chance to Relax   pg 162

Chapter 16 – Treasures Await   pg 170

Chapter 17 – Approach of the Winter Solstice   pg 181

Chapter 18 – A Problem Exists   pg 190

Chapter 19 – Winter Solstice Ritual   pg 199

Chapter 20 – Revelation   pg 208

Chapter 21 – Conclusion   pg 222

Foreword

My original 'Goal' when first laying my fingers on the keyboard was to publish a Sportsman's Adventure Novel, based on lessons learned from some of my most memorable days afield. Nearly four-years into the project, I found myself confronting an agonizing case of writer's block; determined to come-up with a truly unique, and iconic ending.

Awakening one-night literally drenched in sweat, I instinctively scrambled to document my dream-state revelation; knowing once I'd fallen back to sleep, the sandman might pay a visit and delete all my memories of it. The barely-legible notes, I was surprised to find scribbled-down on my nightstand the next morning, provided the perfect, multi-layered plot twist I'd been looking for to end my story.

I hope you find the literary adventure you're about to embark upon entertaining and encourage you to enlighten all your social media friends to my fictional tale! ...Enjoy!!

#Pass it on

#greatest compliment to an author

www.facebook.com/GardenOfOdin

www.GardenOfOdin.com

I always have fun,
only variable degrees of it!

Chapter 1

~Introduction~

The statement above is just one of countless insightful quotes and personal revelations, scribed onto now-faded parchment nearly three-centuries ago, by a highly wise and Worldly man. The individual I'm referring to, happens to be my Great-great-great-great, great Grandpa Bart.

As legend beholds; in order to deny Father Time, the ability to cast an ever-worsening speech impediment upon his progeny, he once gave us orders to "always refer to him as 'Grandpa B'!"

Using an eagle feather tipped with a razor-sharp piece of shark-tooth scrimshaw, Grandpa B is said to have written the profound Manifesto without pause. His countless words of wisdom, documented across the page in fine-flowing calligraphy, have essentially been my guide on 'How to live my life' for as long as I can remember.

The exact year in which he wrote the document is unclear; but, with its heavily-worn edges and deeply-faded lettering, it's easy to tell several-generations of Grandpa B's progeny have regularly sought guidance from his 'Words of Wisdom.' The intricately carved quill pen, and tattered scroll continue to sit atop my home's massive fireplace mantle; put there by Grandpa B as a perpetual reminder, to forever live by the 'Code' he placed before us.

Grandpa B also kept a much larger 'Personal Journal,' to document his daily thoughts and observations. Stored in a weather-beaten leather saddlebag, it continues to hang prominently from a solid-gold railroad spike embedded into the left-side of our fireplace mantle. His personal memoirs have indeed provided my family with successful direction on how to handle many 'bizarre' situations encountered over the years.

Grandpa B never allowed anyone to make entries into his Personal Journal. My ancestors therefore began using our family bible as the 'Family Journal,' to document historical events and other notable personal revelations. The overstuffed bible continues to sit prominently atop a limestone-slab shelf, embedded in the right-side of our fireplace mantle; and is now jam-packed-full of memoirs, from past and present family members, including many entries of my own.

From terribly faded, hard-to-read passages scribbled into the ancient leather-bound bible, by his beloved wife Anne, Grandpa B once lived a very dangerous and adventurous life as a Pirate. Supposedly, not just any Pirate; but a highly-feared Captain of a notorious crew of buccaneers, noted by Grandma A as having been "The Scourge of the Caribbean" back in the early 1700's.

Upon his planned retirement at an 'elderly' Pirate's age of 39, Grandpa B left his life of Piracy behind by retreating to our secret Valley; a mystical place he discovered early-on in his career, during one of his first-of-many inland expeditions.

Settling into our Valley for the remainder of his years, Grandpa B embarked on a life-long mission: "To create a safe-haven for weary souls, a place where absolute privacy could be guaranteed forever."

Grandpa B also noted in one of his earliest journal entries, while making plans to settle into his new place of retirement, having "given due consideration, to the future impact of permanently severing ties with the outside World." Being an extremely intelligent man, he ultimately decided doing so would not be the wisest, 'long-term' course of action to pursue.

Proving to be a true visionary, he wrote: "Without proper planning and due-diligence in execution, some scalawag adventurer will one-day discover, and ultimately divulge to the countless rats of society, the existence of me sanctuary. I must therefore nurture strategic alliances with those of ultimate power and influence; World leaders possessing the inherent ability to forever keep secret, the existence of Odin's Valley."

While Grandpa B was smart enough to embrace change, he did so with an iron fist. Laying out meticulous protocol for his progeny to follow, Grandpa B dictated in his journal exactly "When," "Where," "Why," and "How" contact with the outside World was to be established and maintained. By adhering to Grandpa B's strict 'Code,' my ancestors and I have been highly successful for centuries in providing a truly 'private' retreat for many of the World's most influential dignitaries.

The Visitor Log Grandpa B implemented well before the turn of the 19th century, contains the signatures of everyone having accepted an invitation to visit our Valley. Heavily-laden with parchment pages in the beginning, the antique binder progresses through to autographs now written upon much thinner, modern-day paper.

The first 'Signature Page' in the log prominently displays the autograph of "Benjamin Franklin" himself. Included is a short inscription by Benjamin, noting the year "1756;" which states: "To the man I owe many things, including my life once spared upon the high seas. May you and your posterity forever enjoy the blessings of Privacy!"

Not much is known about what transpired while Benjamin Franklin was here the first time; or the subsequent half-dozen other times he visited throughout the years. Surprisingly, only a single-entry exists in Grandpa B's journal about his first visit; where it states: "Finding myself in need of his trustworthy pen and compass, I've invited my good friend Benjamin to consult on a secret project. With many years due diligence put forth in design, I pray he confirms the engineering plausible."

Given the time frame, I've always wondered if Mr. Franklin's consultation was needed to validate the engineering designs on the house Grandpa B was building; or, if his entry gave reference to a much-deeper political meaning?

Over the many decades, we've had hundreds of Presidents, Kings and Queens; even a handful of Dictators, who've been invited to visit our humble abode. The list is extensive, but Dignitaries are not the only names found documented in our Visitor Log.

Dozens of Worldly musicians have also been invited to come play here throughout the past-century. A select handful of these musicians have graciously accepted my invitation to stay and play here permanently. Living under the protection of the Valley, they get to enjoy performing an occasional gig alongside the house band I've put together; never to be harassed again by the 'Paparazzi.'

It's quite remarkable, the amount of compromise and gratuity those of power and prestige are willing to extend, when seeking relaxation, entertainment; and, most importantly, invisibility from the 'All Seeing Eye.' By removing all political pressure, our guests get to relax and completely shed the stress associated with their official 'Titles.'

The absolute privacy our guests get to enjoy sometimes gets strategically manipulated a bit; most often occurring, when a looming instability between global superpowers demands immediate emergency-intervention measures be taken, to prevent catastrophic loss of life.

By purposely pairing rival dignitaries together in a relaxed neutral environment, we've been able to consistently promote platforms for open discussion, where Leaders of opposing countries can peacefully work-out their differences.

It is quite remarkable, the number of successful resolutions to some of history's most notable, and many times 'Unknown' global crises, that've been secretly settled with a simple handshake; while watching the house band laying-down some killer blues, up on-stage in our Grand ballroom.

Chapter 2

~The Valley and its Neighbors~

My family's estate lies hidden in the center of one of the most inhospitable mountainous regions found within the Americas; far from areas, where Mother Nature has forever lost her virginity to the encroachment of humanity.

Due to the thin atmospheric conditions found here, stars on a clear night shine brighter than the high-beam headlight of my Father's 1938 knucklehead; a Harley Davidson motorcycle he actually procured brand-new, and somehow managed to smuggle it into the Valley suspended below a home-made, hot-air balloon.

His so-called 'Favorite Toy' was brought into the Valley strictly against the will of my ancestors, who were adamantly against having their way of life influenced by 'Instruments of the Modern Age.' The bike was the first-of-many motorized vehicles and equipment, that have since been introduced to improve the quality of our lives.

The existence of my family's estate is not plotted on any Commercial map; and in fact, on high-resolution charts maintained by intelligence agencies Worldwide, our Valley 'Officially' does not exist.

With thousands of thermal springs flowing vigorously throughout the Valley, a highly dense, water-vapor cloud continuously rises to bombard the sky; effectively distorting visual-clarity from the World above. The mushrooming fog somehow creates a mysterious shroud of invisibility, fooling even highly trained experts charged with monitoring the World's most-sophisticated satellite imagery. Ironically, images captured from satellites circling high-above, show our Valley as being a deep lake inhospitably nestled between two-converging mountain ranges.

The region includes several perpetually snow-capped mountains and has always been fearfully avoided by aviators. To this day, the FAA warns all commercial and private aircraft to bypass the area for 'Safety Reasons,' due to extremely-turbulent weather conditions, that frequently occur in the airspace over our Valley. With all this being said, flights in-and-out of the Valley are relatively safe in good weather; provided the pilot stays low on approach and departure.

Legend perpetuates Grandpa B as having strategically ensured his privacy centuries ago, by rendering all mountain trails leading into the Valley virtually impassable. Today, in order to reach my estate on foot, one must prove themself to be an extreme adventure junkie, with an undeniable 'Death Wish.'

Throughout the centuries, only a mere-handful of men and women have been able to successfully make the journey on foot to reach our humble abode. Not surprisingly; those adventurers somehow surviving the perilous journey to get here, have all opted to make Odin's Valley their permanent home.

Even with the invention of aviation making it feasible to safely leave and return to their past lives, no one successfully orienteering into the Valley has ever wanted to leave. Pledging to keep the existence of our Valley a secret, I've allowed these lucky few to permanently stay and enjoy the many amenities our Valley provides. All I ask of them in exchange for staying here, is to occasionally assist in farm-related chores, and other business-related activities.

The privacy, seclusion, and unparalleled security my estate provides is what makes our secret Valley one of the most highly-coveted 'Retreat' areas in the World. Only the World's most elite dignitaries, and celebrities are aware of its existence; and, even though many think they are aware of it, no one really knows the Valley's true location.

Several well-documented tribal cultures have actually perpetuated ancient legends about the Valley. Akin to being granted an invitation to visit one of the World's most secretive areas; like 'Area 51,' everyone receiving an invitation to visit this mythological place impulsively accepts our invite, without hesitating to consider the consequences. It's much like being offered an induction into the 'Illuminati,' a secret society believed to still hold major power and influence, throughout the highest levels of today's World governance.

Our vast estate encompasses a ten-mile-long Valley, including all areas around it for many miles. Grandpa B reported in his journal having found the Valley, using a map he acquired early-on in his career as a Pirate. Upon his first visit here back in the early part of the 18th Century, he determined the Valley to be a two-mile-wide sinkhole created canyon, with shear limestone and granite-laced cliff-walls rising-up between 140'-200' high, the entire-length of the basin.

Realizing no easy pathway existed to get down into the Valley upon first discovering it, Grandpa B wrote the following passage in his tattered journal: "No other place on earth can I conceptualize offering more protection and privacy, than this Garden of Eden. A secure fortress I will construct here, to protect my family from those seeking vengeance on me seafaring days left jubilantly behind."

Grandpa B first had to engineer a way to gain access into the Valley. A drawing I came across in one of his earliest journal entries, actually documents how he was able to engineer a removable-pulley system; one that could easily raise and lower provisions, livestock and equipment, without negatively impacting the aesthetic-beauty, and ultimate-protection afforded by the Valley's continuous, sheer-cliff walls.

The drawing also included a map marking the location of his first log cabin, strategically built atop an elevated mound in the middle of Odin's Valley. A most intriguing notation I found on the map, gives reference to Grandpa B having engineered the river to split, and form a nasty-gauntlet of rapids around the original homestead; providing his family a superior level of protection, in the event of an attack.

Artesian springs can be found erupting from nearly every crack and crevice throughout the Valley. The most prominent of these springs spews out vigorously from a narrow fissure in the rock-faced wall; approximately six-meters directly below the house my family has lived-in for generations. The beautiful waterfall it creates, cascades seemingly forever into the black-sanded lagoon at the base of the cliff.

Thousands of thermal springs continuously erupt, forming countless fast-flowing streams throughout the Valley; the closest-one originates a mere fifty-feet to the right, of where my house sits overlooking the Valley at the base of Sasquatch Mountain.

When Grandpa B built this; his second house, he amazingly engineered a way to tap into these thermal hot springs. Since doing so, he and his progeny have been able to enjoy the luxury of hot-and-cold running water 'On Demand' throughout our entire home.

Areas where the thermal springs erupt, quickly turn into small tributaries that eventually merge together with other cooler streams. The water from these eruption areas is so hot, you can literally hard-boil an egg in minutes. In a handful of locations, just the right mix of hot-and-cold water can be found; creating sauna-like pools, where guests can relax and enjoy the many therapeutic benefits these thermal wellsprings provide.

The countless number of springs found here, eventually all merge together into a series of streams flowing into Lake Odin, located at the far-end of the Valley. With high-cliff walls on both sides, extending all the way down to the opposite-end of the Valley from where my house sits, Mother Nature offers nowhere for the water to exit.

Normal laws of physics dictate the Valley should continue to fill with water, until it eventually overflows the Eastern rim of the canyon; but amazingly, Lake Odin has never risen to crest higher-than twenty-six inches over normal 'Full Pool' level, throughout all of recorded history.

Conversely, Lake Odin historically only falls below Full-Pool one-time per year; occurring like clockwork, during the Annual Winter Solstice event. When this happens, every spring throughout the Valley abruptly stops flowing, precisely one-hour before the sun reaches its highest point in the sky.

Moments after the artesian wells suddenly go dry, the fleeting silence is eerily foreboding. As streams begin losing volume, millions of fish swimming in huge schools throughout the Valley start thrashing about in an ever-increasing panic. The sound grows exponentially, as hordes of fish suddenly find themselves in shallow areas; forced to erratically jockey for position, in the continuously-diminishing pools of water that remain.

Like the finest Swiss watch, every artesian spring throughout the Valley quickly resumes full-flow rates, immediately after the grandfather clock in my study chimes the hour of 1:00 p.m.; provided the 'Toast to Odin' has been properly given upon the stroke of Noon.

Since recordkeeping began two-hundred years ago, Lake Odin consistently drops nearly two-feet during the Winter Solstice event.

Full-pool level is quickly regained, once life-giving waters from the thousands of artesian wellsprings unexplainedly come back to life.

There has only been one recorded incident, where Lake Odin dropped a record 'forty-eight' inches. This ironically occurred when Dad was late in returning one-year, with the specially aged batch of raspberry ale he'd gone to retrieve for our Winter Solstice Toast. The keg of vintage ale had fallen-off the truck, after swerving to avoid a deer enroute to the festivities. Having smashed to the ground, the accident left not one-glass of properly aged raspberry ale needed to perform the ritualistic 'Toast to Odin.'

Knowing he had one extra 'Special Reserve' barrel stashed away in the cellar of the original homestead, my father made an emergency run to retrieve the last keg. While the Toast was delayed for nearly an hour, waters ceased flowing for a longer-than-normal duration; miraculously resuming full-flow rates, immediately after the Winter Solstice 'Toast to Odin' was properly given.

Waters that flow through the Valley offer aquatic life an immeasurable supply of food and shelter, making for some truly amazing Crappie and Bass fishing. Wildlife abounds, with a wonderful balance of Nature existing throughout the Valley; attributable to Grandpa B's strict conservation rules adopted centuries-ago.

Since I've been involved with wildlife management in the Valley, the estate has produced year-after-year, pound-for-pound, one of the best hunting and fishing preserves found throughout the World.

Besides the many deer, elk, and other wild creatures inhabiting the Valley, where my home sits nestled in utter seclusion; the closest neighbors of the human persuasion, can be found residing in a small village, approximately fifty miles to the East. Comprised of three family clans, they live harmoniously-together in relative isolation from

Society.

The Miller's, Jannssen's, and McCallister's, as they proudly call themselves, are what snooty-people might call a bunch of 'Inbred Hillbillies.' While their family trees do fork occasionally, most branches would look like interwoven vines, if you were to actually trace their lineage on paper. They live off the land, and don't take kindly to trespassers interfering in any of their 'Personal Business.'

I keep a close-eye on the clans for security reasons, by regularly visiting them under an 'Alias' every month. My primary goal during each visit, is simply to assure they remain oblivious to our Valley; located only a handful of mountain peaks to their West.

Ironically, they think I'm the 'Law Man' from the big city in the East; because of the way I first initiated contact with them several-years ago, in my 1960's-era Huey helicopter. Arriving under the pretext of having to make an emergency landing, I wasn't sure how they would react. Sporting camouflage fatigues; while donning my lucky 'CAT' (**Cat**erpillar Tractor Company) baseball cap, I remember hoping our first-contact would go well. Needless to say, I was ready and prepared for negotiations to go horribly sideways, at any-given moment.

So that my first visit would not appear to be an intentional act of trespass onto their land, I remember having faked engine trouble, by squirting a small amount of oil onto my engine. The chopper immediately started smoking profusely; presumably forcing me to execute an emergency landing, on the riverbank below their village.

Making it look as if I was having serious control-issues upon descent, I proceeded to safely set the chopper down. With every member of the village watching curiously from above; I perpetuated my ruse, by hopping-out and pretending to fix the problem.

For protection, I had a fully automatic Mac-10 loaded and

concealed within arms-reach; ready to use in self-defense, should any of the shotgun wielding clansmen heading hastily-down the hill towards me, make even the slightest attempt to initiate a firefight.

Within killing range, they all stopped and began grinning from ear-to-ear, with mouthfuls of missing and rotting teeth. I remember, as if on cue, a supped-up car began revving its engine repeatedly from the settlement above. Slowly and deliberately advancing in my direction, I remember the hot-rod sounding like rolling thunder, as it rolled ominously down the steep hillside towards me.

At that very moment, I was never so glad to have covered all my bases, by bringing a previously-ruptured oil hose along to validate my story. Instincts knew it might help prevent blowing my cover; should any of the villagers possess knowledge of engine mechanics and wish to investigate my 'Emergency' landing.

The chromed-out, Canary-Yellow, 1969, Z-28 Camaro, sporting jet-black side pipes as big as semi-stacks, slowly rumbled down the steep hill, advancing to within twenty-yards of me, before eventually coming to a stop. The driver of the car then proceeded to roar his engine several-times, causing the clansmen to gather around the hot-rod like envious NASCAR fans. I remember my trigger-finger starting to itch; seeing them all laughing and smiling, in anticipation of a showdown between me and the car's driver.

Watching the door open, a tall withered old man with a snow-white beard stepped out. Taking a long-drawn-out stretch, he then turned and looked in my direction. I remember him vividly, as he stood proudly next to his car with bearded chin raised; bellowing out in a stern voice, that resonated across the waters of the river behind me: "I am Leland Henry Jannssen, eldest of the Jannssen clan. My ancestors live peacefully in this here Valley with the Miller and McCallister clans; but we don't take kindly to no trespassers! You'd best leave

16

right quick; for your safety be in serious peril, should you fail to heed me warning!"

The armed clansmen all started eerily laughing; making me momentarily contemplate ending the confrontation, by reaching for protection. Instead of introducing them to 'My Little Friend;' like Al Pacino did in the movie 'Scarface,' I opted to reach for the blown-out oil hose. Perpetuating the ruse, of what I wanted them to believe had stranded me there, I remember lifting the faulty oil hose high in the air.

Responding to Leland by name, I'd said to him: "I've already fixed the problem and will be happy to leave immediately; but I'd be forever in your debt, if you'd allow me use of your nearest outhouse."

I remember the elder busting-out laughing, while motioning for me to come towards him; saying, "I can git us both up dat hill a tad-bit quicker, dan you can git up der on foot."

Abandoning my security blanket with mixed reservations, I quickly made my way to his chariot with tightly-clenched buttocks, and hopped in. With a surge of power never felt before coming from a gasoline powered engine, the G-forces unexpectedly unleashed by his supercharged motor plastered me backwards in the passenger-seat, resulting in a trip of extremely short duration up the hill.

Barely making it out of the car without having an accident in my pants, I proceeded to run towards the outhouse. Once the door had slammed shut, I remember letting out a moan sounding much like a woman in the final-stages of childbirth.

After surviving the gut-wrenching stench inside their outhouse, I was put through a barrage of questions by Leland; where, I quickly discovered him to be the eldest of all the clansmen. Once Leland was absolutely convinced that I hadn't come to steal anything, or try to levy a tax on his people, he most graciously offered me a swig of moonshine from his massive ceramic jug.

About the time our jug was reaching empty, along with several other jugs being passed around to the adults and older adolescents of the community, Leland leaned over and asked me in a drunken slur: "what dem der ledders C..A..T.. on yur cap stand fur?"

I remember leaning into Leland; and, after short pause, jokingly answering back in a secretive whisper, "Catch All Thieves." My response nearly gave old-man Leland a heart attack. Unexpectedly falling backwards off the tree stump he'd been perched upon, Leland landed hard on the flat of his back, temporarily knocking the wind from his lungs.

After regaining his breath, but still opting to remain sprawled out on the ground, Leland erupted in jubilant laughter that quickly infected the entire community. With all three clans joining in, they continued to roar obsessively with laughter, until every-last member was either completely-out of breath or passed-out cold from excessive drunkenness. Once Leland finally stopped laughing, I felt compelled to ask how he and his ancestors had come to settle into this remote part of the wilderness.

Leland proudly responded by, telling me how his ancestor had been the first-mate of a large seafaring-group of buccaneers. They'd been on a mission inland, under the direction of one of the most notorious Captains to ever set sail on the high-seas.

The story passed-down through generations of his family states; that during a gale-force winter storm, which quickly and unexpectedly descended upon their expedition, the captain had instructed his crew to "Stand Fast" in this Valley. Having given strict orders to wait for his return, their beloved captain is said to have ventured ahead into the storm, looking to find a safer place for his crew to take shelter.

Shortly after departing with a majority of the crew's cargo and supplies, half the mountainside gave way; presumably burying their captain, under a hundred-fathoms of rock and rubble. More than a month of relentless digging and searching by the crew took place, resulting in a futile attempt to recover whatever they could of their captain and precious cargo.

Having been left unprepared for winter, members of the crew were freezing and nearing starvation. Reasoning their captain had perished in the landslide never-to-return; several-members of his crew departed in dishonor, from what they perceived to be a 'God-forsaken' land.

The fate of those deciding to depart was quickly sealed, after Odin sent a torrential snowstorm to descend upon them; generating a deadly avalanche, that killed every-last soul daring to disobey their captain's order to "Stand Fast."

Out of fear and respect that their beloved captain might one-day possibly return, Leland's ancestor and two other loyal shipmates 'Stood Fast' and stayed. They learned over time that life in the Valley could be downright enjoyable; especially after the last oak barrel's been filled, and there's still lots more whiskey to be made.

Several-hours after I'd taken the last hefty swig from Leland's jug, sense of feeling finally returned to my face and extremities. Confident in my ability to safely navigate an aircraft once again, I remember waving goodbye to Leland and his clansmen, while ascending back-up into the heavens in my helicopter.

The whole-way home, I couldn't stop pondering the sobering history lesson given to me by Leland; marveling over how closely his stories paralleled and gave relevance, to the many passages left in our family bible.

Now feeling responsible for their well-being, I stop by on the first Tuesday of each month to check on the clans. Arriving precisely at Noon each time, to avoid surprising them with an 'unscheduled' visit; the entire village now comes-out of their dilapidated shacks, to welcome me with open arms.

They routinely escort me around their property, while proudly showing-off what they've been able to grow in their gardens. I always find it amusing how they routinely take me on multiple detours to avoid letting me see one of their largest barns; said to be owned, by a reclusive 'Charlie' Miller. Sitting naturally camouflaged and tucked-away in a small valley, the barn smells eerily similar to an area of our Valley known as 'Skunk Den Hollow.'

The clan elders and I ritualistically share a lengthy swig of moonshine during each visit. While Leland's unique, over-sized jug gets passed around multiple-times, we routinely discuss politics and other Worldly events that have occurred since my last visit.

The clansmen always appear Zombified, each time I feed them information on how well-off they all are; compared to city-slickers struggling to survive the daily pressures of modern-day Society.

It seems most of the information they gather from the outside World, comes from an old solar-powered radio acquired years ago from a fleeing traveler; who hastily departed before Leland could finish giving his classic 'Introduction' speech. The small device gets extremely-poor reception; only picking up a single bluegrass station, that offers little in the way of commentary.

Apart from my visits, the only visitors Leland's clan regularly interacts with are a uniquely special group of ladies, who religiously perpetuate the hippie culture. Their entourage stops by for a social visit each-year on eve of the harvest moon, to dance and entertain the

20

clansmen; always departing the next morning with enough moonshine, and other organically grown consumables to satisfy their entire commune's needs back home till next harvest moon.

I keep my monthly visit as brief as possible, with my mission being to determine if any unexpected visitors from the outside World have visited their Valley in the past month. Once-in-awhile, a hiker gets reported as having continued West-ward towards my Valley; usually fleeing for their life in the wrong direction, after hearing Leland's classic introduction speech. When this occurs, I make it my mission to return them safely back to civilization, with nothing more than a grim story perpetuating the mountain range's 'Curse.'

Chapter 3

~View through the Looking Glass~

Most mornings you'll find me finishing up the last of my morning chores, by delivering fresh eggs to Chef J in the kitchen. Once done, I ritualistically nestle myself into the captain's chair to savor the orgasmic aroma of gourmet coffee brewed to perfection.

There's nothing like a mug of freshly-ground java, steeped in scalding water extracted from one of our Valley's many thermal wellsprings. Thanks to one of Grandpa B's many ingenious inventions, our family's been able to enjoy this hot water 'On Demand' for centuries.

Making use of the ancient wooden spigot Grandpa B custom installed over our kitchen sink centuries ago, the beer taper-like device dispenses blistering hot water over fresh ground coffee; producing near atomic-strength java.

Once the coffee finally cools down enough to avoid incurring severe burns to the inside of my mouth and throat, I habitually chug down the entire contents of the mug; instantly sending a warming sensation throughout my entire body. The ensuing rush of caffeine quickly pulsates through my veins; getting me motivated and ready, to go-out and enjoy another exciting day in paradise!

The over-sized coffee mug happens to be a uniquely designed ceramic stein, handcrafted by Grandpa B back in 1791. It's one of eight-pieces of pottery mentioned in his journal, as having been made using the kiln he custom installed down in our basement. The excerpt from his journal states: "The mug I have so finely crafted to mark my good fortune is designed to be used in ritualistic celebration, when giving 'Toast to Odin' on the cusp of each Winter Solstice."

While stating he made "Eight pieces of pottery" in his journal; over the years, I've sadly only been able to confirm provenance on seven of these eight-pieces. Each of the seven discovered pieces randomly displays his unique maker's mark of a "*B*," subliminally inscribed on each piece in such a way; that, you really don't know the mark is present, until it suddenly reveals itself. His unique 'Maker's Mark' is crafted similar to that of a 3-d hologram; a symbol you must stare at from a specific angle, before the image suddenly becomes forever recognizable.

We may never know what the eighth-piece of pottery is, that Grandpa B made. While his journal ironically documents many trivial things in explicit detail; besides his mug, he unfortunately failed to disclose designs for any of his seven other hand-crafted pieces.

Grandpa B designed many other truly-unique items throughout the home he built. My favorite recliner, referred to as the 'Captain's chair,' happens to be one of these truly unique items. Custom built as a permanent feature of my home's massive bump-out window, the chair sits centered on the inner-most edge of the window's framework, offering a panoramic-view of the Valley below.

Permanently affixed to the base, the chair allows you to look out through a giant oval-shaped glass window, comprising nearly the entire floor of the window's bump-out area. The massive piece of looking glass starts out nearly five-inches thick around the outer edge, widening to over ten-inches thick at center. Grandpa B documented the uniquely-shaped glass, as having been one of two identical oval-shaped windows he once salvaged off a pair of 16th century Spanish treasure galleons.

The base of the custom-made recliner sits crafted from an exceptionally large wooden ship's wheel, allegedly removed from the very ship the oval-shaped 'Looking Glass' came out of; unfortunately, no engravings exist on the wheel to divulge the ship of origin.

Grandpa B designed the chair, so the wheel can be easily turned and locked into corresponding positions with the sun; each pre-set position enabling the person sitting in the chair to watch the sun's shadow, in its daily trek across the Valley floor below.

The rest of the chair is hand-crafted entirely from Elk Antlers, interlocked in such a way, that the chair literally holds you in like a harness. The unique framework provides the utmost in comfort and visibility, with each setting allowing me to look-out over the many features of the Valley virtually unobstructed.

The forward-most setting of the captain's chair is the only position allowing you to look straight down through the looking glass. Giving a false sense of feeling like you're about to fall out of the chair, this tilted forward setting provides a spectacular view of the cascading waterfall, and other unique areas directly below the house.

Through countless hours of relaxing in the chair, I've found the most enlightening time to gaze down at the Valley floor is shortly after the grandfather clock finishes chiming the arrival of 'High Noon.' Immediately after the last chime subsides, the sun's shadow being cast from the peak of Sasquatch Mountain begins its predictable journey outwards from the base of the cliff. With each passing minute, visual effects through the looking glass regularly tantalize my brain with detailed images from below.

Staring-out at certain objects through the unique curvature of the oval-shaped glass, I sometimes begin seeing things as if they are magnified. Bringing remarkable clarity to specific areas down on the Valley floor below; these same locations quickly return to normal viewing clarity, once the mountain's shadow passes-by.

As the V-shaped shadow fully engulfs each visual hot-spot below, I systematically switch the setting of the chair to the next position. This always seems to produce a whole new series of magnified areas, that come into focus through the looking glass. It's simply astounding, the amount of craftsmanship and functionality Grandpa B put into designing and installing the chair.

I can honestly say, there are few homes built anywhere containing the craftsmanship, and special design features found throughout every niche-and-corner of the fortress-like castle he created. There are literally dozens of these highly functional features, which Grandpa B design-engineered hundreds of years ahead of their time; for instance, the multi-angle shower unit he was able to custom install for us in the master bedroom.

While everyone else in the 18th century was forced to bathe in a tub, requiring buckets of hot-water to be added in-order to maintain a desired temperature, Grandpa B ingeniously engineered a way to take a shower while enjoying adjustable, hot-water on demand.

By far though, the captain's chair is my favorite feature of our home. The uniquely-designed bay window it's mounted too, provides an unbelievable panoramic-view of the entire Valley below. While sitting in my recliner, I love looking out over the two-mile-wide Valley; strategically laid out with an extensive-labyrinth of giant Ash trees throughout its center.

Each tree was meticulously hand planted by Grandpa B back in the mid 1700's, to fence in livestock and strategically protect his property. Over the centuries, the Ash tree labyrinth has grown to well over a hundred-feet tall, creating a seemingly-impenetrable living wall at its base.

Designed to provide ultimate protection for the original homestead, Grandpa B knew the labyrinth would additionally create several truly phenomenal hunting areas. With only a few locations where wildlife can access food plots planted within the labyrinth's maze of corridors, movement of both large and small game animals becomes highly-predictable.

Grandpa B wrote about these areas in his journal, saying: "The labyrinth will one-day produce several bountiful honey holes to hunt over. Me progeny with due diligence in plotting these points should never find difficulty in putting food on the table."

Passageways into each tillable field within the labyrinth were originally only wide enough for a horse, and small plow to enter through; but decades ago, my father took it upon himself to widen these limited access areas, so that much larger farm implements could gain access.

One morning last fall, while making my way towards the bay window to scout wildlife movement down in the Valley, I accidentally knocked our huge family bible off the fireplace shelf. This happened after tripping over 'Mocha,' my aging chocolate Labrador, who'd strategically-positioned herself within a warm beam of sunshine to take her morning siesta.

The ancient Bible crashed loudly onto the unforgiving, hardwood floor, causing its fragile binding to split wide-open; subsequently exposing a deeply-yellowed parchment letter hidden under the front cover. I remember slowly bending over in apprehension to pick it up, instantly realizing the document must've been secretly-placed into the bible as a time capsule, well over two-centuries ago.

The letter I found contains many areas, where mildew has severely-degraded the parchment. Obviously written after Indians had attacked the property back in 1769, one of the more legible paragraphs reads: "In all my years on the high-seas, I have rarely seen as brave and determined attempt to achieve success in battle, as witnessed with these redskin savages. While each snare throughout the labyrinth worked perfectly as designed, these warriors continued forward with the courage and determination of a crew reminiscent of my former entourage. I find it puzzling they depart in celebration, after being severely-depleted in number, with ner a scalp to display on any spear. We remain safely locked away in the cellar beneath the homestead. It is my intention to wait a few days longer, before departing the safety of our sanctuary."

Another legible passage in the letter states Grandpa B's intention to build a future stronghold; one that would overlook the Valley and pay tribute to the ordeal he'd just endured. The passage reads: "I will build an impenetrable fortress on the high-cliff wall at the far end of the Valley, designed as a monument paying tribute to dates of triumph over me enemies." An odd passage leading me to believe, an excessive-amount of Raspberry ale had probably been consumed at the time of his journal entry.

The centuries-old inscription certainly provides valuable insight, on the early days of Grandpa B living in the Valley; but it doesn't begin to explain the many other 'strangely worded' statements inserted into our family bible by my ancestors.

One of the most obscure passages found in our family bible is believed to have been inscribed by my Granny A, because of her horrible handwriting skills; where it states, "The Jackal pausing to scratch an itch which the distracting flea hath inflicted, affords the rabbit freedom along the river's edge." When I first read this, I thought

Granny A had lost her mind while writing the passage.

Why had she written this strange entry in our family Bible? I've asked myself this question countless times, until suddenly watching Dad from the captain's chair, slowly making his way through the Valley, hot on the track of a huge buck we'd nicknamed 'Bullwinkle.'

As the grandfather clock finishes striking two o'clock in the afternoon, the looking glass suddenly focuses in on the massive buck making its way past the 'Cornerstone' tree; one of the largest Ash trees found within the Labyrinth. I watch with anticipation, as my father closes in on the monarch buck sporting a double drop-tine, pal-mated rack of unbelievable mass and proportion.

Watching a raven land forebodingly in a nearby tree, Dad begins cursing profusely at the undesirable omen; becoming momentarily distracted in his pursuit of Bullwinkle. Suddenly putting relevance to Granny A's strange passage found earlier, I watch in disbelief as the buck takes advantage of the distraction, using it to slip past my father along the river's edge.

Dad eventually returns dumbfounded, as to how Bullwinkle was able to successfully elude his previously fail-proof, corralling maneuver. Upon entering the house, he heads straight for the family bible with pen in hand; ready to document his most recent experience, like my ancestors have done for centuries.

Coming to the profound realization, that every "entry" in our family bible has some degree of relevance, I vow to never again discount the validity of any passage found in the bible; no matter how insignificant it may appear to be.

The next morning, my father and I have an in-depth discussion on how Bullwinkle somehow gave him the slip. Dad starts swearing up-and-down, that the buck 'just disappeared into thin air;' quoting another obscure entry written by Grandpa B, which reads: "The quarry held captive in a most desperate hour was allowed passage to freedom, using a cloak of invisibility provided by one of nobility."

Realizing the argument with my father is quickly becoming a lesson in futility, I gracefully shrug my shoulders and submissively utter, "OK, maybe you're right?"

Suddenly declaring he's heading back down to the water's edge to follow tracks left in the sand by Bullwinkle, my father proceeds to ask: "You wouldn't mind going along with me, would you? I could use your tracking skills, to help prove the buck used a 'Cloak of Invisibility' in eluding his demise?"

Realizing his seriousness in believing the 'quoted' passage to be the factual reason for the buck's prolonged life, I find myself holding back an urge to laugh. Politely declining his invitation, I remind him it's time to conduct our Annual sweet corn harvest.

Still trying to keep my composure, I tell him: "Don't worry, I already have plenty of volunteers lined up to help harvest and process this year's corn crop. With your assistance not being needed, you'll have plenty of time to figure out how Bullwinkle managed to escape past you undetected, within an embarrassing twenty yards." Razzing Dad a bit further, I go on to say: "I respect you not wanting to stop until you've successfully harvested Bullwinkle; especially, since his escape may have tarnished your reputation as a skillful hunter."

You can tell my words cut deep into my father's pride, with an obvious rise in blood pressure causing the veins in his forehead to become more and more prominent, with each pulsating-beat of his heart.

Trying to calm Dad down before he suffers a stroke, I offer him a chance to win the coveted 'First Taste' of Raspberry Ale at this year's Winter Solstice event; the challenge being, he must successfully earn a space for Bullwinkle on our trophy room wall, before the first measurable snowfall. Considering the wager as an opportunity to restore his reputation, Dad gladly accepts my challenge.

Even though it's only mid-August, a freakishly-early snowfall event regularly occurs in September every two, or three-years. Being nearly a decade since the last event occurred, I stand an excellent chance to win the bet and secure 'First Taste' rights for myself this year.

With honor and pride putting weight to my bet, my father will undoubtedly be consumed with the challenge. At least I won't have to worry about him getting in my way for the next few weeks or months, given the intelligence Bullwinkle has already proven to possess.

Chapter 4
~Save the Sweetcorn~

Raccoon population numbers throughout the Valley have nearly tripled over last year's numbers; apparently due to the highly successful breeding season they enjoyed this past spring. In order to keep Mother Nature's harmonious balance, between these egg-stealing predators and our Valley's highly vulnerable game bird population, I've formulated a plan to reduce raccoon numbers to a more acceptable level.

With lunar charts calling for peak wildlife activity to occur just after sunset, I anxiously put on my hunting gear. If all goes as planned, I'll be putting a sizeable dent in the local raccoon population very soon.

My plan includes taking our two walker hounds, Mandy and Keesha, down to Bandit Hollow. The thirteen-year-old litter mates are two of the best coon dogs I've ever had the pleasure of trailing behind, in all my years of hunting.

Constantly competing to outperform each other, the hounds consistently tree at least a dozen raccoons on any given night out in the woods. They've even been known to tree twice that many on cloudless evenings; when their adversary's ability to remain hidden in the treetops gets taken away, by the billions of stars illuminating the heavens.

The local raccoon population is undoubtedly preparing to raid the four-acre patch of Peaches-n-Crème sweet corn, planted early last spring by residents of the Valley. The sweet, fragrant aroma of the ripening corn always draws in scores of critters looking to gorge themselves on their favorite seasonal cuisine.

Raccoons love to strip the husks off every ear of corn they can get their greedy little paws on. After taking a bite or two from each ear, they insatiably move on to the next stalk, leaving a majority of their plunder on the ground to simply waste away.

Just one animal can lay ruin to multiple rows of corn, making it imperative I act quickly to fill this year's raccoon harvest quota. My plan is to permanently remove at least a dozen of the bandits, and hopefully scare away the rest of the marauders getting ready to pillage our fields. If my mission is successful, I'll literally be saving thousands of harvestable ears of sweetcorn from falling victim to these ravaging scoundrels.

Before hopping onto my ATV, I check my flood lights to ensure the battery is fully-charged. Firing up my machine and releasing the clutch, the sound of the engine barely drowns out the hounds baying excitedly to begin the chase.

Instead of kenneling the dogs like I should've done, I release the dogs, allowing them to run freely behind me. They're a site to behold, watching them race to keep up with my ATV; their long, floppy ears flapping in rhythm with each lumbering gait.

My high-beam headlights suddenly pick up a ghostly silhouette of a big raccoon, scurrying across my path about fifty-yards ahead. Instincts tell me my plan to reach the sweet corn patch without detour is about to abruptly change.

Racing past where I'd seen the masked bandit disappear into thick-brush only moments earlier, I try distracting the hounds by throwing mud and loose gravel at them with my studded tires. Knowing how sensitive their noses are, I ready myself for the abrupt detour I'm inevitably about to take.

Mandy is the first to cross over the pathway, where I'd just seen the masked bandit run for cover. Slamming on the brakes, Mandy causes a rear-end collision with Keesha, who is already baying at the scent-trail left behind by the raccoon. With legs flailing, and torsos twisting and turning, each hound frantically skids and rolls about; until finally aligning themselves in the direction their keen noses are pulling

32

them towards.

Once traction in the gravel is re-established, both dogs bolt away in hot pursuit of their quarry. Baying like clockwork every five-seconds, their guttural resonances pierce through my eardrums with each howling sequence.

Skidding to a halt, I shut off the ATV and listen closely to the multitude of sounds emanating from the darkness. Based upon distinct 'tonality changes' occurring in each dog's baying sequence, I can tell they're quickly closing in on the raccoon. Continuing to analyze sounds, the duration between howls suddenly changes, from every five-seconds to every three-seconds; then, to every two-seconds. Shortly thereafter, a frenzy of yelps and long-drawn-out bays lets me know they've treed the raccoon, seemingly no more than fifty yards away. By their unmistakable vocalization patterns shifting into a furor of excited barks, I can tell the coon is just beyond their reach.

The really-big raccoons; ones that've been around for many years, are extremely savvy to various escape routes available throughout the treetops. They seem to know all the pathways to freedom, where the hounds cannot easily follow.

Experience is telling me, I need to hurry and cut off any escape route the raccoon might have within the next few-minutes, or the coon will inevitably slip away and be gone; leaving behind two unconsolably-whimpering canines to deal with. Evaluating the problem of having two giant rows of impenetrable Ash trees between me and the dogs, I quickly calculate the shortest pathway available to reach the raccoon, before it manages to find an escape route.

Not wasting a moment of time, I immediately re-start my ATV and lay-hard into the throttle. Building up enough speed to make it through the fifty-plus yards of swamp laden trails ahead, experience is telling me this will be the easiest-part of my journey. With mud and water flying everywhere, I relentlessly plow my way through the bog.

Eventually making it back onto solid ground, I throw all my weight into making an abrupt hard-left turn, the moment I reach the first-break in the trees. Cranking back hard on the throttle, I take off as fast-as-possible towards the hounds. Even over the roar of the engine, Mandy can be clearly heard with her long, drawn-out howls ending in a harsh gravelly tone.

Keesha's vocalizations are even louder than her sister's, with each baying sequence ending in a shrill screech; reminiscent of fingernails being raked across a chalkboard. Their bays echo back-and-forth through the trees, making it sound as if both dogs are going absolutely nuts! Catching a brief glimpse of glowing eyeballs in my headlights, it appears I'm about reach the pair of hounds about twenty yards ahead.

As my spotlight lands on the dogs, I witness Mandy standing picturesquely with both back-feet planted firmly in the ground. Stretching her front paws up the tree as high as possible, she's baying repeatedly to let me know the raccoon is still there.

Turning off my ATV, I begin laughing at Keesha's repeated attempts at climbing the tree. Her efforts appear futile, as she continues to fall backwards onto the flat of her back, several-times in quick succession. Most dogs would give up, but Keesha is no ordinary dog. Her determination to get at the raccoon is unwavering.

I've found over time, that yelling at Keesha to "Settle Down" is absolutely useless; for every time I find her at the base of a tree, hell-bent on getting at a raccoon, she blatantly disregards my commands. The only action, that works on getting her to stand down, is to shoot the damn-thing out of the tree.

With a flick of the switch, I turn my spotlight on, expecting to see the glowing yellow-eyes of a raccoon; but instead, I see four-sets of eyeballs staring back at me. The pathetic-looking group of juveniles all sit huddled together, defiantly chattering away from a small-pocket of the tree, about fifteen-feet off the ground.

Taking aim between the uppermost set of glowing eyes with my Ruger lever-action .22, I fire the first shot. Before having a chance to chamber a second round, a frenzy of gray shadowy-figures begins descending the tree in mass exodus. Hastily following after their suddenly deceased comrade, who falls to the ground with a resounding 'thump,' the remaining raccoons unknowingly race to their demise.

Instinctively cutting down the first fleeing refugee, Keesha grabs the doomed raccoon in her tightly-clenched teeth, immediately preceding to thrash it about like a rag doll.

Mandy then rolls the next descending raccoon with her front paw. Grabbing the third fleeing furbearer in her jowls, she viciously re-enacts Keisha's execution of the first unlucky raccoon to reach the forest floor.

As the only escapee to initially make it past the gnashing teeth of the hounds attempts to flee, my spotlight quickly zeroes in on it. Taking aim, I ready for a shot; but remove my finger from the trigger, after seeing Keesha pounce on the last surviving raccoon. The short-lived escape, quickly ends in its mortality.

Praising my hounds for their quick and decisive victories, I give each dog a treat. Tossing the raccoon carcasses into the holding bin strapped to the back of my ATV, I fire up the Polaris and resume my mission. Before reaching the outermost border of our sweet corn patch, I've already taken three additional detours; further reducing the local raccoon population by four adults, and two juvenile delinquents.

Hopping off the ATV to close the gate behind me, several raccoons can be heard chattering away over the sound of my idling engine. The critters seem to be issuing a 'Warning' to the hounds; sounding as if they were saying, "We won't be leaving without a fight!"

Mandy and Keesha accept the challenge, by bolting ahead of my headlights into the shadows. With a furor of growls and yelps, mixed with hisses and snarls resonating throughout Bandit Hollow, the two hounds invade the raccoon's territory. It doesn't take long for a retreat to be declared, as scores of raccoons begin ascending in mass from the forest floor.

Quickly scanning the treetops, I can see over a dozen sets of glowing-yellow eyeballs staring back at me. For nearly a minute-or-two, a turkey shoot ensues; as I aim, fire, and rapidly reload several-rounds in quick succession. After sending over a half-dozen corpses falling to the ground, the embattled raccoons eventually realize their 'Safe Zone' in the treetops offers far-inadequate protection.

The remaining contingent of masked marauders all decide to make a run for it simultaneously. With the last crackling report from my rifle fading ominously throughout the Valley, scores of raccoons can be heard plowing over corn stalks, sounding much like stampeding cattle in their haste to elude further confrontation with the sting of my bullets.

Yelling at the dogs "Go Get-em!" Mandy and Keesha don't know which way to begin heading. With all the overlapping scent trails laid down by the retreating enemy, my dog's olfactory senses appear to be short-circuiting. I find it quite amusing, watching them gulp air through flared nostrils; desperately trying to establish a distinct-direction of pursuit.

Laughing uncontrollably at this point, I watch them run erratically back-and-forth repeatedly. Baying in ever increasing frustration, they appear to change direction with each gasping breath. As if suddenly giving up, they simultaneously turn and begin galloping back towards me, with obvious expectations of receiving a reward for their recent victories.

They're a sight to behold as they skid to a stop in front of me, panting and drooling with tongues darting in-and-out repeatedly. Mandy begins baying incessantly for me to throw her a bone; while Keesha rolls onto her back several-times in quick succession, begging for the first reward.

As I toss them each a dog biscuit, Keesha rolls from her back to snatch the bone in mid-air; that was originally intended for Mandy. She then turns like a lightning bolt, racing to gather up the second treat I'd thrown to her, lying yet unseen by Mandy off to my right.

With both bones hanging from either corner of her mouth, Keesha takes off in the direction of home with Mandy in hot pursuit. Not more than twenty-yards into their journey, Mandy swipes the feet out from under Keesha, in an attempt to retrieve her rightful-bounty.

Before the ensuing wrestling match winner can be decided, chattering laughter from one of the raccoons hiding in a nearby tree catches Mandy's attention. The ingrained hatred for her arch enemy immediately trumps the dispute over the prized bone; and, within a millisecond, Mandy howls out what sounds like 'First Dibs' on a more desirable prize, somewhere up-ahead in the darkness.

Keesha instantly drops both drool-covered bones into the mud, racing along-side Mandy to be the first to reach the heckling raccoon; but the cagy critter certainly gets the last laugh. Being a wise old coon, it quickly scurries away through the treetops to the safety of hard-to-reach, inner areas of the labyrinth. Eventually realizing the futility of continuing their pursuit, both hounds return towards me with obvious-expectations of receiving another hand-out.

After refusing to reward them for their recently failed quest, Keesha suddenly remembers where she'd left the two-previous rewards; immediately running back to the mud-puddle she'd dropped them into earlier for safe-keeping. Only getting to retrieve one biscuit, before Mandy arrives to claim her rightful bounty, both dogs head-off together as friends. Having narrowly-avoided a dog fight, I decide to call it a night, and head for home.

With a highly successful coon hunt completed, I'll sleep better tonight, knowing an ample amount of sweetcorn remains harvestable.

Throughout the next few-weeks, residents will be engaged in ritualistic celebration; processing enough sweetcorn, to satisfy our culinary demands until next harvest season. During this time, we annually deplete a majority of our surplus Raspberry Ale reserves, by repeatedly offering-up toasts to Odin for yet-another bountiful harvest.

The end of sweet corn season quickly leads into our annual raspberry harvest; from which, we produce enough 'Nectar of the Gods' to quench everyone's thirst throughout the entire year. With the raspberry crop projected to be a record harvest this season, my primary focus turns to making sure I have enough hardware and supplies on-hand, to process all the plump-n-juicy berries we'll soon be picking.

Chapter 5

~Time to make Nectar~

Flights into and out of the Valley can be quite exciting, especially when Thor decides to grace us with his presence. He always likes to make his presence known, by throwing torrential sheets of rain and lightning at wayward travelers; but, if Thor happens to be in an exceptionally-bad mood, guests will experience what I call a 'sphincter factor' of ten, the whole time they're in the air.

I'm betting from the highly-volatile weather system I've been flying through, that Thor has returned to pay us a surprise visit; and as expected, is extremely pissed-off at what he found waiting for him.

It was only a matter of time before he'd return to find the surveillance system and security lock, I recently installed on the garden gate; put there to ensure Thor's raids on the garden, never-again jeopardize our ability to meet Odin's annual harvest quota.

Navigating with white knuckles for a majority of my ten-hour flight back home, I repeatedly deny death his long-awaited dues. After somehow managing to reach my home tarmac in one piece, I wearily land the heavily laden Huey with far-less than perfect precision.

The moment my landing gear touches ground, I exhale a huge sigh of relief before quickly throttling down the chopper. Turning off the monitor; while simultaneously unbuckling my safety harness, I exit the helicopter with extreme resolve to once again place my feet back onto solid ground.

The whole way home, I'd been tracking on radar a potentially threatening 'Category Four' hurricane. With the immense frontal system creating disaster zones up and down the entire coastal region, forecasters are thankfully not predicting the storm to turn inland; but with hurricanes, you never know what altered path they might unexpectedly decide to take. Grandpa B always said hurricanes were much like Grandma A; unpredictable with a mind of their own.

Whenever a hurricane even remotely threatens to strike our Valley, my family respectfully seeks Grandpa B's journal for his words of wisdom on "How to prepare for a hurricane." His prophetic teachings on what to watch for in predicting a storm's path and severity, have helped prevent several fatalities throughout the centuries.

During his days of Piracy, Grandpa B is said to have had a sixth-sense in predicting the weather; reportedly possessing a refined skill of using atmospheric events to sneak up and raid ships, when they would be most vulnerable and unprepared for battle. Grandpa B actually noted in his journal, about how he once ingeniously approached a treasure ship from behind a wall cloud; successfully boarding, and negotiating surrender with its humiliated Captain, without losing a single-member of his crew to English cannon.

Grandpa B's journal addresses several other interesting 'Topics' on hurricanes. My favorite is his decree on 'What to do when you find yourself in a hurricane,' it reads: "Always anticipate for the worst; but more importantly, always have a contingency plan for when it gets worse than ye ever thought possible." The passage reminds me each time I read it; the sobering lesson, to 'never ignore the potential damaging effects of any storm threatening to hit the Valley.'

When it comes to protecting our harvest, my father always reminds me to act before you have to react; by remembering that "Weather Forecasting is the only profession, were one can be wrong more than half-the-time, while somehow continuing to maintain what many consider to be a highly successful career." With this in mind, I'll

40

be taking every precaution to ensure the successful harvest of this year's raspberry crop.

Knowing what actions must be taken, it doesn't take long to formulate a plan of action for in the morning. No matter what the weather conditions are upon getting out of bed, I'll be heading down to Quail Den Hollow; the mission being, to fill every-last harvest bin too overflowing with red-ripe raspberries. Laying my head down on a pillow, it takes seemingly forever for me to slip into dreamland.

Quail Den Hollow is an open area over a mile long, and nearly half-as wide; located smack-dab in the middle of the Valley, where Grandpa B built his first log cabin. As the name bestowed upon the Hollow suggests, the quail population has always been very prolific throughout this area; but the most important natural resource found in Quail Den Hollow happens to be the enormous patch of red raspberries grown there.

Every spring, residents of the Valley take on the formidable task of pruning all the stalks within our patch, to ensure plants remain healthy and yield enormously-large berries. The unique strain of raspberries we harvest every fall ends up producing some of the sweetest 'Nectar' found anywhere in the Universe.

Since record keeping began, documenting the volume of berries harvested Annually, this year's crop is looking to beat all records; provided the hurricane currently wreaking havoc on nearby coastal areas, doesn't decide to take an unexpected-turn towards our Valley. With berries currently at their peak of ripeness, even a small storm hitting us now would severely impact the amount of harvestable fruit.

Only one time in recorded history has there ever been a hurricane descend upon the Valley during harvest time. The year was 1742, when Grandpa B wrote in his journal: "With the berry crop now completely destroyed in the year of our Lord 1742, I regret not being able to produce ner one pint of nectar to quench me pallet till next harvest moon. My greatest fear be three-years hence upon the Winter Solstice, when we be forced to offer up our Annual 'Toast to Odin' using improperly aged ale."

It's funny; but throughout all of Grandpa B's journal, I can find only a single entry documenting the consequences for failing to have 'Properly Aged' ale on hand for the toast in 1745. The entry reads: "The year without proper toast brings enlightenment to the importance of giving due homage to Odin. The entire Valley has become a parched landscape. Many sobering lessons have been learned this past year; one being, to ner forget the importance of keeping a 'Special Reserve' barrel on hand for the Winter Solstice Toast, ensuring it be vintage of precisely three-years."

As the alarm clock resounds in sync with the first stroke of 5 a.m. on the grandfather clock downstairs, I spring out of bed and quickly throw-on a set of warm clothes. Although only managing to get about an hour-or-two of actual sleep, adrenalin pulsates through my veins as I prepare for the Annual Harvest Day Ritual.

Heading hastily downstairs to the lower-level garage, I throw open the door and take a long, drawn-out stretch. Inhaling deeply the fragrant aroma of roses lining my driveway, I gaze-out over the dew-laden landscape with heightened awareness.

The growingly evident piles of bird droppings being deposited onto my roses by continuous waves of migrating blackbirds are telling me, that a majority of the raspberries down in Quail den Hollow are now ripe-and-ready for picking. Eagerly loading my harvest bins onto the trailer, I carefully secure the cargo while preparing for departure.

Anticipation mounts, as I contemplate how each fermentation

barrel will soon be sitting in my cellar, filled to within inches of the top with our highly delectable 'Nectar of the Gods.' Our raspberry ale is made by adhering to a strict fermentation process outlined in Grandpa B's 'Secret Recipe,' which legend perpetuates was bestowed to him by Odin himself.

Out of all the kegs that will eventually be tapped into throughout the upcoming year, none are more coveted than the 'Special Reserve' barrels put away for proper aging. A smile forms across my face, as I suddenly remember having not just one; but two of these barrels safely stashed away for this year's Winter Solstice Toast.

Each year on the Winter Solstice, upon the last stroke of Noon; without exception, we are to fill our mugs with vintage ale, and raise the following Toast: "We give praise to you Odin for the many bountiful treasures your life-giving waters bestow upon the Valley. Once your thirst has been quenched for yet another year, we plea you be gracious in returning the life-spring waters; that they may once again belch-forth steadily from Mother Earth."

Grandpa B was a very wise and well-spoken man, always having a foreboding sense of importance in his flair for words. With the sense of urgency placed on using these 'Exact' words during the Toast, we therefore heed his decree by uttering the words verbatim each year.

In order to ensure a successful harvest before the nearby, potentially rogue storm might unexpectedly descend upon us, I ready to take-off on my Annual berry picking mission. Laying into the throttle, my ATV immediately roars to life. Hugging the terrain, I veer sharply around Gobbler Knob; heading into the first of several bogs I'll need to traverse, in order to reach Quail Den Hollow.

Entering Mallard Bay Bog, hundreds of Canadian geese begin

sounding off in a classic 'Alarm Call' cadence. Readying for a quick get-a-way should my ATV continue to head in their direction, they soon relax after realizing my presence poses no immediate threat.

Tens of thousands of Mallard ducks taking refuge in their appropriately named bog react to my intrusion altogether differently. As if being directed by a symphony conductor, they simultaneously take to the air in mass. The deafening sound of their wings beating in unison nearly drowns out the noise from my ATV, as I scream hastily through the waterway with trailer-in-tow.

For several-seconds, I find myself literally driving in the shade, until the entire flock swings South in precision formation to invade Coot Hollow; but once I've passed through the area, they abruptly swing-back to the sanctuary of their home base.

Free from bog running for now, I proceed to enter Whitetail Hollow; a flat area, choked with thick patches of elephant grass and bulrush. While the ten-foot-wide pathway is clear, I dare not run at full-throttle knowing deer regularly bed down in this area. Collisions with deer have been the cause of several, near-fatal accidents over the years; and I certainly don't want to become a grim statistic, by foolishly pushing my luck.

Dozens of does and several small bucks can be seen dashing across the pathway ahead of me, frightened by the sudden noise that disturbs their slumber. Disappearing quickly into the dense foliage on the opposite side of the pathway, they leave behind only their tracks in the saturated mud.

A large doe suddenly jumps out directly in front of me. Swerving to avoid hitting her, the graceful animal bounds directly overhead, barely clipping one of the harvest baskets I have in tow. Landing back to earth, the doe waves her tail at me; as if saying,

44

"Sorry…goodbye!" before disappearing into the dense underbrush.

The minor collision causes several empty baskets on my trailer to begin shifting perilously to the left. With my load destabilizing more-and-more with each new bump in the road, I'm eventually forced to throttle-down for an unscheduled pit stop.

Reaching a man-made clearing in the middle of the flat up ahead, I hurriedly hop off to re-secure my load. Before proceeding onward, I looked around to survey several large cedar trees strategically planted around the perimeter of the open area decades earlier. To my pleasant surprise, every tree in view exhibits a large, freshly made rub; with two of the largest trees being completely girdled around at their base, by a dominant buck in the area. I immediately make plans to hunt the area on my earliest opportunity.

Hastily proceeding onward into the second-half of the grass-filled flat, I make it no more than sixty-yards before screeching to another halt; stopping literally inches from running into a young buck standing motionless in my path.

The yearling appears to have excellent genetics! Already weighing in at roughly a hundred pounds, it continues to sport several fading spots throughout its sleek coat. For several-seconds, the button buck stands nearly eye-to-eye with me; until eventually issuing a short bawl from his gaping mouth. It then bounds gracefully out of sight with a single leap, easily clearing the ten-foot-high patch of elephant grass to my right.

Cautiously proceeding onward, I soon see another doe in obvious estrous; being followed closely behind by a much-larger, 8-point buck. Each animal reacts in unison to my approach by crashing headlong into the dense wall of foliage to my left, instantly disappearing out of sight.

Several-yards from reaching the outer clearing of the flat, I foolishly gun the motor in expectations of making better time: which causes yet-another doe to jump out in front of me. At the last split-second before collision seems imminent, the graceful animal bounds directly overhead, nearly taking-off my baseball cap in her flight to freedom.

Thankful for having eluded injury, I stop for a moment to re-secure my cap; before slowly making my way out of White-tail Hollow. Once clear, I crank-back hard on the throttle to make it over Gobbler Ridge, before racing off towards the bog of 'Fortune and Fate;' the last area one must travel through, in order to reach the Labyrinth.

The bog of Fortune and Fate is the decreed 'Name' given to the swamp, by Grandpa B. In his journal, he states: "This final bog granting access to the labyrinth shall henceforth be called 'Fortune and Fate;' a befitting omen to the many perils facing those who traverse its waters."

Grandpa B somehow designed the bog to provide a smooth, solid, rock-lined pathway approximately three-meters wide. The submerged pathway lies mere-inches below the surface, absolutely invisible in the murky water.

To safely traverse the bog, one must avoid the many areas of quicksand and other pitfalls dispersed throughout the bog; thankfully, Grandpa B left strict 'Instructions' for his progeny to follow on how to safely navigate through this area.

The passage in his journal states: "One must humbly enter the bog of Fortune and Fate between the two pillars of Blackbeard's Golden Galleon, traveling focused on the Cornerstone in an unwavering line till one clears the bog. A stern WARNING! Do not stray from the path, or your fate be sealed with dire consequence!"

It should be noted the 'Two Pillars of Blackbeard's Golden Galleon' refers to a pair of massive Red Oak trees on the far-Western edge of the bog. The pair of centuries-old trees literally dwarf all the other trees nearby.

I used to be somewhat apprehensive when traveling through the Bog of Fortune and Fate; but after successfully traversing the submerged pathway thousands of times, I rarely give second thought to the possible pitfalls that might still exist.

Flying along on my ATV between the two giant Oak trees, I hydroplane a bit upon entry into the bog. Eventually gripping the raised edge of the pathway, my studded tires slowly redirect me back onto the trail. Focused with unwavering attention, I head straight for the Cornerstone tree in the distance. Making my way through the bog as quickly as possible, I eventually reach the entrance to the labyrinth.

Catching Dad out of the corner of my eye as I'm going in, I can see he's totally engaged in his relentless pursuit of the elusive Bullwinkle. From reports he's been feeding me periodically over the radio, the buck has already eluded him multiple times, using what he claims to be a 'Cloak of Invisibility.'

It takes seemingly forever for me to stop laughing, as I navigate through the remaining bogs and corridors of the labyrinth to reach the inner-sanctum area. Once reaching the lush-green fields found there, I know Quail Den Hollow is only moments away. Soon seeing its vast array of crimson-red raspberries spread out before me, I significantly slow my pace.

On final approach to the patch, the sound of my ATV causes thousands of blackbirds feeding on the berries, to suddenly rise-up in mass exodus. Based on years of experience encountering this exact same scenario, I know precisely how current events are about to unfold.

Scrambling to cover myself up with a tarp, I do so just in time to avoid getting plastered with bird crap.

Passing directly overhead, after having their migration feast interrupted, wave after wave of blackbirds begin strafing me with the precision of a squadron of B52's on a daylight bombing mission. Their red-staining excrement unloads upon me, in a sustained barrage lasting well-after the final bird passes by overhead.

I remember my first experience with the birds many years ago, while joining Dad on my inaugural berry harvest mission. OH, what an initiation it was! Compared to my first encounter, I'd come out relatively unscathed this time. Knowing the tarp will be needed again to cover and protect my load when ready to leave; I shake-off the tarp, and temporarily stow it away.

Taking every precaution to scare off any bears that might be feasting nearby, I noisily beat my harvest bins together after removing them from the trailer. Placing each container along the outer edge of the berry patch in even intervals, I now have everything in place to begin the Annual harvest. Upon first inspection of the berries, a majority appear to be perfectly ripe, with nearly every crimson-red morsel being plump and juicy.

Putting gloves on to avoid the needle-sharp thorns, I'm now ready to begin the Annual berry picking ritual. Holding the harvest bucket in my left hand, I grasp the first of several-thousand plant stalks firmly with my right.

The procedure I use for harvesting raspberries, consists of first gently shaking-off the loose berries found at the end of each plant stalk; doing so, over the wide-mouth rim of my harvesting bucket. After the ripest berries fall off into my container, the remaining fruit is stripped-off into the bucket, by rapidly flailing my fingers down each stalk in a less-than-perfect, but highly effective picking motion.

This 'finger flailing' routine allows me to harvest the maximum number of berries in the least amount of time. While a few berries will inevitably be left unpicked on each stalk in my haste to harvest them, I know nothing will go to waste.

There have been only a hand-full of years, where I can remember Mother Nature requiring us to meticulously pick every-last, red-ripe morsel we could find; in order to meet our desired quota of Raspberry ale for the upcoming year. This year however looks to be a bumper crop, with nearly every berry at its peak of ripeness!

Just as the picking crew finally arrives to help with the harvest, I finish filling my first harvest bin. The next few containers I personally load take a bit longer to fill, as I occasionally find myself uncontrollably stuffing my face with handfuls of the berries. After a few-hours more of intense picking, the seasoned crew has every-last harvest bin literally filled to overflowing.

With the sun directly overhead, only about two-thirds of my berry patch has been picked. Loading the last of over four-dozen harvest bins onto the trailer, I strap them down securely before heading for home; eager to begin the process of fermenting the berries.

With a little under two acres remaining unpicked, you'd think I'd be making plans to return; but doing so would be a complete waste of time. By the time I'd be able to make it back to the patch, after acquiring all the additional supplies needed for processing, very few harvestable berries would remain.

Currently at their peak of ripeness, Mother Nature's creatures will certainly feast heavily on the remaining unpicked fruit. Knowing nothing will go to waste, I have no regrets in leaving the unpicked berries behind.

After double-checking to make sure each heaping-full bin is properly secured and safely covered with a tarp, I proceed back home at a much-slower pace than when I first arrived. My Father taught me many-years ago when transporting a full-load of red ripe berries, to always proceed with extreme-caution in order to minimize loss of volume.

Not more than a hundred-yards into my journey back home, a massive-flock of blackbirds patiently awaiting our departure rapidly descends upon on the remaining, un-picked fruit left behind.

Several-minutes into my journey home, I suddenly realize my berry-soaked picking gloves remain draped over the well-pump, back at the raspberry patch. Knowing a return trip to retrieve them would subject me to yet another strafing by the birds, I elect to leave my gloves for Mother Nature to launder-out the berry stains.

With Dad frantically radioing to inform me about a substantial rain event quickly approaching the Valley, I don't waste any time in getting back. While I don't mind traveling through the bog of Fortune and Fate on a sunny day, attempting to see landmarks on the opposite side of the expanse can quickly become near-impossible, once rain-soaked winds envelop the area.

After successfully navigating my way through the bog of Fortune and Fate, storm clouds can be seen quickly amassing in the distance; making me extremely glad I didn't go back for my gloves. Had I done so, the entire berry harvest would've been put at risk, by being forced to weather out the storm overnight, under the limited protection of the Cornerstone tree.

Quickly making my way back through the tall grasses of Whitetail Hollow, I observe not-one deer attempting to cross the pathway ahead. This instantly raises a 'Warning Flag,' knowing every-last animal has sought refuge from the weather.

Experience has taught me to respect, and never dismiss even the slightest-variation in normal patterns of wildlife movement; for Mother Nature's creatures seem to have an inherent 'Sixth Sense,' in predicting the severity of an approaching storm.

Clearing White-tail Hollow heading into Mallard Bay Bog, I can see storm clouds have gathered overhead, and are beginning to exhibit an eerie, jade-green hue; more significantly, not one Mallard or Canadian goose has taken flight. They all appear to be hunkered down, like the whitetail deer behind me; readying for what's looking to become a rather-significant weather event.

No longer worrying about losing any volume in the berries, I hit the throttle; racing through 'Mallard Bay' bog as fast as my ATV will pull the loaded-down trailer behind me. Lightning strikes no-more than a quarter mile away; sending a shiver of apprehension racing up-and-down my spine. Cranking back even-harder on the throttle, I round Gobbler's Knob in the final dash for the safety of home.

With my father frantically waving me in towards the open doors of our garage several-hundred yards directly ahead, a look to my right has me witnessing an extremely rare funnel cloud descending into the Valley.

Racing for the safety of my ever-inviting garage, the vortex disappears back-up into the swirling clouds, moments before the storm delivers a lightning bolt; striking mere-yards behind my trailer. I thankfully do not lose any of the precious cargo, let alone my life in the ordeal.

Once inside, Dad slams the garage door shut behind me. He then falls to the floor, laughing his ass off. After seeing my sheet-white complexion in one of my rear-view mirrors, I begin cursing and swearing at him for his inconsiderate attitude.

Upon regaining his composure, Dad stands up and gives me the biggest bear hug one could ever experience; telling me in a reassuring manner: "Relax, what's to worry?... you're OK.... that's all that matters!!"

Releasing the grasp around me that's been cutting-off my air supply for what seems an eternity, Dad drops me to the ground like a sack of potatoes. Quickly tearing the tarp off the trailer, he begins checking on the condition of our berries. With a whoop and a holler, my father re-embraces me in another celebratory bear hug, shouting: "Yes! Thank You Odin! The berries are all fully ripe, and unharmed!"

Choking-up enough air in my lungs to offer my own celebratory cheer, I sound eerily similar to 'Alvin the Chipmunk' being squeezed to the point of suffocation. Suddenly realizing his own strength, Pop eases his grasp moments before I'm about to pass out. Quickly regaining full-consciousness, I hurriedly perform my own inspection of the berries.

It appears very-little in volume has been lost; even after my mad-dash for safety! If my calculations are correct, I'll have more than enough berries to win my bet with Dad; the wager being, to have every-last keg filled and fermenting in the wine cellar by morning.

As the storm rages outside for hours, Dad and I meticulously follow the Secret Ancient Recipe throughout the entire extraction and mixing process; as predicted, we end up with all-fifty oak barrels topped-off and sealed. As the break of dawn begins illuminating the Eastern horizon, I perform the last task by cleaning-up my workspace.

Amounting to almost twice-as-much produced than in previous years, it still doesn't come close to the eighty-plus barrels per year; that Grandpa B is said to have annually processed for his own personal consumption.

With all the Raspberry Ale needed for the upcoming year safely stored-away to ferment in the cellar, I'll soon be able to focus all my energy on getting ready for the upcoming guest season; but first, I plan to spend the next few-days harvesting fall crops, hoping to fill our pantry shelves with enough produce to sustain everyone through, till next harvest season.

Chapter 6

~The Onset of Winter~

With an iridescent-orange sun slowly sinking into oblivion behind snow-capped mountains to the West, my wintering flock of whooping cranes suddenly erupt in shrieks of excitement. From every corner of the valley, they welcome home several late-arriving family members. The exhausted travelers answer back jubilantly, upon catching first-glimpse of the bountiful feeding grounds that have instinctively beckoned them home for nearly a thousand miles.

The ensuing responses begin building into what becomes a tumultuous cadence of echoes; with seemingly every Whooping Crane in the Valley calling out from their own private, fish-filled cove. The ritualistic uproar resumes with each new arrival, until the last returning member finds its mate. Once this happens, vocalized outbursts become reserved for issuing warning of impending danger, as the entire colony begins settling into their winter residence.

The small plots of real estate they lay claim too, is where each bird will reside throughout the change-of-seasons, growing gluttonously fat on fertile waters teeming with baitfish, and other small crustaceans. Come spring, every member of the flock will be plump, healthy, and ready to make the long, perilous journey back to their summer breeding grounds.

Several resident loons laugh back-and-forth to each other; as if mocking the visiting cranes unfounded claims to water rights. Their calls echo resoundingly against the canyon walls, as scores of hungry deer begin rising from their bedding areas, eager to feast on millions of newly fallen acorns now blanketing the Valley floor.

An extremely abrupt, and freakishly violent windstorm ravaged through the upper-end of the Valley earlier in the day; catching me totally off-guard, and unprepared.

I happened to be down in Skunk Den Hollow planting a sizeable plot of barley and wheat, when the violent frontal system arrived without warning. It was so surreal, watching winds in advance of the front violently snapping off treetops, as the storm descended upon the Valley like a rogue tidal wave.

A barrage of walnuts was soon being whipped around by the swirling winds, reminiscent of baseballs being thrown about during a major league warm-up. For protection, I'd huddled myself between two of the largest protruding roots found at the base of the Cornerstone tree. Dodging projectiles hurling past me at super-high velocities, I remember watching Mother Nature's ravaging winds create swirling panoramas of leaves; at one point gaining in mass to over a football field wide, and hundreds of feet in the air before eventually dissipating.

After the frontal system had passed, nearly every tree throughout the Valley had been stripped bare of its colorful, fall tunic. Only a few of the mightiest burr oaks, which traditionally refuse to relinquish hold of their leaves until late winter, managed to retain a few clumps of withering foliage on their centuries-old skeletons.

As quickly as the storm had arrived, it was gone. With millions of colorful leaves falling to the ground, the picturesque scene reminded me of a snow globe having been vigorously shaken, before being allowed to settle-back to earth. Mother Nature had literally transformed the Valley from a picturesque backdrop of vivid fall colors, into a canvas-full of barren trees, in just a few-short minutes.

Climbing out from a depression between the roots, which in all-likelihood saved me from sustaining any serious injuries, I found myself bruised and tattered. After brushing off my jacket, I eagerly returned home to have Anne nurse my wounds.

While driving through the panorama of fall colors littering the trail in front of me, I come across an area where wild hogs have heavily rooted up the pathway. With guests scheduled to be visiting these areas in a few short weeks, I certainly cannot risk putting anyone's health in jeopardy.

Before reaching the parking garage, I've already cleared my morning schedule to go survey the extent of hog damage; hopefully coming up with a fail-proof plan, to eliminate every-last nuisance bovine from the area.

Chapter 7

~Wild Hogs~

Wild hogs were first-introduced to the Valley after an extremely rare 'F-3' tornado ripped through our hog confinement pen; down in a low-lying area, befittingly known as 'Skunk Den Hollow.' The small valley was forever altered by the destructive funnel cloud, which killed over a hundred pigs, before granting freedom to nearly-twice that many more.

According to Grandpa B's journal, Skunk Den Hollow actually earned its befitting name, after he'd been 'heavily doused' by pissed-off skunks; an agonizing five-different times, while planting the Labyrinth's Southwestern quadrant. After losing his sense of smell for nearly a month, Grandpa B decreed the desecrated area to be "the perfect location for raising livestock."

One of my favorite excerpts from Grandpa B's journal references his encounters with the skunks, where he wrote: "Little black demons with white war-paint across their backs be everywhere! With so many of these wretched smelling inhabitants waiving their tails throughout the Hollow, the insertion of livestock will ner wreak havoc on the environment; any more so, than does the noxious stench emanating from these foul, vindictive creatures."

Before the freed pigs could cause any major damage to the Valley's sensitive ecosystem, all but about twenty piglets were rounded up. Only the smallest ones were able to avoid capture; doing so, by slipping undetected into Odin's Garden through a locked gate.

Once the crew rounding up the freed bovine had passed-by where the piglets were hiding, the entire litter managed to squeeze back through the gate's heavy-iron bars. Immediately feasting on hordes of acorns nearby, the piglets quickly fattened-up to where the gate effectively barred them all from re-entering the Garden. Odin is said to have intervened; for had even one destructive piglet remained trapped inside unchecked, catastrophic damage would've been inflicted upon the Garden.

Descendants of these bovine quickly turned feral, becoming extremely wise to the array of escape routes available to them throughout the Valley. For years, my father and I tried to eradicate the hogs entirely from the Valley, but a few elusive creatures always somehow managed to avoid the crosshairs of our rifles.

We eventually realized it would take several months of relentless pursuit, to completely eliminate the hogs from the Valley; given the sixth sense of danger they seem to possess, when being hunted. In interest of time and effort required, we decided to simply set a quota on how many hogs needed to be harvested each year, to ensure population numbers remain in check.

The quota for each quadrant is set, based on actual head counts taken during my annual aerial survey. To get the most accurate survey data, I always conduct my reconnaissance missions immediately-after a heavy snowfall blankets the entire Valley floor. When this semi-rare meteorological event happens, usually occurring only once or twice per year, I'm forced to act quickly before the snow melts.

Taking to the air in my helicopter the moment weather breaks, I follow an established grid pattern, while logging head-counts on each 'species of interest' living in each quadrant. Because the newly-fallen snow makes it practically impossible for many of the larger animals to hide, I'm able to gather extremely accurate data on herd populations throughout the Valley. I then use this data to determine how successful reproduction rates have been for each species throughout the past year.

In addition to wild hog numbers, our annual census includes taking head counts of deer, elk, and several other elusive creatures found throughout the Valley; all being done to ensure herd populations remain balanced, and healthy.

Similar to racoons, but in much larger numbers due to the size of their litters, hog populations will occasionally spike in a given area; potentially threatening the successful harvest of an important food supply, or cash crop. When this happens, my only option is to quickly eliminate as many nuisance animals as I can, from these sensitive areas.

Flying over an area we call the 'Corral,' I can see hogs have somehow gotten in and destroyed a sizable area of our corn crop. For years, I've considered the Corral one of the safest places throughout the Valley to grow corn, and other life-sustaining vegetables. Setting course for home, my thoughts run through hundreds of plausible scenarios; trying to come up with a viable plan to eliminate the destructive bovine from this sensitive area, before even-more catastrophic damage can occur.

Opening the front door of my humble abode, I head straight for the captain's chair. Trying to relax with limited success, I eventually find myself surveying the area nearest the corral, using the original antique-brass telescope Grandpa B once used to spot ships out on the horizon, during his seafaring days.

The telescope expands to nearly three-feet long, allowing me to zoom in from considerable distances with remarkable clarity; similar to how an eagle soaring high-overhead possesses the uncanny ability to spot a tiny-little field mouse, as it scurries across the forest floor below.

Damage appears to be occurring where the Corral abuts up to the main creek; near the area I found rooted up on the trail last night, while making my way back home. If I'm going to have enough harvest-able corn left standing, to fuel all my vehicles and motorized toys throughout the upcoming year, I'll need to act quickly.

I suspect the hogs have somehow found a way to breach the near-impenetrable wall of Ash trees; due to there being only one 'known' access point into the Corral. The gated opening I'm referring to, is only accessible from an area deep within the inner-sanctum of the labyrinth; and once you've entered it, the pathway leads you down a long-narrow corridor, befittingly nicknamed the 'Gauntlet.'

The Gauntlet happens to be noted in Grandpa B's journal, as being responsible for the annihilation of all-but-one of the Indians, who attacked and burned his original cabin to the ground. With every snare set by Grandpa B throughout the Gauntlet; said to have "systematically unleashed death and despair upon the departing savages," his revenge must've been gratifyingly sweet.

An excerpt from his journal about the event, states: "Out of the original raiding party of nearly three-scores of savages seeking to remove me seed from their sacred Valley, ner but one set of tracks do I find departing the labyrinth."

Regressing back to the facts lending credibility to there actually being a breach in the labyrinth, I consider the following: If the nuisance bovine are accessing the Corral area using the Gauntlet, surveillance cameras would've picked up their presence on film; plus, no visual damage exists within the horde of tomatoes growing next to the Corral entrance, a favorite food source for the hogs.

With all the damaged crops being located at the far end of the Corral, it becomes obvious the pigs have somehow managed to breach the once considered 'Impenetrable' labyrinth wall. If I'm to stand any chance of being able to eradicate the entire mob, before any further damage occurs, I'll need to locate where they're gaining entry from.

Just before sundown, on the third-night in-a-row of relentlessly scanning the Corral through my telescope, I finally discover the precise location being breached. Back-tracking the trail of a hog that suddenly comes into view, I quickly focus in on another massive sow struggling to worm her way into the Corral; through what appears to be an ever-widening access hole.

The breach under the labyrinth wall happens to be located near a tree we call the 'Hanging Tree.' The massive Oak tree possesses a very-large protruding limb, extending straight-out horizontally like a person's arm for over twenty-feet, before reaching up skyward with its fists full of acorns. My ancestors and I have used this uniquely shaped limb countless times over the centuries, to hang harvested game safely out-of-reach of predators seeking to score an easy meal.

From where I'm sitting in the captain's chair; under normal-conditions, the limb would be blocking view of the passageway being used by the hogs. If it weren't for a strong gust of wind from an approaching storm, causing the limb to sway back and forth significantly, I would've never spotted the breech. By last count, before multiple streaks of lightning begin racing ominously across the ever-darkening horizon, fifteen gray-shadows have successfully made their way into the Corral.

With rain quickly obscuring my view of the Valley below, it's clearly evident the hogs will become trapped in the Corral until shooting light by the rising water; provided heavy rains persist throughout the evening as predicted. If I can reach the Corral, and be locked and loaded when the rain is predicted to end shortly after daybreak, it should literally turn into a shooting gallery.

Gathering up all the supplies and materials I'll need to carry out my mission, I look forward to refining my marksmanship skills. If my plan is successful, I'll soon be filling the freezer with enough bacon and hams to satisfy our culinary needs for several-months.

Hog populations were somewhat low, according to my last survey back in early February; but, it remains uncertain, as to how successful their breeding season was this spring. The dilemma I find myself confronting, is still having several-other 'sensitive areas' needing nuisance animals removed. Eradicating the entire mob of hogs will come close to exceeding harvest quotas set for the year; nevertheless, I must protect my corn, and other sensitive crops nearby at all costs.

Having one of my favorite tree-stands located within easy range of the labyrinth breach makes it easy to come up with a plan to eradicate the nuisance bovine. The stand offers the ultimate in comfort and protection from the elements. Nicknamed the 'Cabin in the Sky,' it sits located within a hundred-yards of where the hogs have been accessing the Corral.

To ensure the pigs cannot escape, I'll need to block their only alternate escape route out of the Corral. This can easily be accomplished, by simply closing the gate behind me after entering the Corral. From the Cabin in the Sky's elevated position, I'll be able to systematically eliminate the hogs from the area, using my M21 sniper rifle.

As expected, the storm arrives dumping copious amounts of rain throughout the entire evening. Making my way through the first flooded area of the Gauntlet in my swamp buggy, I soon find myself grinning from ear-to-ear.

The 'Swamp Buggy' happens to be a supped-up Monster truck, that I use to get around; each time Mother Nature lets loose with one of her 'Meltdowns,' and floods the Valley. My most relied upon and trusted 'Toy,' is the only vehicle capable of safely navigating through almost any inhospitable road condition one might encounter after a heavy-rainfall event.

Normally, I'd be using my ATV to reach the Corral; but with the immense amount of rain falling, I know taking the 'Toy' is my only option to guarantee a successful mission. In a few of the most severely flooded areas, I actually begin considering future upgrades to improve my swamp buggy's performance; the whole time praying I'll make it to my final destination.

Somehow managing to navigate through in just a little over ten minutes, I reach the Gateway into the Corral. Jumping-out to close the massive cast-iron gate; effectively sealing the fate of every-last hog trapped inside the Corral, I suddenly find my entire body slowly sinking into a quagmire of mud.

Practically sucking my knee-high boots off, with each trodden step taken in my mission to close the gate, I eventually make it back to the vehicle. Nearing complete exhaustion upon climbing up into the driver's seat, I suddenly find myself instantly re-energized at the thought of soon returning to the Cabin in the Sky, located a little-over five-hundred yards directly ahead.

Arriving at the stand, I park my vehicle directly below the access panel into the cabin. Reaching up and grasping hold of the ladder, I pull it down until it rests firmly on the inside floorboard. Quickly climbing up the ladder, I slow my ascent upon reaching the next-to-last rung. A foreboding premonition of what I might soon discover, sends goose-bumps up-and-down my spine.

Poking my head up through the entranceway, a quick glance around reveals no 'new' damage has been inflicted to the inside of my cabin. The last time opening the hatch, I had the unpleasant surprise of discovering the cabin completely redecorated by a family of raccoons. The little shit-mongers had torn into the cushions of my sofa, leaving shredded foam stuffing and feces strewn everywhere! Pleasantly surprised this time to see everything in its proper place, I finish carrying-up all the supplies needed to complete my mission.

The deluge of rain that's been continuously falling throughout the night finally subsides, mere moments before the predictable approach of daybreak casts a faint-glow across the entire Eastern horizon.

I calculate having at least an hour-or-two to get settled in, before flood waters eventually recede enough to begin exposing the hog's only available escape route. Opening a shooting window, I listen intently for the slightest sound of movement, while slowly surveying my surroundings.

Watching in awe as the morning mist hangs over the saturated field in front of me, I find myself marveling at the countless, swirling columns of rising steam. Appearing eerily similar, but in a much-larger scale to what I witness each morning within the over-sized rim of my coffee mug, the swirling vortex's have me mesmerized.

Shaking off my trance, I begin scanning the Kill Zone to confirm seeing several large silhouettes moving about in dawn's early light. Hearing the hogs rooting feverishly in the mud near the edge of the corn, it's clearly evident they have no idea I'm about to 'Rock their World!'

Slipping my rifle onto the sandbags in front of me, I peer through the scope; patiently waiting for daylight to bring the grayish silhouettes into focus. Several-minutes pass, before I'm finally able to positively confirm the identity of my first target; a large female,

64

standing closest to the corn. Setting my cross hairs on her upper shoulder, I slowly squeeze-off a round. Dropping the sow abruptly in her tracks, the remaining mob instantly scatters in all directions.

With most of the herd running for shelter in the corn as expected, I take aim at one of the largest boars, and gently-squeeze the trigger. Leading it perfectly, the bovine rolls head-over-heals several times, before coming to a dead-stop within inches of my first kill.

In all the noise and confusion, the hogs seem uncertain as to which direction they should flee. With their comrades falling all around them, I'm able to tally up six additional kills, before the pigs eventually reach safety in the standing corn.

Waiting patiently, I know it won't take long for the hogs to realize the Gauntlet is no longer a viable option for escape. Instinctively knowing the bovine will eventually regroup and make a mad dash for the breach in the labyrinth, I expect this to occur once floodwaters have receded enough for them to escape back through.

Many-minutes later, while shaking the last bitter-dregs of coffee from the thermos into my wide-open mouth, I look out to see water levels are beginning to drop rapidly. Knowing it won't be long before the hogs attempt their escape, I ready my assault rifle for another round of target practice.

Numerous grunts, followed by a chorus of high-pitched squeals, tip me off; mere seconds, before the herd's mass-exodus ensues. With a couple of the biggest porkers leading the way, nearly two-dozen animals of all sizes bolt from the corn; creating an undulating wave of gray, white, black, and brown, as they scurry their way through my established kill zone.

Darting back and forth, the pigs all predictably head in the general direction of the newly re-opened 'Vortex of Safe Passage.'

While this is exactly the move the pigs were expected to make, I find myself momentarily caught off guard by the sheer number of hogs remaining. The entire mob must have gotten trapped inside the Corral, by the deluge of rain that dumped over nine inches of continuous rainfall throughout the night.

Picking off the largest animals in the group first, I'm unable to eliminate all of my targets before being forced to reload. At last count, seven small piglets led by one lone sow are lucky enough to make it safely to freedom.

Mad at myself for not being able to eradicate the entire mob, I climb back-down into the Swamp Buggy. After re-securing the ladder, I start the vehicle and quickly head-out to assess the overall success of my mission.

Knowing I've fired a total of twenty-rounds, I'm confident in having successfully inserted hot-lead into each of my targets. 2,4,8,9, 12,... I begin counting, as I approach the corpses strewn about in groups of up to four animals. On final count, twenty-one pigs lie dead in the mud.

"Twenty-one kills, with only having fired twenty-rounds! Sometime during the mayhem, I must've taken out two with the same shot," I think to myself! The proud moment is the only thing keeping me from relentlessly persecuting myself, for having allowed several of my targets to escape. Knowing the bovine will inevitably return with friends, I grimace at the additional work now required to ensure a successful corn harvest this season.

The first thing I'll have to do after butchering the hogs is finish rebuilding the starter motor in my D8 bulldozer. Once I can get the old CAT dozer running, I'll come back to permanently seal up the hole where the hogs have been accessing the coral.

Using the swamp buggy, and the many hemp ropes I've brought along; each hog is quickly hoisted high-enough to keep them safely out of most scavenger's reach. The large, protruding branch of a tree we call the 'Hanging Tree,' provides the perfect gallows to do this from.

After suspending a dozen pigs from the massive Oak tree's; now heavily laden branch, I move to another tree about thirty-yards away to finish hanging the remaining corpses. Inspecting each carcass for where my bullet has entered and exited, trying to determine the amount of meat I'll be harvesting from each animal, I suddenly make a startling discovery!

One of the smaller piglets exhibits a series of four-deep gashes along its entire side, as if made by an attack from a rather-large predator! Seeing no visible bullet wounds on the animal, I quickly surmise the hog has recently been attacked by what appears to have been a Mountain Lion!

Searching for tracks, I quickly confirm my suspicions upon finding several-large panther tracks in the mud surrounding the hog's corpse. A chill runs up-and-down my spine; suddenly realizing, the mountain lion may still be trapped inside the Corral.

I've been aware of the cat's existence in the area for the past few-months, with several night-vision security cameras regularly being activated during the midnight hour. Due to the elusive animal's strictly nocturnal behavior, I've unfortunately never been lucky enough to experience the pleasure of spotting the cougar 'Live' in the wild.

The moment I begin reaching for the safety of my rifle, the cougar suddenly bolts from the corn, heading straight for the same passage-to-freedom used earlier by the hogs. I instinctively raise my rifle to get a closer look at the rare Black Panther dancing back-and-forth before my eyes; but have no intention of taking a shot at the beautiful animal.

Following the fleeing feline through the scope, I'm able to determine the panther is an extremely pregnant female. Her labored leaps and bounds through the thick muck, make me feel compassion for her flight-to-freedom.

Keeping the lioness focused in my crosshairs, I watch in awe as the magnificent animal relentlessly struggles to free herself from the grip of the mud. With every twisting leap and bound she painstakingly takes, it's readily apparent the cat refuses to succumb to the same fate; as that, of the recently expired bovine.

Knowing the entire time her ultimate destination is to reach the escape route used earlier by the hogs, I find her actions very intriguing. In all her aerial acrobatics and backbreaking lunges, she never once divulges the direction of her intended escape route. Her movements are truly elegance and grace in motion. I watch in awe, as the cougar eventually disappears through the same vortex of safe-passage used earlier, by the few hogs lucky enough to escape.

After hanging the last corpse several-feet in the air from my makeshift gallows, I head back home in the swamp buggy to get my wagon and butchering knives. Expecting to harvest several-hundred pounds of delicious pork, it'll be a race against time before the meat begins to spoil, with temperatures expected to reach into the mid 60's by noon. Knowing it'll take the better part of a day to finish processing all the hogs, I quicken my pace.

Getting back to the house just before 9 a.m., I ready my backhoe to assist in retrieving the meat. After securing a large chest-freezer to the front bucket, I hop into the operator seat and quickly hoist the unit wrapped in chains high into the air. Recently having converted the freezer to run off my tractor's twelve-volt battery, I'll be using it to immediately cool down the meat, and substantially reduce the risk of spoilage.

Hurriedly driving the backhoe back to the Corral, my empty chest freezer sways rhythmically back-and-forth like a metronome; ironically, in perfect sync to one of my favorite songs, 'Burning down the House', currently jamming away at full-volume thru my earbuds. Knowing the whole way back I'll be forced to travel at a much slower pace, with a heavily loaded freezer dangling in front of me, I relish in the speed I'm currently able to travel.

Passing through the Corral gate, I quickly survey the hordes of tomato plants growing there. It's funny, but around the end of June, I remember having been legitimately concerned the plants might not produce many tomatoes this year.

We certainly experienced an unseasonably cool, late spring; but once the hot summer temperatures kicked in, with temperatures holding steady in the upper 80's and lower 90's, the tomatoes seemed to literally explode in growth overnight.

Staring out in amazement at blood-red fruit hanging heavily from every plant, it won't be long before residents of the Valley will be spending a few-days in the kitchen, juicing and canning the massive horde of Beefsteak and Roma tomatoes nearing their peak of ripeness.

Cruising gingerly past row-after-row of Jalapeño and Habanera peppers, the 'Scoville' units contained within the patch starts to burn my nostrils; lending high-expectations of being able to produce some truly 'Hot' salsa this year.

Traveling on, I look out across row after row of Bell peppers and Hungarian waxed pepper plants loaded down with scores of yellow, orange, and red fruits ready to be picked. Just past the peppers, the last remnants of our sweet corn patch remain untouched, and appear to be drying-out nicely in the sun.

I'd harvested a majority of the sweet corn months earlier; but intentionally left several critically important rows of seed corn standing, to propagate our superior strain of sweet corn next year. The stalks are standing erect and drying-out nicely, despite all the rain we've had. Breathing a sigh of relief, I continue onward; thankful the hogs have yet-to-inflict any apparent damage to the field.

Looking ahead, I can see the approaching stand of pig-corn planted throughout the last-half of the Corral. Slowing my pace, I begin surveying the extent of actual damage brought on by the hogs. My gut twinges painfully, upon seeing nearly a full acre of corn completely uprooted and destroyed.

Arriving at the hanging tree, I park the backhoe, by immediately dropping both stabilizer arms into the soggy ground. Swinging the bucket around to position it alongside the largest-corpse suspended from the Hanging tree, I hop off the controller's seat, and begin using a step-ladder I've brought to climb-up into the excavator's bucket. With a butchering knife in my right-hand, and a battery powered reciprocating saw in my left, I begin the butchering process.

Within minutes, I've skinned and quartered the first hog. Slowing down momentarily, I try my best to remove the bacon-laden belly fat with minimal loss or damage. Filleting out the ribs my mouth begins to water, as I make plans to barbecue them over red-hot, apple-wood coals.

In what can only be described as a 'Virtual Moment,' I envision myself devouring every-last morsel of deliciously tender meat, from each delectable rib. Eventually deciding it would be a good idea to pay closer attention to my knife, I wash away the virtual BBQ flavor in my mouth with a swig of nectar from my flask, quickly refocusing my attention on the task at hand.

After processing five of the largest hogs, my bucket is already full. Climbing down from the bucket and onto the backhoe, I reposition the bucket over the freezer, and begin strategically packing meat into the frost-lined container.

Once my bucket is unloaded, I visually confirm having gotten off to a good start on filling the freezer. Already nearing one-third full, I pause to calculate a single-trip packing strategy for harvesting all of the remaining hog meat.

Validating my packing strategy, I reposition the backhoe, and hurriedly get back to butchering the remaining hogs. After placing the last ham into my now completely full freezer, I wrestle the lid closed and secure the lock. Breathing a huge sigh of relief; all that needs done now is to dig a deep hole and bury the carcasses.

Jumping back into the control-seat of the backhoe, I prepare to execute a quick burial of the remains. If all goes well, it won't be long before I'm headed for home, with a heavily loaded freezer suspended in front of me.

Skimming the surface of where I plan to entomb the carcasses, several-inches of sloppy muck are removed, before eventually reaching a thick layer of rich, black topsoil. Resulting from centuries of being fertilized by cattle grazing in the area, the composition of the soil looks to be simply outstanding! Quickly resurveying the area in front of me; I resume the dig, by plunging my bucket deep into the earth.

Upon reaching a depth of nearly six feet, I strike a dense layer of clay. The clay appears to be mixed with rocks and other debris, which quickly bogs down the hydraulics of my backhoe. Depressing the clutch a split-second before killing the engine, I decide to stop and survey the status of my dig.

71

Looking out at a large mound of backfill, it appears the pit I've dug will be sufficiently deep enough to effectively bury all the bones, and waste trimmings. After picking-up and disposing of all-but-one of the carcasses into the mass gravesite, I can't quite reach the last corpse with my tractor in its current position.

Instead of re-positioning my backhoe, I decide to hop-off my tractor and save time, by manually tossing the last remaining scraps into the pit by hand. While disposing of the last remnants from the kill, my left foot slips in the mud, causing me to take several quick, off-balanced steps backwards. With every attempt to regain balance ultimately failing, I land squarely on my back against a heaping mound of mud-laden earth.

Lying motionless for a moment, trying to collect my wits on what has just happened, a sharp pain begins emanating from my left shoulder. I soon find myself thinking: "Whatever I've landed on, it is certainly not a forgiving object."

Reaching around to see what's making my shoulder feel as if it's just been dislocated, I grasp what feels like a large, wooden mass. Turning around to identify the object of unknown origin, I see a thick wooden artifact with man-made carvings protruding from the mud.

Numerous thoughts begin racing through my mind, including: "Who buried this thing? Why had the object been hidden here? And, most importantly, what could it be?!"

Removing clumps of mud and dirt away by hand, my pace of digging rapidly increases the moment I discover bits of gold-inlay on the artifact in front me!

Clearing as much of the loose dirt away as possible, I expose the first-half of the massive wooden object. It appears to be a lavishly engraved yoke, once used to support a rather-large bell; a bell, that I suspect still lies buried in layers of mud yet-to-be stripped away!

Exposing letters carved into the wooden object, I'm eventually able to spell out: "NEP" With additional letters still waiting to be unearthed, the suspense is killing me. I suddenly feel as if I'm playing the game 'Wheel of Fortune;' speculating the remaining letters may eventually spell out "Neptune," once fully exposed. With wild-anticipation, I can hardly contain my thoughts, as to the importance of my find.

Knowing it will require an excessive amount of time to successfully unearth the entire object by hand, I momentarily contemplate using power equipment to assist in the dig; but decide against taking any action, that might inflict further-damage to the artifact.

With sunset quickly approaching, and knowing my prize waiting to be unearthed isn't going anywhere, I hurry back home to research the importance of the soon-to-be exhumed object. If I've solved the puzzle correctly, by properly interpreting 'Neptune' as the name found on the bell's yoke, the provenance of the piece could tell volumes about my ancestry.

I've always had the suspicion, that my Grandpa B was the infamous Captain Bartholomew; a highly successful Pirate famous for his escapades in the Caribbean, during the same timeframe as Grandpa B's swashbuckling career.

Speeding through the labyrinth as quickly as my backhoe will take me, the trip back home is a bit bumpier than expected. With a glance at my watch, rounding the last corner heading into the homestretch, I realize darkness will soon be settling into the Valley.

Pulling my tractor up next to the house, I put the vehicle into neutral and shut the motor off, before slowly relaxing back in the driver's seat. Gazing up in wonderment at the soon-to-be star filled Universe; I watch intently, as the last rays of sunlight disappear from the uppermost-atmosphere.

The absence of cloud cover this evening allows me to focus in on the blackness of space, and the countless constellations shining ever-so-brightly. Watching a pair of shooting stars chase each other across the sky, my mind starts to race upon analyzing the significance of my recent discovery.

The sound of a beaver slapping his tail in the distance, instantly brings me back to my senses. As if suddenly picking up a strong radio signal in my head, my brain begins broadcasting instructions to get-off the tractor. Gently setting the freezer down onto my garage floor, I slip down-off the tractor, and hurriedly plug the freezer into a more stable electrical current.

Entering the house, I instruct my newly-installed, virtual assistant computer program; named 'SHEILA,' to "Activate." The voice recognition software works beautifully, as I rattle out the command: "Please give me all information available on the 'Neptune,' a ship suspected of being in operation at the turn of the 18th century." With only a momentary delay, the results of my query are ready.

SHEILA begins disclosing the facts I've requested, stating: "The Neptune was a heavily loaded Spanish treasure galleon bound for Spain. It is reported to have fallen victim to Pirates on February 9th, 1722 under the flag of Captain Bartholomew." Continuing on, SHEILA reveals that "Captain Bartholomew was later killed the next day, on February 10th during the heat of battle. His crew wrapped his dead body in chains, throwing it overboard to deprive their inevitable captors, the honor of being able to display Captain Bartholomew's head as a trophy."

I find myself laughing, as pieces of the puzzle seemingly all come together at once. If the yolk I've found actually came from the Neptune; then, it would prove Grandpa B had successfully faked his own death, to escape the watchful-eye of vigilantism.

My entire life, I've suspected Grandpa B as having been the notorious Captain Bartholomew; but I'd always discounted the theory, due to historical reports of Captain Bartholomew's "death" in battle. It was obvious from his journal he'd once been a Pirate Captain, but I could never prove Grandpa B was; in fact, the most successful Pirate to ever set sail on the high seas.

Laughter fades into silence, upon suddenly realizing the significance of my find lying back at the dig site. With my heart racing in anticipation, I ponder what treasures might be found from last treasure ship Grandpa B is reported to have plundered? Better yet, how many other ship's treasures might I find; being he successfully raided over four-hundred ships, during his career as a buccaneer?!

The aroma of fresh deer chili prepared the night before has been tantalizing my senses since walking-in the door. As the grandfather clock in the study chimes the hour of six, I'm reminded its dinner time. Reaching the commissary, I immediately grab Grandpa B's oversized ceramic bowl, and serving ladle.

Both the bowl, and serving ladle happen to be two-more of the acclaimed eight-pieces of pottery; which Grandpa B is said to have designed and hand-crafted, using our kiln in the basement. The uniquely-designed ladle makes it easy to strain the broth away; allowing me to quickly fill the bowl with the meatiest portion of the chili. The steam rising from the cooling concoction tries offering a subtle hint for me to slow down, but it's too late. The spoon has already conveyed the first-ounce of chili, past my awaiting teeth.

Closing my mouth like a trap door, my pursed lips peel every last trace of chili from the spoon, as I remove it from my mouth. The moment I begin chewing the succulent tender bits of venison and savory kidney beans, my lips start burning with an intensity of a raging fire; a fire that'll soon engulf my entire digestive tract, if I don't drink something quickly to stop the burn.

Reaching for my flask of raspberry ale, the first gulp of sweet nectar immediately extinguishes the inferno in my mouth, like a burnt match-head being tossed into a glass of water. As the cooling ale travels down my throat, I can feel it quickly nullifying the intense burning sensation growing in my gut.

Unfortunately, from past experience; I know once the Ale gets absorbed into my small intestine, it will regretfully leave my colon vulnerable to the scorching after-burn of the chili peppers. I will certainly experience gastric distress later, for eating the chili; but I don't care! The chili is simply awesome!!

Quickly polishing off the chili, I soon find myself scraping up the last remnants of savory broth from the bottom of the bowl. With my belly stuffed full of food and ale, a siesta is sounding better-and-better with each passing minute.

Relaxing back in the chair, I expect to close my eyes only momentarily; but end-up falling asleep for several-long hours. During the countless vivid-dreams that ensue, nearly every treasure hunting scenario I could possibly encounter over the next 24-hours, plays out in my subconscious mind.

Chapter 8

~A New Twist~

Like the finest Swiss timepiece, my internal alarm clock goes off exactly one-minute ahead of the 4:20 a.m. wake-up call, that SHEILA always likes to provide me with each morning.

Squinting through bloodshot eyes at my diamond encrusted wristwatch, synced to go-off as a precautionary back-up alarm, the glowing-gold numerals draw my stare. Anxiously observing the second-hand advancing slower than a snail's pace towards the next sparkling gemstone, I find myself unable to wait in suspense any longer for the imminent alarms.

Once again denying SHEILA the somewhat twisted pleasure she seems to get in coming up with innovative ways of waking me up each morning, I wearily announce: "I'm awake, cancel the alarm; and please, reset my wake-up call for the same time tomorrow morning."

SHEILA responds in a clearly disappointed tone, "You would've loved the John Phillips Sousa march I was getting ready to play for you. Why do you always rely on that outdated watch, when I can easily provide you the exact time upon request?"

With my eyes fighting to stay open, I respond somewhat gruffly at first: "My analog watch serves its purpose just fine; besides, using it always brings back fond memories."

The Rolex was given to me as a 'Thank You' gift by President R, after the fall of the Berlin wall. Ronnie was certainly grateful for facilitating an environment where he and Mikhail could work out their differences, without any political pressure.

As far as President G goes; well…, let's just say he was exceedingly grateful to get away from the watchful eye of the Kremlin for a few days; reported by the media as being "off on a fishing trip, somewhere high-up in the mountains of Georgia."

Reminiscing about how perfectly my secretly arranged meeting of the two men unfolded back in 1989, I can't help but wonder what might have happened, had the crappies not been biting as-well-as they did that day, so many years ago;...let me explain:

I'd taken it upon myself during the peak of spring spawning season, to invite both Ronnie, and Mikhail for an unforgettable weekend of giant slab-crappie fishing; without either President knowing who their fishing partner would be, until arriving dockside.

By sequestering the once politically-portrayed enemies together in a small rowboat for hours-on-end, they were able to enjoy an unbelievable platform for private discussion. Landing fish-after-fish in the boat, until it was literally about to sink from the added weight of their catch, the two World leaders worked out their differences, and quickly became good friends.

What a fish fry we enjoyed that evening! I must say Ronnie really surprised me, by keeping up with Mikhail mug-for-mug on the Raspberry Ale. Between the two-of-them alone, they finished off an entire keg, by offering-up relentless, back-to-back salutes towards 'A New Era in Friendship.'

Mikhail admitted to me later, that they were actually engaged in an 'unofficial' drinking competition; trying to see who could get the other to pass-out drunk first. When the keg ran out, they ended-up calling it a 'Draw.' It was truly a sight to behold watching them support each other arm-in-arm down the hallway, singing "God Bless America" in off-pitch harmony, while slowly staggering back to their assigned suites.

It took several-months for Mikhail to facilitate an environment of change within his government; but, on November 9th of that same year, Mikhail's government eventually reached a peaceful resolve, allowing the Berlin wall to come down without any further bloodshed.

Suddenly realizing I've slipped off into another dream, I re-open my weary eyes. With an enduring blank stare at my sparkling watch, I ponder the thought of how many more diamonds and jewels I might be looking at by the end-of-day. Time feels like it's standing still, until yet another minute quietly slips away.

Coming to the realization, I must have fallen asleep at the computer last night, my butt remains firmly planted in a swivel chair that's beginning to shift slowly-away from the computer desk. Discovering my face to be literally-infused within several keys of the keyboard, I allow my body to remain momentarily slouched over in a rather-contorted position.

While my mind is awake, I let my body revert back to 'snooze' mode for a little-while longer. As the right side of my body begins tingling from the return of blood flow to my upper extremities, I finally start to feel the watchband strapped to my wrist. Eventually able to move my hand, I slowly lean my arm against the desk to steady myself.

Once I've pried my face from the grid of the keyboard, I deliberately shift my feet in search of the floor, trying to regain a sense of stability. The instant bare toes make contact, with the insanely-cold marble tile, my once weary eyes instantly bulge wide-open.

Slowly attempting to orientate myself within the dimly lit study,

I find myself gazing momentarily-perplexed at my reflection in a nearby mirror. A chuckle comes over me, upon noticing several crater-like imprints etched into the left-side of my face. With the palm of my hand, I slowly attempt to massage-out the checkerboard pattern from my cheek.

Experiencing a bit of navigational difficulty from my newly-found legs, after making the decision to rise, I begin heading towards the kitchen with unwavering conviction. The tantalizing scent of deer chili catches my nose, triggering intense hunger pains deep-within my gut; but the primary goal of my mission remains unwavering.

Turning the lights on upon entering our galley, I find myself temporarily blinded by the intense glare radiating off the stainless-steel jungle in front of me. It's a rather large kitchen, that's proven numerous times to be the perfect-sized facility, in meeting all our culinary demands during the Annual Winter Solstice festivities.

Realizing my ceramic coffee kettle is regrettably still downstairs, I tear apart the pantry looking for the rarely-used 'Instabrew' coffee machine. After finding the backup device stashed away behind some pots and pans, I fumble to separate a single coffee filter from the newly-opened pack. Eventually separating a filter from the bundle; I carefully place it into the machine, and begin dumping-in generous amounts of freshly-ground java.

Providing myself with a special treat, I've decided to break into my 'Special Stash' of coffee; gifted to me a few-years back, by a former high-ranking official from Venezuela. After initiating the brewing process, impatience has me removing the coffee pot, well before the machine's filter has had enough time to purge all its liquid content. As each tardy drop exits the filter, they sizzle and evaporate instantly; falling in ever-diminishing frequency, onto the scorching-hot burner plate.

Half-hour chimes begin resonating from the grandfather clock; reminding me with each strike, why I've decided to get up at such an ungodly hour.

Anticipation of soon unearthing treasure fuels my energy level, strengthening my resolve to return and exhume the wooden artifact. Having no idea how long it will be, before returning home with prize in-hand, I decide to quickly prepare myself a hearty breakfast.

Tossing butter in the skillet, along with a handful of shredded morels, I stir occasionally until the mushrooms are properly glazed. Quickly cracking three jumbo-sized eggs into a separate bowl before adding them to the mix, I toss in ample amounts of crisp apple-smoked bacon, finely-chopped ham; and then top it off, with a fist-full of finely shredded cheddar cheese. Within minutes, I'm sliding a sizzling-hot omelet out of the pan, and onto my dinner plate; which now looks a bit undersized for the portions placed upon it.

Devouring my omelet in near-record time; I slip on my hunting clothes, and quickly head downstairs to the garage. After reading a note from Fast Eddie, letting me know he's delivered the excavator back to the dig site as requested, I eagerly hop onto my ATV to take-off on another fun-filled adventure.

Laying heavily into the throttle, I release the clutch; causing mud and gravel to fly everywhere. Spinning freely at first, my tires soon gain traction; launching me like a bat out-of-hell on my way back to the Corral.

The heavily rutted pathway created by my mud-running adventure the night before, makes for an interesting obstacle course. Each time my front tires cross over a rut, they spin freely for a moment, before gripping into a more-solid area of the pathway.

Navigating through the flooded pathways, I swerve from left-to-right; and then back again, trying to see how many fishtails can be performed within each new rut. As my studded tires suddenly grab hold of solid earth, it immediately launches me forward at a much-higher velocity.

Making my way into the gauntlet, the mass of interwoven tree branches overhead reminds me of a commercial fishing net; heavily laden with its bountiful-catch of stars in the early morning sky. It doesn't take long, before lights from distant galaxies begin slipping through the net; eventually fading into obscurity, with the relentless approach of dawn.

Having left the Corral gate wide-open last night to save time in getting back to the dig site, I fly past the massive iron structure. Moments later, I'm quickly throttling down, while skidding sideways for the last few-yards of my journey; coming to a complete stop alongside the hole, where the artifact awaits my shovel.

Hastily climbing off the ATV, I can see the panther has visited multiple-times during the night. Its tracks are everywhere! For nearly a dozen-feet around the outer edge of where the hog carcasses lie buried, the ground is matted-down solid with panther tracks. The cat must've circled the pit a thousand-times; appearing to have approached the area from multiple angles, while searching for its stolen feast.

My attempt to keep wildlife from getting at the carcasses has been successful, but the telltale stench of rotting flesh lets me know I've neglected to bury them deep enough. Knowing the noxious odor will inevitably continue to worsen, I get ready to add more soil over the gravesite; hoping to avoid repeated bouts of gagging, throughout my day of treasure hunting.

The backhoe fires up the moment I push the starter button, sending thick-black plumes of smoke high into the air. Smoke from the stack quickly dissipates, as the engine begins purring like a kitten.

Scraping topsoil from areas to my left, I deposit additional dirt over the carcasses, until the putrid stench of decaying flesh is no longer detectable. I then turn my attention to confirming the bell's provenance.

With a pick in one hand and a brush in the other, I begin peeling away clumps of mud and gravel. Fully exposing a "T" and then a "U," my confidence in soon unearthing an "N" grows proportionately with my level of excitement. Feeling my heart pounding in my chest, I dig carefully; trying not to inflict any damage to the artifact.

Uncovering the first part of an "N," I disappointingly discover the bottom half of the letter has been damaged by the backhoe. The tooth of my bucket evidently gouged-out a deep chunk from the wood. With the yolk already damaged; and having enough of the artifact exposed to get a chain wrapped around it, I decide to use the backhoe in expediting its removal from the mud.

Wrapping the chain around the yolk, I hop into the operator's seat to begin the slow process of pulling it free from the muck. With tension mounting on the chain, the earth reluctantly relinquishes its grasp on the wooden artifact. Ever-so-slowly, it begins to move.

Once the yolk is fully exhumed, I set it down and hop-off the backhoe. Taking my knife from its sheath, I begin scraping away cakes of mud from the intricately carved wooden object, eventually confirming the last letter to be an "E!"

Falling back against the mound of dirt and clay, a wild sense of realization and intense anticipation instantly envelops my entire body. Amazed to have just visually confirmed the artifact as being from the 'Neptune,' the magnitude of my discovery is truly overwhelming! Reaching into my pocket, I pull out my flask and take a long, celebratory swig of raspberry ale to give Odin his due praise.

I'd hoped the bell would still be attached to the yolk upon pulling it free of the mud, but the bell is nowhere to be found. Had the bell detached from the yolk, upon first disturbing it with my backhoe? Is there more treasure to be found buried alongside the yolk? Questions relentlessly start racing through my mind.

Wanting to make sure no further damage occurs to any of the artifacts waiting to be found, I proceed to meticulously sift through each shovel-full of soil. After searching for over an hour, and finding nothing, I eventually shift my attention to digging deeper in the area where the yolk was removed.

Mother Nature reminds me time is quickly ticking away, as the shadow from Sasquatch Mountain suddenly leaves me standing in the shade. Exploring alternative ways to expedite the digging process, I begin using my backhoe to more quickly excavate the site; intending to resume digging by hand, the moment any treasure is discovered.

Plunging my bucket into the bottom of the pit for the first time since the yolk was removed, I immediately hit something hard; causing my hydraulics to bog down, and quickly killing the engine. Immediately returning to my original plan of conducting the dig by hand, I place a ladder in the hole, and hurriedly descend into the pit.

Hopping off the last rung of the ladder, my boots sink deep into quicksand-like muck, until eventually landing on something solid. No longer sinking any further, my adrenalin skyrockets as I begin digging ferociously by hand; trying to confirm the provenance of the object I'm standing on. Within a few minutes, I've uncovered a four-square-inch surface area, of a much-larger metal object. Seemingly forever later, I've unearthed enough to positively-identify it as being a ship's bell.

Still not having found any clues to confirm its provenance, I begin stripping away the last cakes of clay-like mud. Soon uncovering engravings in the metal using my knife to dig into the crevices, I trace out an "E," and then a "P" in lettering synonymous to the era. Minutes later, I officially validate the bell as being from the Neptune.

What a great time to celebrate, I think to myself; taking another long swig from my flask to give Odin his due praise. Sitting in the bottom of the pit, looking up at the bell in amazement; thoughts of how Grandpa B managed to get the bell here, have me wondering: "If he was able to bring a heavy bell like this into the Valley, just how much additional treasure might there be nearby?"

Suddenly remembering the words of Leland Henry Janssen, in which he stated, "The Captain and crew were said to have made numerous trips to lighten the load of their ship prior to the captain's demise," I get excited! Hopefully I've found the very spot, where Grandpa B buried all his treasure; but my gut's telling me, he wouldn't have hidden his entire 'retirement fund' in one-single location.

Reality sets-in, upon realizing I'm about to embark on a treasure hunt of a lifetime; or one that might actually take a lifetime, to discover all the treasure Grandpa B has hidden throughout the Valley. "First things first," I say to myself, mentally preparing to find the first cache of treasure buried somewhere beneath my mud-laden boots.

A chill raises every hair on my arm, as I contemplate a journal entry found earlier mentioning "Honey Holes to dig over." Looking down at the earth, I instinctively know I'll be once again scouring through Grandpa B's journal tonight; trying to find additional clues, that might help in locating the bulk of his buried treasure.

Deciding to not lift the bell out of the hole just yet, I begin scraping away mud with my trowel; one-quarter inch at a time. Eventually removing over a foot of soil from the bottom of the pit, the bell now sits completely unearthed. Still not having found even the slightest hint of treasure, my confidence in finding the 'Mother Load' begins to wane.

Wanting to have the bell out of the hole before calling it a night, I decide to expedite the removal process. With the backhoe's hydraulics struggling to lift the heavy object, I slowly raise the bell out of the hole; setting it down onto an old wooden pallet, which starts to crackle and pop from the weight suddenly placed upon it.

After repositioning the chains through the pallet and around the bell, I lift my prize high in the air and head for home. Having plenty of time to think while making my way back to the house, I begin reviewing my treasure hunting options. It doesn't take long to come up with a plan of action, for returning in the morning.

The strategy I come up with, is to dig down to a depth of at least six-feet; then outwards at least ten-feet from where the bell was exhumed. If there truly is any treasure to be found, it should certainly be located within these digging parameters.

Finding myself tossing and turning all night long, sleep is hard to come by. Up long before the sun, I head with resolve towards the dig site, as Mother Nature slowly begins adjusting her dimmer switch on the Eastern horizon. After visibility has been restored to objects freed once more from the veil of darkness, I eventually reach my destination.

Resuming the archaeological dig immediately upon arrival, I carefully begin sifting through the pile of sand, that once supported the bell in the center of the pit. To my amazement, I quickly discover a meticulously carved meerschaum pipe!

Experiencing a sudden adrenaline rush, I continue digging deeper-and-deeper. Several minutes pass before finding myself

86

standing in waist-deep water, no-longer able to effectively remove any additional sand from the pit. Soaked to the bone, and quickly reaching the point of complete exhaustion, I reluctantly decide to postpone my search.

Pondering where the missing treasure might be located, I think to myself: "Surely, Grandpa B didn't just bury the bell, leaving a single-meerschaum pipe as a 'Clue' to follow! But, if he did; what relevance does the pipe have, in helping to locate his hidden treasure?" Only time will tell its true significance!

Chapter 9

~The Plot Thickens~

Sleep is nowhere to be found, as I gaze up at the plethora of stars shining brightly out my bedroom-ceiling's massive skylight; a twin-sister of the giant-portal window downstairs. In a flash, and then yet another, falling stars illuminate the skies. The celestial display is simply breathtaking, with clusters of meteorites occasionally passing through as many as several constellations, before eventually breaking-up in Earth's atmosphere.

A lone meteorite with a super-bright tail exhibits longevity deep into the horizon, causing me to prepare for imminent impact; a moment later, I find myself giving thanks to Odin for simply being able to make yet another wish. Distant galaxies beckoning my stare soon have me contemplating the magnitude of space, and the microscopic role we as humans play in the Universe.

Trying desperately to conduct a prolonged examination of the back of my eyelids, I eventually concede neither eye will remain closed for more than a few-minutes at a time. Abandoning all hope of falling asleep under the stars tonight, I reluctantly vacate the space beneath my down-filled comforter.

Migrating downstairs, as I regularly do when sleep is hard to come by upstairs, I'm hoping to relax and quickly nod-off in the comfort of the captain's chair. Laying my head down on the pillow, my last conscious thought before falling fast asleep is wondering what kind of dream-state adventure I'll be pulled from; once the first-beam of radiant sunshine comes pouring through the massive bay window in front of me.

Drifting off quickly, I slip into a vivid dream that has me swimming effortlessly through clouds. Silver linings swirl just beyond my grasp, while reaching out to catch them with each imaginary stroke. After completing several virtual laps around the Valley, I eventually settle back down to earth; when a thought-provoking theory, as to where Grandpa B may have hidden his many treasures, suddenly pops into my brain. No longer able to keep my eyes closed, I find myself staring out the window, trying to debunk my latest theory.

The premise of my theory focuses on a statement Grandpa B wrote, that "Every word and number I scribe hath truth and specific purpose." Could statements in his journal, originally perceived as 'Babbling Rhetoric,' actually be offering directions on how to find his treasure?

Already wide-awake by the time the first rays of the sun begin streaming through the multitude of windows before me, I take precaution to ensure remembering my dream-state revelation, by writing everything down onto yellow 'post-it' notes.

Continuing to document additional passages discovered in Grandpa B's journal, that might possibly harbor a clue in locating his treasure, at least a hundred post-it notes are soon plastered around the perimeter of the massive bay window.

I've experienced many 'Visions' through the looking glass, where areas of the Valley below mysteriously come into crystal-clear focus. Almost as if looking through a telescope, the smallest of features down on the Valley floor occasionally become magnified. A handful of times, I've actually been able to identify the exact location becoming magnified within the Valley.

My pulse quickens, as another plausible theory races through my mind; that being, 'Could each area becoming magnified through the looking glass, actually be a resting place for some of Grandpa B's treasure?' Wanting to test my theory, I head down to an area known for regularly becoming magnified through the looking glass.

Reaching the familiar spot, I immediately begin digging in the black sand with my backhoe. Within minutes my hydraulics bog down, as the bucket takes hold of a solid object beneath the surface. Retracting the bucket from the hole, I jump down from the operator's seat with shovel in hand, and feverishly begin digging.

With each shovel-full of sand I toss from my dig site, nearly half-as-much settles back into the hole. After digging relentlessly for nearly an hour, expectations are confirmed, when my shovel suddenly strikes hard into a solid object. My heart skips a beat, before instantly racing like a jackhammer.

It takes nearly three more hours, before I've completely unearthed another ship's bell; this one being much smaller than the Neptune's. Looking closely for a name on the bell to give provenance to my discovery, I'm able to decipher the name 'Samuel.'

Not having found any treasure around the Neptune's bell, my sixth-sense is telling me I won't be successful in finding any additional treasure around this bell either. Refusing to give up, I continue searching for treasure with hopeful, but somewhat-limited expectations. After digging several-feet around the perimeter of the bell, and nearly half as deep below the water table, I'm startled to discover another finely engraved meerschaum pipe buried in the deepest recess of the bell.

What could the significance of the pipes be? I highly doubt it to be mere 'Coincidence,' in discovering a meerschaum pipe at both locations where a bell has been unearthed! This calls for another intense review of Grandpa B's journal! For the next few days, I scour through Grandpa B's numerous entries, methodically analyzing every possible clue he might've left.

The perimeter of my bay window eventually begins looking like a thatched roof, with scores of post-it notes plastered everywhere in layer-after-layer of yellow, and red. Many fewer in number, the red notes specifically give reference to Treasure, Grandpa B's love of smoking, and any mention of "Bells."

As the sun comes up on the morning after finishing my in-depth review of Grandpa B's journal, I awake in the captain's chair looking around in awe at what I see. The number of clues is quite overwhelming, with the montage before my eyes resembling a thousand-piece jigsaw puzzle.

Beginning with a review of the red notes, I ponder the most relevant statements. The clue I suddenly find myself focusing-in on, references both Grandpa B's love for his pipe; along with a strange reference to 'bells,' which reads: "Each time the finger dictates where to place me seed in the ground, I smoke to a successful planting. Make no mistake; bells silenced by monks will ring once again, on days when time is right for harvest."

While sensing deep in my gut this statement holds deep significance, I find it hard to interpret its true meaning. With so many thoughts racing through my mind, compounded with the fact of still having scores of chores to do in preparing for the upcoming guest season, I'm starting to feel a bit overwhelmed.

Chapter 10

~Arrival of Guests~

With invitations already sent out for the upcoming guest season, I'm once again forced to put my treasure hunting pursuits on temporary 'hold.' For the next few months, all residents of the Valley will be busy executing their individually assigned tasks and duties; collectively ensuring superior service, and personalized accommodations are provided to each of our invited guests.

Our 'Prime Directive' issued centuries ago by Grandpa B dictates; that "Every guest, without exception is to be provided unprecedented service, privacy, and hospitality throughout their entire stay."

When guests arrive, they get to enjoy leaving all responsibilities of their 'Life in the Spotlight' behind. Rarely are they bound to a schedule, while visiting our secluded resort nestled high in the mountains; making it an extremely relaxing vacation, for those lucky enough to receive an invitation.

I find myself holding back laughter every time the media reports a World Leader as "participating in high-level talks at a particular Summit;" when they are actually here enjoying our hospitality.

With my first group of guests scheduled to arrive early tomorrow, I've been forced to shift into acquisition mode. Currently in final approach of arriving back home, I'm loaded down with all the supplies needed to accommodate their many special requests.

Landing my heavily laden Huey on the tarmac, residents rush up to quickly unload the massive amount of cargo. The long list of provisions I've been acquiring from various Ports of Call, will be used to feed and pamper our guests like 'Kings and Queens' during their visit; ironically, the first group of invitees this year actually includes two such guests holding said 'Title.'

A majority of the food served to our guests Is actually grown and raised onsite, helping to assure we provide the freshest meat, and produce imaginable; but inevitably, there are always a few culinary items requested by our guests that must be imported to the Valley. The list of requested items can be quite extensive, and sometimes highly-exotic. From the most expensive Beluga Caviar, to the finest-aged wines and liquors, no attainable request is to be denied.

Culinary items are not the only things guests ask us to provide. Every once-in-a-while, there are certain requests for 'Accommodations' that can be extremely difficult, and highly challenging to fulfill; like a request made last-year by a Saudi Prince. The prince had requested his entire harem, comprised of over two-dozen of the most beautiful women on earth, be flown in prior to his arrival. Instructions provided by the prince, were to have all his ladies settled in; ready to fulfill his every desire, during the long-awaited weekend retreat.

His delayed departure nearly two-weeks later, set a benchmark for being the 'Longest Non-permanent Guest Visit' on record. He was extremely grateful for being allowed to enjoy the unprecedented extended-stay. To show his gratitude, he actually offered select members of my staff choice of companions, from several ladies of his harem expressing a desire to stay here permanently.

With it already being a little after two-thirty in the afternoon when I arrive back home, the sun will undoubtedly be setting behind Sasquatch Mountain, well before the last of the provisions are finally unloaded. Supervising the unloading, I can see the long V-shaped shadow cast from the summit's peak beginning to pick up speed, in its daily-trek across the Valley floor below.

The shadow will eventually reach the far-end of the Valley around 4:20 pm., after it routinely dips its finger into Lake Odin. Grandpa B once decreed 4:20 p.m. as being the official time to celebrate sunset; reminding us to always give due praise to Odin, for providing yet another wonderful-day in Paradise.

With my trip taking a little over two hours longer than originally planned, the long, perilous journey in the enclosed cockpit of my chopper has left me gagging on my own stench for quite some time. Throughout my entire flight, I've been looking forward to enjoying a long-hot-steamy shower, as a reward for successfully completing my mission. Reaching the bathroom at the top of the spiral staircase, I toss my heavily-soiled clothes down a nearby laundry chute.

Simultaneously turning the ivory knobs of the 'Cold' and 'Hot' water, stopping precisely at the 'Noon' position, perfectly temperate 105-degree water begins cascading from a trio of over-sized ceramic shower heads. The shower feature was designed and engineered by Grandpa B to provide a deluge of water from all angles; similar to riding out a hurricane, while standing on-deck at the ship's wheel.

Stepping in quickly, the pummeling water immediately begins scouring the dirt and grime from my body. Once my fingertips resemble shriveled up prunes, I engage the 'Auto Shut-off' feature, and slowly step out of the steam-filled shower.

As the rhythm of raindrops falling onto the shower floor quickly subsides, a not-so-silent alarm suddenly announces the arrival of our guests, by blaring out the beginning of Kansas's iconic song 'Leftoverture.' Leaving cascading clouds of steam behind, I exit the bathroom and hurriedly race to get dressed.

Positioned to provide a clear view of passengers exiting their respective helicopters upon arrival, activated surveillance cameras begin broadcasting high-definition images across my bedroom's giant plasma TV. As planned, six guests have arrived on schedule for their weekend retreat and are now entering their awaiting limousines.

Moments after the first chauffeur presses the West gate's doorbell to announce the arrival of our guests, I broadcast "Welcome to Odin's Valley" over the speaker system. Opening the heavy iron gates via remote control, I wait for the second limo to continue passing through the already open gate, before instructing Sheila to deactivate all security measures along the route. Once arriving at the house, drivers are to park in predesignated parking areas.

It takes my guests several minutes to make their way through each habitat area, eventually arriving at the parking coordinates given earlier to each driver as an extra security protocol.

The first security protocol put into action, was giving both chauffeurs the code words "One and Done;" meaning, if they both stop to buzz the gate upon arrival, one or more of their guests has failed the retina scan secretly conducted upon entering the limousine.

Additional instructions were also given for drivers to park in an alternative parking area; if for any reason, either driver perceives a breach of security to be taking place. The alternate parking area was meticulously designed to offer a 'Totally Secure Zone' in protecting our guests; or conversely, arresting any intruders should our security ever become compromised.

Having 'State-of-the-Art' protection devices and protocols in place, has already proven once to be highly-effective in protecting our guest's privacy, as well as ensuring our Valley's secrecy to the outside

World. The occurrence happened back in 1922, when two undercover revenue agents posing as US Congressmen tried unsuccessfully to conduct a prohibition raid on our Valley.

At that time, President H could not express enough his deepest regret, and sincerest apologies; claiming the two men in his entourage had acted independently, trying to make a name for themselves during the prohibition era. Odin's revenge for breaking our 'Visitation Contract' unfortunately fell heavily on President H the following year, when he suffered a fatal heart attack.

During their journey through the Valley, arriving guests will have just enough light to clearly see the hunting areas most will be hunting from in the morning. Knowing the significant amount of wildlife, that they undoubtedly will see moving about in this last hour before sunset, I begin to chuckle.

I always enjoy watching guest reactions, when first time introductions are exchanged. Most visitors invited here to hunt for the first time react like giddy kindergartners, after being told areas they recently drove through will be their hunting playground for the next few-days.

In case our guest's long journey has left them overly parched, I pull an extra barrel of nectar from the wine cellar, and ready my support staff to provide the warmest of welcomes. Handing Mocha the key ring for the captain's quarters, and Roscoe the key ring to the galley, my entourage and I exit the elevator upon reaching the lower level. Walking with eager anticipation down the pathway to the parking area, I remind Roscoe not to drool all over the Queen like he did the last time.

As my first guest of 'Royal' acclaim is assisted out of the limousine by her chauffeur, Mocha presents the beautiful lady her set of keys, by patiently waiting for the Queen to remove the brass ring from her mouth. Once receiving the royal pat on the head, Mocha finally proceeds to chew the earned reward I'd slipped inside her cheek earlier.

While Roscoe is an excellent bird dog in his own right, the German Short-hair Pointer's attention span is short-lived, when it comes to remembering 'Royal Protocol.' He's already begun to chew his treat, before handing his keyring off to the next guest exiting the limo.

The intended recipient begins laughing, as he watches Roscoe performing a trick. Flinging his set of keys high in the air, Roscoe quickly takes a couple chews on his treat, before catching the key ring back in his mouth each time. Once he's finished consuming his intended reward, Roscoe gently offers the brass ring to the awaiting palm of the King. His Majesty pats Roscoe on the head, praising him for his jester-like performance, before graciously accepting the handkerchief I offer to wipe-off his now drool-filled hand.

After our remaining four-guests exit the second limousine, my entourage and I escort everyone into the house. Taking the elevator up to the main level, we soon enter our massive trophy room; adorned with the most-impressive mounts ever harvested throughout the Valley.

The eyes of my guests open wide like saucers, ogling over the unbelievable mass of each mount on display. There are White-tail deer, Bear, Wild Boar, and several enormous Elk adorning the walls; each mount being an 'Undeclared' World Record in its own right.

With the King gravitating towards a massive Elk hanging majestically across the room, he eventually reads the name proudly displayed on its engraved placard. Seeing his trophy for the first time, since harvesting the magnificent animal last-year, his Grace runs-up and gives the mounted elk a prolonged-hug.

I can tell he'd give anything to be able to announce to the World his accomplishment of being in the '500 club;' but, as it would undoubtedly bring unwanted attention to our Valley's superior genetic pool, we do not allow anyone to divulge their hunting success stories to the outside World.

Embracing the King in a hug that would melt butter, the Queen nibbles on her husband's ear, before whispering a proposition that immediately cures his momentary bought of depression. With a provocative wink, and jingle of the keys presented to her by Mocha, she gently coaxes her husband towards the suite meticulously prepared for them by Anne.

I remind the lovebirds their dinner will be served in a few short hours; and, that tomorrow's hunting itinerary will require everyone to be present by 6:15 a.m. for breakfast. His Majesty smiles in acknowledgment, before disappearing behind closed doors.

Here for an unforgettable bachelor party, my remaining four-guests have all made themselves comfortable in the adjacent lounge; where their bartender Megan, has been instructed to make them feel right at home.

Easily diverting their attention during the royal swooning, Megan announces she has a round of 'Blow Jobs' ready and waiting for them. Bailey's Irish Cream and Kahlua, topped with whipped cream; whoever invented the tasty concoction, along with the provocative fashion the shot is to be consumed, was a true genius.

Showing them how to consume the beverage, Megan is soon licking away the residual cream with the tip of her tongue; her moistened lips glistening from the overhead bar lights. After generously pouring several-rounds of various other concoctions, the gratuitous guests soon have Megan's tip jar filled to overflowing in appreciation of their fun-filled education in Mixology.

As the grandfather clock strikes six o'clock, wonderful aromas begin emanating from the kitchen; prompting me to announce with jubilation: "We will be having a special treat of freshly harvested fried Morels, personally prepared by Chef J to compliment the Fried Chicken you'll soon be enjoying."

"Fried Morels!?;" The bachelor of the group responds, "How did you manage to get fresh morels this time of the year?"

I answer with pride, "The Valley has an ecosystem that produces morels year-round in various areas of the Valley. Hundreds of pounds are harvested each year, and rarely do we find ourselves in short supply."

Just then, the door to the master suite creaks open. Sticking his head out, the King asks: "Did I hear you say Morels will be served?" Seeing me nod to confirm his inquiry, the King grins saying: "Oh how I've missed Chef J's morels! How soon will we be eating?"

I respond, "Mona will be serving your Majesty and the Queen in bed, with the first course arriving in just a few-short minutes."

Before I can finish my words, a hand slips out from behind the door. Taking hold of his Majesties tussled hair, the Queen slowly pulls her husband back into the room, responding in a sexy, sultry voice: "Please, give us a few moments to build up an appetite for dinner." As the door closes, you can literally hear a pin drop.

With heightened anticipation, everyone readies for the first course to be served; minutes later, doors to the kitchen open abruptly. My four remaining guests relax-back comfortably in their chairs, as two of the prettiest ladies in the Valley enter the room adorned in shear-silk togas. Each of the goddess-like creatures, a green-eyed blonde named

'Mona,' and a brown-eyed brunette named 'Grace,' carry in sliver platters loaded down with heaping piles of golden-fried Morels.

I quickly respond, "Dig in guys! This is just the first course. Your next course will consist of steamed asparagus drizzled with lemon juice, topped-off with fresh sauteed-garlic shrimp; so 'fresh,' they were literally swimming in the ocean this morning!"

Mona slips away towards the King's chamber, knocking once on the door before slipping inside with her tray-full of morels. Moments later, she quickly and quietly slips back into the kitchen to retrieve the remaining courses.

As Grace leans over to set the heavy platter down in front of her guests, the four men begin undressing her with their eyes. She glances momentarily at each of them with a sexy smile, before asking: "Which one of you would like to have first taste?" Three of the four men immediately raise their hands.

The fourth-member of the quartet, our bachelor, quickly sizes-up his competition before strategically raising both hands towards the ceiling. Grace flirts with each man, trying to decide who will be the first to savor the delectable morsels adorning her tray. Telling the lucky winner to close his eyes and open his mouth, she takes the first golden-morel and slips it past the bachelor's awaiting lips.

The other three guests are so engaged in waiting for their own taste, that no one notices Mona slipping back into the King's chamber with the remaining dinner courses. The lingering aroma of fried chicken, from Mona's brief pass through the room, has Grace's enchanted guests looking like puppy dogs waiting for their next treat.

Grace's pager goes off, letting her know the remaining courses for her guests are ready. As she slips into the kitchen to retrieve her food, the bachelor and his friends are left to contemplate, what each will say to capture Grace's favor upon her return.

Light floods in, as Grace re-enters from the kitchen. Hurriedly setting down the overloaded tray onto the nearest table, she stretches in relief from the lightened load. With Grace's sensuous figure silhouetted through the shear fabric of her toga, little is left to the imagination. Appetites quickly escalate, as the bachelor party begins consuming food from her platter, in what can only be described as a 'Free-for-All' feast.

All four guests eventually relax back on their barstools, each with Buda-like stomachs filled to capacity. Bidding everyone good night, I announce: "I'll see everyone in the lounge tomorrow morning bright and early. Sleep well and enjoy yourselves fellas!"

As I exit the room, Grace winks at me saying, "Don't worry, I'll take good care of them!"

Reaching the study, I sit back in the captain's chair, gazing out at the giant full moon sitting directly overhead in the night sky. My attention eventually shifts to looking out across the moon-lit Valley floor below; wondering what treasures I might've discovered by now, if guests had not-yet arrived?

My eyes wander continuously back and forth, trying desperately to envision where Grandpa B's treasure lies buried. After taking a giant gulp of nectar from my mug, I set the captain's chair in its most laid-back position, to begin the meticulous process of re-analyzing every-last excerpt from Grandpa B's journal.

Reviewing the hundreds of passages I've found, that might provide any sort of clue in helping to locate Grandpa B's treasure, the massive amount of data has my mind in a whirl. Before I know it, gravity is once again pulling down on my eyelids.

Chapter 11

~Life is but a Dream~

Awakening like clockwork as the first rays of sunlight begin pouring through the massive bay window in front of me, I begin scanning the room in a near-transcendental state. Slowly inhaling the crisp morning air, through my nose till my lungs are filled; then exhaling-out with slow-steady precision, every muscle of my body is totally relaxed.

Several minutes pass, before starting to sense something in the room isn't quite right. Slowly turning my head to the left, watching prisms of light shift and refract all around me, my entire body suddenly becomes rigidly tense.

Experiencing both horror and disbelief, I find myself staring at Grandpa B's ceramic mug hanging precariously upside-down from the uppermost antler-tine of the captain's chair. With each rhythmic pass of the oscillating fan, the priceless mug rocks back-and-forth; threatening to crash to the floor at any given moment.

Better judgment has me resisting the urge to reach out and quickly secure the family heirloom; for my right-hand has not yet regained full-dexterity from having slept on it wonky all night. The tingling in my fingertips intensifies; reaching the point of being painful, as blood circulation slowly returns to my appendages.

A feeling of intense remorse envelops me, upon gut-wretchedly discovering the unconsumed contents of my mug, spilled everywhere across the surface of the looking-glass below. "Perfectly good nectar wasted" is all I can think, as my parched throat nurtures a festering regret for its loss.

Grandpa B's journal sits across my stomach; opened to the last page I must have been reading, upon falling asleep in the chair last night. With sunlight illuminating the manuscript, I attempt putting relevance to an obscure passage found on the page before me.

From past experience, I've come to the realization that every entry in Grandpa B's journal has some degree of relevance, no matter how vague the inscription may appear to be. Choking back the urge to laugh, as I slowly re-read the following passage that's caught my attention, it states: "Minutes and seconds past Non shall forever put revelation to dates of conquest I celebrate each year. Be vigilant to keep clear visions from the looking glass, for Mother Nature will one-day give up her virginity to the finger, which tickles her bosom at precisely the right-moment in time."

Grandpa B loved to include provocative statements like these in his journal; but, as I slowly pull myself out of the chair and look down at the floor, all I can think once again is: "What a waste of good nectar!"

Using my shirt as a rag in an attempt to restore clarity, it quickly becomes apparent visions through the looking glass are extremely cloudy this morning. With the grout around the edge of our portal window having softened into mud, my soiled garment does nothing but smear the looking glass with increasing regularity.

Not yet willing to concede defeat, I reach into a nearby drawer for a handful of washcloths to assist in my cleaning efforts. Using a wide circular motion, similar to putting wax on a car, I become obsessed in restoring the window's clarity.

Just as I start to worry about weakening the integrity of the mortar, that's held the looking glass securely in place for over two-centuries, interesting etchings begin to emerge from within the window's framework.

With rapidly increasing furor, I continue wiping away the softening mud, that's been secretly hiding the engraved message for countless-years. When my arms can scrub no more, I relax back in the captain's chair to take a well-earned rest.

A bead of sweat begins trickling down my brow, as I take a break to contemplate the potential magnitude of my find. Laid out before me are thirteen numerical sequences; clues hidden centuries ago under the thick layer of grout by Grandpa B.

"These clues have to be the key to breaking Grandpa B's code," I think to myself; but initial observations are telling me, it will take a considerable amount of research to figure out the true significance of each numerical sequence. With thoughts racing through my mind like a runaway stampede; the eerie silence is broken, when our grandfather clock begins chiming the hour of 6:00 a.m.

The first resounding hourly chime brings me instantly-back to my senses. Before the second chime can strike, I've instinctively vacated the captain's chair; heading towards the elevator with intense conviction.

Guests will soon be arriving in the banquet hall, each expecting to be served a 'Breakfast Feast' of legendary proportion. Wanting to make sure my staff is fully prepared; I pick up the elevator phone and call down to the kitchen. Gleefully answering the phone, "Hello!" Chef J assures me everything is ready. My stomach starts to rumble, in anticipation of soon filling my belly with her legendary 'Breakfast Duck Casserole.'

Immediately mobile once the elevator door opens to let me off on the main floor, I quickly make my way towards the banquet hall; the whole-way there, relentlessly pondering the significance of the numerical-engravings, now photographically etched into my brain.

Having spent countless hours researching Grandpa B's journal, about his many escapades throughout the Caribbean; as well as studying other well-known Pirates in operation during the same timeframe as Grandpa B, an in-depth search through my memories produces a promising observation.

For twelve of the thirteen numerical-sequences uncovered, I believe the last eight-numbers in each sequence might actually correspond with dates in history, where a treasure ship was reported to have been successfully raided on the high seas. Still unclear is the significance of the first four-numbers found in each of these twelve sequences. All I can hope is to one-day experience an epiphany, that instantly provides the key to solving Grandpa B's treasure map.

Remembering the thirteenth sequence to be "04201222," the clue is only eight-numbers long and follows no recognizable pattern. With its prominent location in the upper-most area of the window's frame, I'm convinced the 'Anomaly Clue' holds major significance in solving Grandpa B's coded message.

Taking a shortcut to reach the banquet hall, I slip into the room just in time to see his Majesty, and the Queen making their way through the main entrance. Expecting the Royal couple to be traditionally late, they surprise me by being the first to arrive. My four-remaining guests enter the room shortly thereafter; each appearing a bit disheveled from the 'Master's Degree' in Mixology, they apparently earned last night.

The banquet tables are filled with steaming-hot chaffing dishes full of meats, eggs, and an assortment of breads; all waiting to be swarmed upon, by our ravenous guests. After giving thanks to Odin, the Queen is politely offered 'First Dibs' on filling her plate. A chuckle comes over me, upon watching our remaining guests drooling like hungry dogs; each patiently waiting for their own first-taste of the meticulously-assembled smorgasbord.

With the utmost grace, the Queen delectably samples a ruby-red strawberry. Chewing ever so slowly at first, it doesn't take long before she's voraciously filling her plate. Taking a clue from her sudden indulgence, the remaining guests follow suit by converging on the banquet table, like a pack of lions around a fresh kill.

Once everyone finishes-up several minutes later, appetites for food are quickly replaced with appetites for adventure. Entering the room, carrying-in a large serving platter loaded with several personalized scrolls, Mona announces; that each document assigns a specific hunting-stand, to its designated recipient.

One-by-one Mona hands out the stand assignments, wishing each hunter "Good Luck" upon delivery. After her platter is empty, she quickly slips out of the room, leaving behind an alluring-trail of her intoxicating perfume.

As if on cue, guests begin breaking the seal on their personalized scrolls, to discover which stand location each person will be hunting from. With a resounding "Whooo Hooooo" echoing throughout the hall, like a great-horned owl calling out in the dark of night, the King celebrates having been assigned the stand location he desired most.

His Majesty will be hunting from one of the tallest Ash trees found within the labyrinth; the same location he harvested his 'Unofficial' World Record elk from, the last time he was here. The protected platform offers luxury in the treetops, providing a bird's-eye view with near-total concealment.

The strategically-placed stand sits located within thirty-yards of an area in the labyrinth, that was widened decades-ago by my father; so that modern farm machinery could gain access to fertile-tracts of land within the labyrinth. Because the opening also provides wildlife easy access to major food sources, the area routinely provides hunters with extremely heavy deer, and elk traffic.

As the other guests reveal their stand placements, one-by-one, stories of past experiences are reviewed for each location. Current and expected wind directions are discussed, along with recently collected trail-camera footage of wildlife movements throughout each assigned area. After the last stand placement has been analyzed, everyone is eager to get out in the field.

Over the intercom, Mona captures the attention of our guests once again, by announcing in her best 'Stewardess' sounding voice: "Shuttles will be ready for departure in exactly fifteen-minutes. Escorts will drop each hunter off at their assigned stand. Once your feet hit the ground, escorts will continue onward without stopping, thus minimizing the risk of wildlife becoming aware of your presence. Good luck once again to each of you!"

With bellies full, and anticipation at a climax; everyone readies for the hunt by checking their weapons, and making sure all gear is packed and ready. Slipping each hunter a small flask of raspberry ale, I issue final instructions before departure; stating, "Always wait for celebration until your kill has been confirmed. Most importantly, never forget to offer praise to Odin, before-and-after pulling the trigger."

The King remarks: "May Odin get due praise from everyone! With any luck, I'll be radioing for assistance in packing out a trophy bull, well before being able to fully digest this wonderful meal." He then heads outside to board his awaiting quad-runner, along with the other guests who hurriedly follow suit. As everyone speeds-off towards their own designated hunting area, my thoughts immediately turn to the etchings discovered earlier.

Expecting to have a couple-hours before hunters might need assistance out in the field, I rush back to the captain's chair to reaffirm, and analyze the significance of the first four-numbers found in each of the twelve similar etchings. With several theories racing through my mind as to what the numbers might represent, only time will tell if one of my theories proves treasure worthy.

Entering my study, I head directly for the bump-out window. Immediately jumping into the captain's chair with heightened expectations, I suddenly find myself utterly dumbfounded.

Expecting to see scores of numbers screaming out clues to my brain, I'm flabbergasted to find nothing in front of me, but a fully-grouted window frame! Not a blasted Thing!!??...Nada!...
...Nunka!!...Zilch!!!..??

Shaking my head, I fully expect to see numeric etchings suddenly re-appear before my eyes. After opening and closing my eyes several-times in quick succession, the framework of the window continues to give no indication of numbers ever having been present! Worse yet, the grout around the edge of the window appears to have never been disturbed!?

Extremely puzzled, I think to myself, "Could I have dreamt, what I know I saw?" It was all so real; so real in fact, I can still feel the soreness in my arms and shoulders, from having relentlessly scrubbed to clear the glass.

Not willing to believe what my eyes are telling me, I grab several towels from an earlier-raided drawer. "Anne must have refilled the drawer" I think to myself, while reaching for my rescued mug sitting safely on the bar. Slowly removing the mug-full of ale from the counter, I hesitate momentarily; once again stopping to consider if I might've actually been dreaming, when I 'supposedly' found the etchings?!

Based on remembering specific details about the hidden etchings found earlier, my gut's telling me the numbers should still be there! Without further hesitation, I pour the entire contents of my mug across the window, hoping to quickly confirm the presence of hidden numbers under the thickly-grouted window frame.

It becomes readily apparent that centuries old grout does not easily soften. After attempting nearly every method for removing grout, short of using a sledgehammer, I've barely begun to scratch the surface of the window frame. Nearly exhausted, I refill my mug; only to empty it once again, by sloshing ale everywhere across the surface of the glass, in an experiment fueled by frustration.

Extremely upset at myself, for having spent the entire morning believing my dream to be real, I begin speculating on the amount of ale it would've actually taken to soften the grout. Even if my incredibly 'believable' experience had been a dream, it clearly would've required pouring much-more ale across the window to significantly soften the grout.

With my eyes contradicting what my brain is trying to tell me, my thoughts turn to questioning, "What if the sequences of numbers are actually still there? Could my inner-psyche be trying to tell me something?" Questions begin racing through my mind faster than my brain can comprehend, before suddenly coming to the abrupt realization: "What does it matter? It was only a dream!...right?!?"

Storming out of the room, I head deliberately in the direction of the helipad to clear my head. Flying the Huey always puts me in a mindset, where I can analyze my thoughts in meticulous detail. While rarely flying across the valley during times when guests are out in the field, I find myself totally consumed in disbelief over the disappearance of the etchings. Hopping into the Huey, my brain tries desperately to wrap itself around the reality of the numbers no-longer being present; if they were actually ever there in the first place!

Before I can close the door to the cockpit, a rifle shot resounds from somewhere down in the Valley; followed quickly by two-more piercing reports in short succession. The first shot left me listening, while the second, and third reports allow me to pinpoint the general direction of the last two-shots.

With rifle reports continuing to echo about the canyon walls as I fire up the chopper, I'd be willing to bet the King has missed his quarry. Hooking my seat belt, I rev-up the motor and prepare for takeoff; unsurprisingly, the very moment my chopper starts to lift from the tarmac, my satellite phone begins vibrating.

Once airborne, I fumble to answer the phone that's been buzzing uncontrollably at my feet since lift-off. Trying to catch it as it dances across the cockpit floor, I eventually get a solid grasp on the slippery little device. Expecting to hear a plea for assistance in tracking down a wounded animal, I answer the phone with an energetic: "Hello your Majesty! So…how many points was he?!"

The King responds, "He was an 8x8, but now he's an 8x7! After my first shot took his G2 tine off, like a hot knife through warm butter, the second and third shots dropped the magnificent animal in its tracks!" Requesting assistance to help pack out his trophy, the King announces: "My bull lies dead approximately twenty-yards South of the entrance into Lambeau Field. Please send someone to assist."

We call the recently harvested cornfield 'Lambeau Field;' because, with all the head butting going on between massive bull elk vying for breeding rights during the rut, it often sounds similar to a pro-football game in overtime begin played there.

Confirming the location where he's dropped his Elk, I suddenly realize the King would've had to make an amazing three-hundred-yard kill shot! With wind gusts I'm currently experiencing ranging between 20-30 knots, I respond over the radio: "You must have made one hell of a shot!" Before the King can respond, I inform him: "I'm within two-minutes of your kill. With the corn out, I'll be able to land practically alongside your bull. We'll be able to hoist him up and out, without having to mobilize a recovery team."

"With the route I'll need to take in reaching my trophy on foot, it'll take me a bit longer than two-minutes to get there. Any way I can catch a lift?" the King responds.

"Have you in sight...I'll drop you a lifeline in the clearing to your right...Let me know when you're hooked up" I respond. Immediately pulling back hard on the yolk to slow-up the chopper, I execute an abrupt hovering pattern over the King's arranged extraction point, and quickly toss a rope down to his Majesty.

Seeing he's hooked up by the thumbs up signal being given, I fully-engage the winch, immediately reeling him in at near break-neck speed. Coming to a sudden halt upon reaching the open door of the chopper, I graciously reach-out to assist his Majesty into the Huey.

Grinning from ear-to-ear, I suspect he's either bagged another record book trophy; or he's simply experiencing a ride-induced seizure. Once the King lets out his unmistakable victory war cry, I instinctively know another highly prized piece of real estate on our 'Hall of Trophies' has just been taken off the market.

The King begins babbling like a baby, trying desperately to

111

speak the words that'll confirm my suspicions. Eventually stopping to take a deep breath, he slowly enunciates the words: "My first shot took off nearly ten inches of antler... If deductions don't rape my expectations, the bull should still score well-over five-hundred points!"

By the time he finishes his words, I've already landed the helicopter in the freshly cut cornfield. Quickly powering down the chopper, I unhook my seatbelt and prepare to help the King retrieve his trophy. The King is obviously overly excited; because, before my blades start to wind down even slightly, he's already exited the chopper! Signaling me to hurry and catch-up with the camera, he takes-off on a sprint!

Watching him jump over cornstalks like an Olympic hurdler, he races to claim his magnificent bull. Running as fast as possible to catch up with the King, my mission is to photograph the proud-moment he arrives to claim his trophy.

Upon reaching the massive animal, his Majesty positions himself squarely between the antlers, smiling for the camera in a truly majestic pose. Immediately after the flash, he pulls out his royal measuring tape to begin scoring the animal. By the time every last inch of the bull's rack is documented, the series of numbers on the paper tally up to an amazing green score of 509!

"Sad to think it would've scored nearly 519, if I hadn't shot part of his G2 tine off with my first shot," the King replies. Shaking off the momentary sadness, he begins looking forward to his second induction into our prestigious '500' club.

Acknowledging his superior marksmanship, I say to the King: "Tell me about how you spotted the bull; and I've got to ask…What went through your mind in calculating that awesome, long-range kill shot?!"

The King takes the opportunity to rehearse his hunting story for the Annual 'Roast' being held at tonight's banquet; where he is sure to bend everyone's ear, by saying: "I was watching the V-shaped shadow from Morel Mountain progressing slowly towards me. Glancing down at my watch, the moment the shadow reached the base of my tree stand, I remember it being precisely two-minutes past the hour of eight. It was at that very moment, I looked up and noticed sunlight glinting off the bull's rack. Confirming the bull's presence through my scope, I quickly calculated the distance, and fired my first shot.

Observing my bullet take off the tip of his antler nearly three-feet directly above its intended mark, I re-adjusted the crosshairs, and fired two additional rounds. Before the bull could shake off the shock of my first bullet severing the tine from its majestic crown, I quickly ended his reign as 'King of the Forest,' by placing two final-rounds through his vitals."

Congratulating the King once again, I go on to say: "That was a hell of a shot you made! Let's get him out of here. Chef J has prepared barbecued elk for hunters coming-in for lunch; which is ready and waiting for us in the banquet hall. After your bull's hooked up and we're ready to go, you can follow me back on your ATV."

As the King finishes securing his trophy below my hovering chopper, using a thick hemp rope attached to my landing gear, I get ready to extract the massive elk. The motor of my Huey strains upon first trying to lift the heavy animal off the ground; but, once the beast is safely suspended in the air, I'm quickly heading back to the house with trophy in tow.

Arriving back at the landing pad, I perform several unsuccessful attempts at laying the elk down gently onto the tarmac. Each time I try setting the massive animal down without damaging its antlers, a strong gust of wind comes up; forcing me to ascend, re-position, and

113

repeatedly wait for my fragile cargo to stop swinging.

The moment I finally get the majestic beast laid-to-rest unscathed on the tarmac, the King races up to the landing area on his ATV to proudly claim his trophy. Acknowledging the successful delivery, I give the King a respectful salute as he un-tethers his prize.

Several residents of the Valley rush-up to help safely carry the majestic animal off the tarmac, and load it into an awaiting hummer for transport. It will take several months to complete the mounting process; but given the animals green score of 509, the record-class bull will undoubtedly be granted prominent placement within our 'Hall of Trophies.'

Bidding the King's pardon, I apologize for not be able to join him for lunch, due to unexpected 'Business matters' requiring my immediate attention down in the Valley. "Raspberry Ale will certainly be flowing tonight in celebration of your triumphant accomplishment," I say to the King; while hurriedly stepping off the tarmac, to commandeer his already warmed up ATV.

Feeling somewhat guilty for the ruse, I tear-off; heading directly towards my favorite spot to relax and shed stress. Getting his Majesty's precious trophy home in one piece has left my nerves a bit frazzled. Hoping to rejuvenate my mind; the plan is to meditate in the warm sunshine, until my next call for assistance comes-in over the radio.

From an elevated position several-meters across, a massive slab of limestone rock is calling my name. Having been polished to a mirror-smooth surface from the gentle touch of water and time, the outcropping of rock sits directly below my house; a stone's throw to the left, of where the waterfall cascades into the black-sanded lagoon below. My favorite place to relax; Grandpa B befittingly named this wonderful geological feature, the 'Meditation Stone.'

After arriving at the base of the cliff, I shut the ATV off and quickly begin climbing the steep, moss-covered steps. Determined to reach the elevated plateau beckoning my presence, it takes only a few seconds to scale the last three meters. Already warmed up nicely by the early morning sun, I soon find myself stretched out comfortably across the smooth rock surface.

Assuming my favorite yoga position, I dare not stay on my back for any extended-period of time. Thanks to the magnification effects of the waterfall, the sun's rays can turn you into a crispy critter very quickly. Only having an hour of time before the Queen has requested use of the Meditation stone, my contingency plan if no calls come in, is to enjoy every-relaxing minute possible until her arrival.

With the Queen suffering from what Grandpa B termed 'Indoor Complexion Syndrome;' or 'ICS,' a condition caused from spending too much time indoors during daylight hours, I dare not forget to politely remind her Majesty about needing to use sunblock, while sunbathing on the Meditation Stone.

We once had a South American dictator here, taking time away from the 'All-Seeing Eye' of his Cartel for a few-days. Confident in having a sufficient base tan, he decided to take a short siesta without requesting a wake-up call. Three-hours later, the overly-baked dictator awoke from dreamland, to an agonizing case of extreme sunburn.

Luckily, we had enough herbal healing salve on hand from Odin's Garden to effectively treat his ailments. Immediately taking the edge off the pain, the medicinal ointment aided in healing his 2nd degree burns; significantly reducing what should have been weeks of recovery time, into a few-short days.

Hearing a distant bark from Mandy, sounding as if she's telling me to 'Turn Over,' I flop onto my stomach. Rolling back to a supine position minutes later, my impersonation of being a hotdog on a rotisserie causes me to chuckle.

Resuming my yoga breathing exercises, Mandy can suddenly be heard baying relentlessly from several-hundred yards down in the Valley; obviously on the trail of another raccoon. For a short while her bays are in perfect sync with my breathing, resounding each time I exhale; but as Mandy closes in on her quarry, her vocalization pattern quickens.

Getting closer-and-closer to where I'm positioned, I lift my head to look in the direction of her last bay. Catching brief glimpses of a masked bandit scurrying along the base of the cliff, it disappears into a hole down below, about thirty yards to my right.

Mandy's bone chilling bays immediately change into muffled droning sounds, the moment she enters the hole in hot-pursuit of her quarry. As minutes tick away, her droning howls considerably diminish in volume.

Sitting upright on the plateau straining to listen for Mandy's next bark, I suddenly hear a barely audible, high-pitched "Yelp!" Silence ensues momentarily, before instinctively vacating the Meditation Stone to go check on her. Fearing she might be in need of assistance, I quickly make my way down the slippery-rock pathway, towards the hole she disappeared into earlier.

Reaching the narrow cave opening at the base of the canyon wall, I listen for any clue as to how far Mandy may have ventured inside. Sticking my head and shoulders into the hole, I can see the tunnel quickly widens into a much-larger cave, about two body-lengths ahead.

Yelling "Come!" at the top of my lungs, I try providing Mandy a clue, as to which direction she should head in finding her way out. Waiting nervously for a response and hearing nothing, I pray to Odin for Mandy to hear me; bellowing out once again, "COME!!" Straining to listen for the slightest clue on her disposition, I suddenly hear a barely-audible, extremely-long and drawn-out howl.

Perpetuating my worst fear, that my dog is lost somewhere deep within the cave, it sounds as if Mandy is calling-out for me to come rescue her. With explicit words flowing from my mouth like a raging river, I realize the only option at this point is to initiate a rescue mission. Refusing to grasp the concept, of possibly never getting to see my dog leaping up to catch a Frisbee in mid-air again, I enter the opening.

I've been spelunking thousands of times throughout the hundreds of narrow caves found on this end of the Valley, and fitting through tight places certainly has never bothered me. What concerns me at this moment, is having no idea how old the batteries are in the emergency flashlight I grabbed off the ATV.

Snapping a limb off a nearby tree to clear a pathway through the mass of spiderwebs in front of me, I crawl head-first into the opening. Soon reaching an area inside the cave allowing me to walk upright, my eyes continuously scan the ground ahead; desperately looking for any sign of a track to lead the way. What I eventually see up ahead gives me serious pause, as there appears to be several tunnels branching-off in all directions.

Thankfully, a lone dog track can be seen leading into the far-right tunnel. Had I not found the faint clue on the predominately solid-rock floor of the cave, it would've been near impossible to determine which tunnel to take; especially, with no-longer hearing any more howls coming from Mandy.

Proceeding ahead cautiously for approximately twenty or thirty yards, I stop and strain my ears for even the slightest clue on Mandy's disposition. What I end up hearing is a series of scuffling noises getting louder, and louder with each passing second.

"Mandy must be making her way back," I think to myself. Turning my flashlight off, I crouch down in a corner; patiently waiting to scare the hell out of her, the moment she goes to pass by.

With random splashes, and the clickity-clack of claws tapping on the rock floor getting closer and closer, it sounds as if Mandy is just about to round the bend a few-yards ahead. The moment it sounds as if she's right in front of me, I let out a yell that shakes the walls of the cave.

Turning the light back on, expecting to see Mandy cowering with eyes the size of softballs; I instead, find myself staring down at an extremely pissed-off raccoon, coming at me with a mouth-full of razor sharp, gnashing teeth.

Yelling at the top of my lungs, trying desperately to thwart its attempt at taking a bite out of my ass, I step aside just in time to watch the critter run past me. Knowing how vicious a raccoon can be when threatened, I instinctively flee further into the tunnel, putting as much distance as possible, between me and the rabid-like animal.

It seems like an eternity before I finally stop running, suddenly realizing I've dropped my flashlight somewhere in the darkness behind me. Extremely lucky to have thus far avoided hitting my head on one of the many stalactites found within the cave, I wait impatiently for my eyes to slowly adjust themselves to the near-total darkness.

A faint-glow ahead beckons me to continue spelunking on further. Making my way hand-over-hand at first, the dim light ahead keeps getting brighter-and-brighter, with each passing yard. With the ever-brightening light ahead looking as if I'm about to reach the earth's surface, my slow-shuffling steps turn into an accelerating trot.

Rounding the last corner I dash triumphantly into the light, expecting to see a glorious blue sky overhead; but instead, find myself standing perplexed and confused?! Staring out at a giant subterranean cavern, the pathway ahead leads directly down to a huge bonfire burning brightly like the sun. Throughout the center of a seemingly endless abyss, the flames nearly reach the ceiling of the cavern.

I suddenly begin sweating profusely; but, not because of the intense heat emanating from the mass of glowing embers below.

With extreme horror, I suddenly realize the bonfire is not a traditional fire; but instead, the flames appear to be a woven mass of burning bodies, all writhing in perpetual agony. As the lava-like mass of bodies quickly starts flowing in my direction, I scream like a newborn baby taking its first breath; running back into the tunnel as fast as my legs will carry me.

Weaving around stalagmites, and dodging under stalactites, the flow of burning bodies pursuing me appears to be losing the race! With fewer and fewer balls of flame hitting my backside, I start believing I'm out of effective throwing range, until yet another wild pitch deals a scorching blow across my neck and shoulders.

The light in the tunnel dims proportionately to the distance being put between myself, and the flow of burning bodies. Taking a quick glance backwards, I regretfully confirm countless burning souls continue to remain demonically motivated in their 'Hot' pursuit of me.

Looking back ahead into the darkening tunnel, I squint in disbelief at what appears to be a dead-end fast approaching. Quickly slowing my forward momentum, I frantically begin looking around for an escape route.

For a split second, I consider the option of engaging in a counterattack; but instincts for self-preservation tell me doing so would be suicide. Turning around to consider my options for escape, I suddenly see three doors of stone positioned side-by-side at the very end of the tunnel! Staring in horror at the demonic flow closing in fast, I disappointingly realize there are no marks or clues visible to help in choosing which of the three doors I should open.

As the light gets brighter-and-brighter with each passing moment, I suddenly see a distinctive shadow being cast from a large stalactite behind me. Interpreting the 'Sign' as being Odin's answer to my recent prayer, the point of the shadow rests squarely on the middle door.

Grabbing hold of the designated door, I strain with every-ounce of my being to break the hard-to-open seal. With an audible release of suction, the door flings wide-open; releasing a wall of water, that immediately envelops my body in a raging tidal wave. As Class-five rapids tumble me head-over-heels backwards into masses of extinguishing souls, I eventually get knocked-out cold from the 'One-Two' combination punch of excruciating pain, and lack of oxygen.

Awaking untold-minutes later, I find myself lying sprawled out in a shallow pool of water at the base of the waterfall. Staring up at a deep-blue sky with water cascading across my legs, I come to the realization I must have fallen asleep on the Meditation Stone, and somehow managed to survive the perilous plunge down the steep embankment. With my body bruised, tattered, and extremely sunburned, I slowly inspect myself for any broken bones.

Getting to my feet, I glance at my Rolex the very moment time advances to the next gemstone. Looking down at exactly one-minute and twenty-seconds past noon, the V-shaped shadow of Sasquatch Mountain is pointing directly at my feet. A few moments later, I stand completely blanketed in shadow.

Instantly becoming numb to the pain emanating from my severely-sunburned backside, I experience an epiphany related to a recent statement made by the King. I knew there had to be a reason I experienced a sudden chill through my body, when he stated "the V-shaped shadow from Sasquatch Mountain was pointing to the base of his tree stand, at precisely two-minutes past the hour of eight!"

Could the spot on the valley floor, where the V-shaped shadow points to at any given moment in time, possibly be the key to finding Grandpa B's hidden treasure? My mind begins embracing the notion, that the first four-digits of each numerical sequence might actually refer to exact 'Minutes and Seconds' past the hour of Noon.

My theory fits perfectly with the transcript I'd awoken to find earlier in Grandpa B's journal, reciting the words from memory: "Minutes and Seconds past Non shall forever put revelation to dates of conquest I celebrate each year. Be vigilant in keeping clear visions from the captain's chair, for Mother Nature will one-day surrender her virginity, to the finger tickling her bosom at precisely the right-moment in time."

Might the shadow be what tickles Mother Nature's bosom, at a 'specific-time,' on a 'given-day' of each year? The sun's shadow changing latitude with celestial precision each day, would be the perfect-way to pinpoint the exact location of each ship's buried treasure!

Could 'Minutes and Seconds past Noon' really provide a location on the Valley floor, where Grandpa B buried his treasure? The shadow is certainly long and pointed enough to resemble a finger! If my suspicions are correct, Grandpa B certainly didn't believe in using a 'Traditional' treasure map!

121

Thinking to myself "It all fits together perfectly like a puzzle," I suddenly realize a major flaw in my highly plausible theory. The numerical sequences engraved in the window frame were unfortunately all part of a 'Dream;' or, were they? With my dream seeming so realistic, I start hopelessly believing the engravings might actually exist under the grouted edge of the window frame!

Chapter 12

~After the Banquet~

Making my way back to the parking garage after tending livestock down in Skunk Den Hollow, an unexpected deluge of rain forces me to pull my ATV over and wait for the slow-moving frontal system to pass. Nearly an hour later, Mother Nature eventually allows me to resume my journey home.

Witnessing a rare, full-double rainbow stretching clear across both sides of the valley, I take off with water flying everywhere. The moment my motor starts to bog down in the soup-like mud, I crank back hard on the throttle; nearly spraining my wrist trying to keep the engine from stalling out.

Roaring back to life, the ATV begins fishtailing back-and-forth; ironically, in perfect sync to my favorite song 'Burning down the House' blaring at full-volume through my earbuds. Once the studded tires finally start grabbing hold of solid ground, my destination quickly draws near.

Downshifting hard, I find myself skidding sideways for the last several-yards of my journey; coming to a complete stop, just before crashing into a newly installed "Packers Fan Parking Only" sign. Obviously placed in front of our house by my football-fanatic Father, the sign can mean only one thing…The Bears must've lost to the Packers; a game I recently wagered my favorite parking space on.

Initially pretending not to see the sign, I eventually decide it would be in my best 'future interest' to acknowledge Dad's rightful claim. Not wanting to take a chance on becoming a recipient of my Father's genetic disposition to wrathful vengeance, I humbly relocate my ATV a few-yards to the right of the sign.

Planting my feet into ankle deep mud, I head deliberately towards our home's ever-inviting 'Welcome Home' sign; a ceramic sign that's hung proudly from my home's lower-level entranceway for centuries. The sign was recently authenticated as being the 'Seventh' piece of pottery discovered, out of eight-unique pieces Grandpa B reportedly hand-crafted centuries ago, using the enormous kiln he custom-installed down in our basement's cellar.

Having welcomed home my family for centuries, we finally ascertained the sign's provenance a mere six-months ago. It happened while Anne was sitting at the kitchen table, looking at a picture she'd taken of the sign. Suddenly able to visualize Grandpa B's 3-D hologram 'Signature' in the photograph, my ears are still ringing from the moment she first realized the provenance of the piece.

Like a kid on Halloween being treated to a basketful of giant-sized chocolate bars, Anne began screaming and pointing at the "Welcome Home" sign in the picture. Not being able to enunciate a single word in her fit of jubilation, all she could do was repeatedly babble, "B...b..b..b..beeEEE!!..."

Eventually visualizing the letter "B" in the photograph, I immediately became infected with my wife's euphoria. Now forever recognizable, it's hard to believe the subliminal signature "B" had never been noticed by anyone, until that very moment!

No one knows how Grandpa B's 'Signature' monogram managed to escape everyone's attention for centuries, but it did! The discovery was simply astonishing; putting shivers up and down my spine, that day of enlightenment earlier this year.

With my phone buzzing in my pocket like a pissed-off bumblebee, I enter my home's doorway fumbling to answer the call before being sent to voice mail. Performing a literal juggling act with the slippery little device, I eventually secure the phone in my groping, outstretched fingertips.

As I'm wrestling the captured phone up to my ear, I can already hear the King bellowing through the tiny little speaker, "So!…What's for dinner tonight?!!"

Without breaking stride, I quickly respond, "Crow, for everyone else but you!"

Lack of words soon gives way to roaring laughter, confirming the King clearly enjoys the 'First Taste' I've given him of what to expect during tonight's dinner banquet. His hunting success story will undoubtedly be celebrated by everyone, with countless toasts of raspberry ale being offered-up throughout the evening.

Knowing how she likes to surprise everyone coming back from their day afield with a 'Special' dish, it's anyone's guess as to what unforgettably-delicious 'Main Course' Chef J will be serving at tonight's dinner banquet. My mouth instinctively begins drooling like Pavlov's dog, the moment I begin thinking about the many dishes Chef J has 'wowed' us with over the years, during our Annual 'Toast to Success' feast.

The best part of the banquet is after everyone has finished enjoying their desert. This is when tradition demands all 'Successful' hunters are to be ceremoniously 'Roasted' for their hunting skills, by all the 'Not-so-successful' hunters of the group.

Grandpa B's reasoning for initiating the 'Roast,' as noted in his journal, states: "While it is encouraged to remove genetically inferior specimens from the Valley's Gene Pool, no Worldly hunter in his right mind will take an immature, healthy animal by choice; knowing their hunting ethics will repeatedly bear the brunt of scathing 'Roasts,' throughout the entire Toast to Success Feast."

Over the centuries, my family has found this 'Privilege of giving Roast' actually provides the unsuccessful hunter an honorable excuse for not filling one's quota; making it more desirable to wait for a trophy, rather than taking the first decent-sized animal that comes along. This Privilege has without question, directly contributed to most of the animals harvested each year being 'World Class Monsters.'

Preparing to end my conversation with the King, I remind him to "Please be on time when Chef J rings the bell to let everyone know her fabulous 'Soup de Jour' is ready." She's earned a reputation for being brutally unforgiving with guests; even refusing to serve those of the highest social status, when she feels her call-to-dinner has been disrespectfully ignored.

The twenty-seven-inch dinner bell, which Chef J loves to ring almost as much as she loves to cook, is documented as being the original prototype used in designing a much larger 'Sister' bell; better known as the infamous 'Liberty Bell.'

Chef J loves to ride the bell's pull rope up-and-down repeatedly, using it to call everyone inside to celebrate the latest gastric masterpiece she's created. The bell can be heard throughout the entire Valley; and, if you're not already sitting at the banquet table by the time she rings it for the last time, you'd better be heading there with the utmost sense of urgency.

Hunters arriving after Chef J has served her main course can expect to be ceremoniously chastised for being disrespectful. Punishment for being late without a valid excuse can be excessively harsh, with tardy guests usually offered only a limited number of entre' selections from Chef J's 'Short' menu.

While selections from her short menu are better tasting than most entrees served at four-star restaurants, it truly is a 'Punishment' to miss-out experiencing the orgasmic aromas that tantalize your senses; each time Chef J serves up a new course from her 'Full' menu.

I decide to double my bet with Dad, on Chef J serving 'Venison Loin Au Poivre' at tonight's dinner feast; doing so, because of having lost the last four-wagers, on which gastronomic masterpiece she'll be presenting next to our guests. Not having served it to us for many months, this amazing dish covered-and-smothered in rich Morel mushroom gravy is one of her favorite recipes to prepare, and one of my most-loved meals to chow-down on.

Having accepted my gambling addiction years ago, I never allow myself to make a bet with anyone else but my father; however, if I could find a bookie foolish enough to take my bet, I'd make a fortune wagering no one will be leaving the dinner table tonight with a less-than-completely overstuffed belly.

With guests currently taken care of, I attempt to confirm my premonition that 'Hidden Numbers' actually do exist beneath the thickly-grouted border of the looking glass. A glance at my watch tells me I have just under one-hour to test my theory, before being considered 'Late' for tonight's dinner celebration.

Jumping excitedly into the captain's chair, my eyes immediately begin scanning the lower-edge of the bay window; and, if my eyes aren't deceiving me, it looks as if the grout has begun to run slightly! The raspberry ale thrown earlier across the window frame in my fit of frustration, appears to have significantly softened the grout, but just how much of it has softened into removable mud is yet to be determined.

With a severe case of Déjà vu, I grab several towels from a nearby drawer, and start to clear away whatever I can of the softened grout. Very little is removed before realizing it'll take much more ale, and plenty of time for it to soften-up, if I ever hope to remove enough grout to expose all the hidden numbers.

Growing confidence tells me the sequences of numbers have to be present, concealed just beneath the hardened surface. With so many pieces of the puzzle fitting together in my dream, how could they not be there?!

Adding a considerable amount of additional ale across the window, I intend to let the grout soften overnight; hoping to be much more successful at removing the centuries-old plaster in the morning.

Refilling my mug one last time, I offer up a toast to Odin, praising him for the opportunity to soon be finding hidden clues in locating Grandpa B's treasure. Before I know it, the grandfather clock downstairs is giving me the 'Fifteen-minute Warning' for the start of tonight's banquet celebration. Leaving to let the sacrificed ale perform its magic on the grout, I head quickly down to the banquet hall in eager anticipation of seeing what dish is being served.

Upon entering the room, Chef J proudly announces her dinner entre'; moments later, Dad humbly returns half of my recent gambling losses, conceding gracefully with a firm handshake, and a significantly lighter coin purse.

Throughout the evening's festivities, my thoughts remain spellbound on what I'll find during my next visit to the captain's chair. Not wanting to forfeit any of my cognitive abilities, I refrain as much as I can from overindulging in the ale; but, with all the celebratory toasts to Odin being raised, I'm clearly not able to think coherently as the banquet nears end.

Finally able to leave without offending anyone, I slip out and instinctively head for the ever-inviting captain's chair. For reasons of health and safety, I carefully make my way up the stairs by means of crawling instead of walking; eventually reaching my destination in the wee hours of morning.

Awakening to find myself naked and basking in the sun with only my sandals on, I feel as if a second dose of radiation has just been applied to my recent sunburn. Instinctively knowing its well past sunrise, my heart starts racing upon realizing guests are probably in the banquet hall awaiting my arrival!

Without pause I dash out of the captain's chair, failing to first confirm whether-or-not the grout has softened any from last night's drowning of ale. Experiencing no hesitation as I make my way upstairs to get dressed, every ounce of my being knows the numbers have to be there. They've waited centuries to be found; consequently, I can certainly wait a few-hours more to expose them once again.

Clearing the last stair, I find Anne putting the final touches on another spotless cleaning of our Master bedroom. As my wife stands before me modeling her sexiest French-maid outfit, I reluctantly find myself hastily trying to change out of my birthday suit.

"Why did you let me sleep so long?... better yet... Why didn't you bring me a change of clothes, knowing my 'Willie' was pointing due East in the chair?" I say to my wife jokingly.

Anne replies with a befitting comeback, saying: "It'd been pointing towards Australia, when I first found you lying there this morning. You were so cute; looking like Cupid holding an arrow, with no bow in hand." She continues with a smile that would melt butter, saying: "I was going to wake you up, by offering to let you use my bow to hone your archery skills, but decided to come back upstairs first and clean up the mess you made."

Realizing the time for 'Target Practice' has long since passed, I respond: "While I sincerely appreciate your offer to give me archery lessons, I regretfully must quiver my broad-head arrow, and focus on damage control for my soon-to-be compromised record of flawless hospitality."

Anne replies, "No Worries! Everyone partied so hard last night, I doubt anyone will arrive at the banquet hall until well past noon. I'm sure your reputation is still intact." She then tosses me the pair of pants I've been looking for, saying: "The archery range is regrettably closed for repairs today anyway. You'd better hurry up and get dressed!"

With an air of disappointment in my voice, I say to Anne: "You do realize you won't be seeing me for the next few weeks. The peak of rut's coming into full swing, and Dad wants me to go with him on another 'Once in a Lifetime' expedition into the Eastern quadrant."

Anne smiles and says, "So what's new? I'm used to you disappearing into the woods this time of year; besides, after I'm done dropping-off the Royal Lovebirds, I'll be taking a detour of my own to the Riviera. You get to enjoy your hunting, and I get to enjoy a week of sunbathing with Mona and all her girlfriends."

Knowing how much Anne has been looking forward to her reunion with Mona's sorority of harem sisters, I say to her: "I'll miss you drawing my bath each night. Your friends will undoubtedly be enjoying the sensual baths you have a talent in preparing."

Anne smiles and responds, "I draw them the way I like them; besides, when I'm with Mona's sisters, I only have to draw one bath for everyone to enjoy!"

"Oh, how I'd love to be a seagull over that beach house," I

quietly ponder, while wrapping Anne in a warm embrace. Giving her a long passionate kiss, my reading glasses start to fog up. As our interlocked lips slowly separate, Anne gracefully slips away and is gone from the bedroom, before my glasses have any chance to clear.

Since the King has successfully filled his quota, he wishes to get back to pressing matters of his Realm. Anne will therefore be leaving to take the Royal couple home earlier than originally planned.

I on the other hand, won't be able to leave on my expedition with dad, until all the other guests have departed the airport later this afternoon. The moment the last chopper lifts off and is heading out of sight, we'll be taking off on another unforgettable mission into the Eastern quadrant.

Deer hunting in that part of the Valley is certainly not as dangerous as walking down the streets of Iran waving an American flag; but it can easily be compared to walking through a zoo, without any fences to protect oneself from predators higher on the food chain.

Grandpa B warns us numerous times in his journal, stating: "Dangers posed by the many snares I set in the Valley fail in comparison to the risk one takes when venturing beyond the labyrinth."

Very few people have ever been allowed to hunt this area throughout the centuries, for Grandpa B always promoted the Eastern quadrant as being 'Cursed.' While I've hunted it for many years, never suffering anything more than a scratch, I always find it a good practice to be packing some serious firepower when visiting the area.

I've encountered many species of wildlife while hunting there, several of which failed in their attempts to have me as their dinner. Each of these animals' heads hang prominently in the West wing of my house, serving as a constant reminder to never trust any life-form that feasts on the misfortune of others.

The labyrinth acts as a natural barrier; similar to how the Great Wall of China was once built by Emperor Qin, to keep the Mongolians out of his country. It helps keep the many exotic animals introduced by Grandpa B permanently sequestered on the far end of the Valley.

Native animals forced to survive alongside exotics higher on the food chain, have already begun to exhibit significant changes in their evolution; for example, the antlers of the native whitetail deer population in the Eastern quadrant have progressively increased in size each decade, since record keeping was first initiated centuries ago.

Grandpa B predicted this change would occur based on the premise; that deer with larger racks would survive longer, than those with inferior racks. Having more time to pass on their genetics, he surmised the deer's genetic code would allow for increased growth of progressively larger antlers, on average, throughout the herd.

Another of Grandpa B's many directives, specifically related to the Eastern quadrant beyond the labyrinth, includes letting natural selection run its course. In his journal, he mandates: "Only _one_ deer per year may be removed through human interaction." Honoring his decree, my father and I are the only two hunters who visit the area, limiting human exposure to a maximum stay of two-weeks; or one animal harvested each year between the two of us. Competition to be the first to harvest each year's targeted species sometimes gets interesting; to say the least.

Proving Grandpa B's theories on Natural Selection, by maintaining strict conservation protocols in the Eastern quadrant, the average antler mass for whitetails living in the quadrant has increased to well over 180-points typical this past decade, with many of the largest bucks exceeding the 230-point typical mark. Exactly four-years ago to-date, I actually harvested a magnificent non-typical specimen, breaking the once thought unobtainable 400-point barrier. Mind you, these are not Mule deer or Elk. These are true Whitetails, of the specie 'Odocoileus Virginianus!'

Just under two-decades ago, my father and I first introduced these superior genetics into the whitetail population on the West-side of the labyrinth. If you think it's hard to harvest a trophy whitetail, try capturing one and keeping it alive; long-enough to successfully relocate it into a much-less violent environment.

While we could pen raise bucks captured in the Eastern quadrant for introduction into our Western quadrant's breeding program, I prefer to release these magnificent animals back out into the wild. There is however one drawback to releasing them out into the wild on this-end of the Valley. Being free to roam and establish their own territories, they can potentially fall prey to a well-placed rifle bullet, that's been lethally air-mailed by one of our guests.

As I walk through the hall of trophies on my way to the kitchen, one such breeding stock animal harvested by the King proudly sits on display; unfortunately, there is no definitive way to tell how many does he was able to pass his genetics onto before being harvested. The monarch Buck obviously passed-on his genetics to more than a just a few does; for genetic tests have already confirmed several of his offspring to be roaming within the labyrinth area.

Reaching the banquet hall, I'm relieved to confirm my reputation for providing flawless hospitality remains untarnished, as Anne predicted; however, I'll need to get moving in the kitchen, if I ever hope to keep it that way. With Chef J having taken a few-days off for vacation before our Winter Solstice event, I've agreed to show-off my culinary skills, by preparing a farewell brunch for my guests about to return home.

I immediately begin preparing mounds of bacon, while searing up several pounds of perfectly seasoned breakfast steak. After loading up two chaffing dishes full of French toast and scrambled eggs, the pots and pans I've been rattling around in the kitchen appear to have effectively substituted for ringing Chef J's dinner bell. Tossing the last frying pan into the kitchen sink, my guests arrive in mass for brunch. With everyone jockeying for position to fill their plates, I'm confident my menu offerings will more than satisfy each guest's culinary expectations.

Once everyone is properly fed, I offer parting salutations, prompting guests to begin heading back upstairs to finish packing. With everyone leaving at the top of the hour, my plan is to immediately take off on my hunting trip, the moment our last guest departs the Valley.

Already being packed and ready, gives me a few short minutes to check on the results of my earlier ale test. With no time to waste, in my quest to confirm clues actually exist under the grout, I hurriedly make my way through the house. Racing around the last corner in route to the captain's chair, my feet hit a recently tanned bearskin rug; taking me on a slip-and-slide ride across the freshly-waxed, hardwood floor.

The last thing I remember before losing consciousness is seeing my feet tap dancing on the rotating ceiling fan. With the back of my head having been bounced across the floor like a basketball by the force of gravity, I cautiously take a few-moments of valuable time to regain a sense of composure.

Glancing at my Rolex, I quickly realize a precious two-minutes of my highly anticipated time for discovery has already been lost. Springing upright, I whip my head around to look in the direction of the portal window. To my excitement, the grout around the looking glass appears to have significantly softened.

Nearly ripping the drawer from the kitchen cabinet, I once again grab a handful of rags to begin removing the grout. It only takes a moment for the soupy paste once resembling concrete, to easily peel back in layers with each circular motion of my towel.

As my scrubbing makes its way deeper into the grout, my finger suddenly gets pricked from a noticeably raised edge. Instinctively shoving my injured finger into my mouth to relieve the pain, I stand in awe upon confirming my premonition to be true.

Resuming my scrubbing, a dozen numbers etched in the framework soon become visible, with many more digits predictably waiting to be discovered. Taking only a few-minutes more to expose the remainder of Grandpa B's etchings, I uncover nearly a gross of roughly carved numbers; all but one-series containing sequences of twelve-numbers as expected.

My watch's alarm chimes a warning, letting me know guests are already gathering on the landing pad expecting to receive a formal send-off. With a flurry of pen strokes, I hurriedly scribble down the mass of numbers onto paper, hoping to have plenty of time on my hunting trip to decipher their true meaning. After writing down the last sequence, I immediately make a beeline for the helipad.

Arriving on the tarmac to wish my guests a safe journey home, parting salutations are exchanged. Executing my last ceremonial task before their departure, I remind them to always remember, "What happens in Odin's Valley, remains in Odin's Valley."

Closing the door behind the last guest boarding the chopper, I pat three-times in succession on the exterior of the aircraft, letting the pilot know he's clear for lift off. As the blades of the Huey pick up speed, swirling gusts of wind nearly strip the camouflage hunting jacket from my back. Running for cover to avoid being further

135

sandblasted by loose dirt and gravel, I duck underneath the landing pad while waving goodbye to my departing guests.

Spellbound faces can be seen plastered against each window, taking in one last extended gaze. A select lucky-few may get invited to return; but for most departing guests, this will be their last-chance to marvel at the wonders of our Valley.

Chapter 13

~An Epic Day of Hunting~

Heading home after watching our last guests depart the Valley, my eardrums begin picking up the faint approach of an incoming chopper. Reaching the house, I hurriedly grab my survival gear from behind the front door; quickly stepping back outside with a fully-loaded sniper rifle strapped across my chest.

Like he used to do in Nam, Fast Eddie swoops in; throwing down a rope that lands perfectly uncoiled within inches of my feet. Tickling my boots, as if telling me to "Grab Hold," the rope dances back and forth; causing me to instinctively reach-out for the line.

Hovering dangerously close to the cliff wall with my father inside the chopper barking out orders, I suddenly realize the 'Voice' in my head telling me to "Grab hold of the rope" was actually Dad, now yelling down over the turbulence of the blades; saying, "Hook up… let's go!" The parody causes me to bust a gut laughing, which apparently is not appreciated at all by my over-impatient father.

In a bellowing voice that drowns out the chopper blades, sounding much like Leland Henry Jannssen when he first introduced himself over the roar of his Camaro, Dad shouts down instructions that resound throughout the quadrant; "I SAID, HOOK UP… OR BE LEFT BEHIND! 3!!...2!!...1!!!" Looking up, I can see by the stern expression on his camouflaged face, that he's not bluffing.

My father can be rather impatient, so his unwillingness to wait for me to make my way too the helipad a mere hundred yards away is no surprise. Realizing my only option at this point is to hook up and get ready for a wild ride, I warily place my life in the hands of a man fearlessly determined to charge fast-and-furious into the untamed-wilds of Mother Nature.

Each year during the peak of the rut, as if falling under the spell of a 'Voodoo Witch Doctor,' my father suffers from what I call 'Buck Fever Overload Syndrome.' The condition seems to worsen during the onset of 'No Shave November,' an Annual Ritual practiced for centuries by the men of our Valley to display their manliness and hunting prowess. With the tidal wave of testosterone being released by the already fully-bearded, lunatic-fringed elder above, I'm not surprised at what happens next.

Somewhere between Dad's countdown of "1" and "Zero," I announce my successful hook-up by attempting to give a 'thumbs up' signal; but before I can extend my thumb skyward, gravity has it flailing helplessly towards the horizon. Winching me up at near-breakneck speed, I can hear my father barking out orders; instructing Fast Eddie to immediately set course for the Eastern quadrant.

With my body resembling a rag doll being played with by a hyperactive child on an overindulgent sugar rush, a bit of Grandpa B's temper comes out; when I begin bellowing at decibel levels off the chart, "CUT THE CRAP!! … BRING ME ABOARD!!!!"

My ascent towards the chopper suddenly comes to an abrupt halt; as I continue to be carried along, narrowly missing scores of treetops throughout my ride. Pretending to have trouble with the winch, Dad allows me to dangle below the aircraft for nearly half-the-distance to my drop zone. After hearing profanities starting to flow from my mouth like a raging river, he graciously decides to finish reeling me aboard.

138

Moments later after making it back into the chopper, I sarcastically congratulate my father for picking the perfect opportunity to return a favor for his friend the King; whom I recently put through a similar 'Joy Ride.' Having been righteously humbled, I blurt out: "Paybacks can be a bitch, can't they?!!"

I can tell it's all my father can do, to keep from laughing his ass off. Desperately attempting to put his 'Serious' face on, Dad sternly announces: "Listen up; and listen up Good! The only reason I brought you aboard; instead of leaving your ass hanging all the way to the drop-off point, is to make sure you clearly understand your mission in 'MY' hunting trip this year!"

"Your hunting trip, what about mine?" I quickly interject!

Placing his hand on my shoulder with a firm look on his face, Dad responds: "Remember our bet, where you agreed to be the 'Dog' this year if you lost?... Well?!" ... Dad's piercing stare remains fixed upon me, until I eventually acknowledge him with a humble nod.

During final approach of dropping me off into the 'Birdhouse' stand, located a half-click West of Lake Odin's Southeastern shoreline, my Father provides me with the detailed rules of my 'Mission;' as governed by Grandpa B's 'Rules of Order.'

To secure my undivided attention, Pop grabs my chin with his strong, calloused fingers; and, in a stern eye-to-eye stare, issues the following instructions: "Regardless of your situation, at exactly 9:15 am., you are to leave your stand. You will then proceed by making a slow push towards me, approaching in a meandering zig-zag pattern. I expect 'Hiney' to attempt circling back around you, using the same 'Cloak of Invisibility' Bullwinkle recently used to escape past me along the water's edge. This should put Hiney directly in front of me." Easing his grip on my chin, my father summarizes by saying: "If all

139

goes as planned, shots will be ringing out a few-moments after you walk past me."

Choking back laughter from his reference to Bullwinkle using the 'Cloak of Invisibility,' I decide to give my Father one last dig, by asking him: "So… Pop…Why do you call the buck you're after Hiney?"

With a reluctant, yet humble expression, he eventually answers back: "Because, that's all I've ever seen of him. In every surveillance photo I have of the buck, he's always running away from the camera waving goodbye with his flared-tail sailing high in the air!"

Gut-wrenchingly laughing at this point, Fast Eddie instructs me to get ready for drop-off. Immediately hooking up to the rope, I ready for departure.

Keeping true to established 'Rules of Order' for this year's hunting mission, I attempt to salvage any hope of being able to fill this year's quota myself, by strategically questioning my Father: "I just want to confirm, the 'Ultimate Goal' of my mission is to get you 'Eye-to-Eye' with Hiney, regardless the situation I might find myself in at 9:15…Correct?" The moment my father nods in acknowledgment, I take advantage of a strategic 'loophole' in our gentleman's agreement.

Using a learned technique on gaining one's undivided attention, I firmly grasp my father's chin, stating with a devious grin across my face: "I have no problem being the 'Dog' that brings you eye-to-eye with Hiney!" Before Dad can crack a smile, I go on to say: "especially if I'm able to harvest him myself, before the 9:15 deadline!"

Without allowing time for a rebuttal, or getting a chance to see what I'm certain will be an epic facial expression, I perform a human microphone drop. Jumping headfirst out of the chopper, I once again find myself dangling precariously from a long, narrow rope.

140

During my final descent into the stand, Dad's explicative words from above can be clearly heard over the turbulence of the blades. Eventually yelling down to me "Good Luck" as my feet land firmly on the roof of the stand, I can already hear Dad bellowing out 'Orders' to Eddie from above: "Take off...Take off!!" With no time to spare, I hurriedly fumble to unhook myself.

Fast Eddie pays back a favor, by delaying an immediate response to Dad's orders; providing me an extremely valuable half-second longer to disconnect my lifeline. Luckily, it's all the time I need; for within a fraction-of-a-moment after getting the hook unlatched, the rope gets ripped from my hand by the departing aircraft.

My Father always likes to be dropped off directly into his stand, which sits along the Western shoreline of Lake Odin. It has all the comforts of home. Perched high in one of the largest Elm trees in the Eastern quadrant, the strategically placed stand offers a panoramic view of several major funnel areas; all of which conveniently converge into a rather-large open area, surrounded by extremely dense underbrush.

Unlike my father, who will wake up in the morning and simply slide open a window to start his day of hunting, I will be cautiously navigating through pitch-black darkness for nearly an hour to reach my deer stand. Positioned nearly a half-mile due West of my dad, my plan is to hunt along the upper rim of a small canyon leading all the way down to Lake Odin. What I like most about my stand, is how the brush-choked hillsides effectively funnel wildlife moving through the area into nearby kill zones.

Settling in for what will undoubtedly be a very short night, I finally get to sit down and review the treasure hunting clues, I wrote down earlier onto the tattered-piece of paper in my hand.

Analyzing each series of twelve-numbers with meticulous

scrutiny, a familiar pattern in the numbers suddenly warrants a much closer look. With all the research I've recently done on Grandpa B's days of Piracy, the last eight-numbers in each sequence appear to correspond perfectly with a specific day, month, and year; in which, Grandpa B is known to have successfully raided a treasure ship on the high seas.

The first four-numbers, if they truly represent the 'Minutes and Seconds past Noon' as I theorize them too, may soon divulge the exact location for each ship's treasure buried by Grandpa B. It all begins to make perfect sense, that Grandpa B would use the absolute precision of time and shadow to create an ever-enduring treasure map.

Before long, dusk arrives on what is expected to be a predominantly moonless night. With the sound of nocturnal animals becoming amplified in the growing darkness, I find it difficult to fall asleep. Curious to see what the weather will be like in the morning, I turn on the NOA weather radio, and listen intently.

The weather report calls for brief passing thunderstorms throughout the evening, with dense fog in the morning quickly dissipating after sunrise. A strong low-pressure system is then expected to usher in much colder temperatures to the area. A smile comes over my face as I start to nod off, knowing I'll be making my way to the stand virtually undetected in the morning, concealed by dense fog blanketing the entire Valley floor.

In what seems like only minutes after falling asleep, I'm rudely awakened from dreamland by a Supernova-like flash of lightning. The immense lightning bolt illuminates the night sky, as if it's the middle of the afternoon; instantly resounding in a deafening clap of thunder, that shakes the entire cabin for several-seconds.

Looking out the window to investigate the aftermath, I can see an ancient oak tree about thirty feet away has received a direct hit from the massive, mega-watt discharge. The deep wound inflicted on the tree smolders heavily for a moment, but is quickly extinguished by torrential rains that ensue.

Shredded strips of bark fly high in the air, viciously ripped from the tree by the fury of Mother Nature. As fragments surrender to the laws of gravity, they begin falling back to earth; literally pummeling my roof in a rhythmic-onslaught, sounding much-like a snare-drum cadence being played overhead. Listening to an extended, double-bass drum solo hammering away up in the heavens, I find myself staring blindly up at the ceiling in complete darkness; waiting for the next bolt of lightning to race across the sky.

Slowly proceeding to check the time on my Rolex, I wearily attempt to focus in on diamond encrusted numerals beckoning my stare. Clearing away sleep from my eyes, I confirm the time to be "4:19 am."

Being only moments away from the time I'd set my alarm to go off, I'm enlightened to the fact, that Mother Nature has just given me one of the most profound 'wake-up' calls of all time.

Pushing the button to deactivate my watch's alarm, I do so just as the buzzer begins emitting a faint vibration. Finding myself wide awake, I slide out of bed and quickly throw on my hunting gear. Glancing up at the stars, which now litter the night sky after the passing of the storm-front, I can see the rain has subsided for the foreseeable near-future.

Making my way outside, I head swiftly towards the area I'll be hunting from. Saturated leaves allow me to move silently along the forest floor, without disturbing any of the local wildlife. Reaching the base of my deer stand by 5:15 am, I take a moment to mentally prepare myself, before beginning my tactical ascent into the treetops.

With extreme stealth, I slowly make my way up the ladder; eventually slithering into my stand, like a snake nestling itself over a clutch of eggs. To my disgust, I soon realize it is not a clutch of eggs I've settled myself onto; but instead, I find my butt firmly planted in a massive deposit of raccoon crap, that was so kindly donated by the stand's last occupant.

Knowing getting up to clean my pants off might cause losing the element of surprise I've worked so hard to attain, I decide to simply deal with it. With my butt firmly rooted in the putrid, natural cover scent, I patiently await the arrival of dawn by listening to the plethora of sounds emanating from the forest floor below.

Mesmerized by the rhythmic crooning of a Great Horned Owl announcing the advancing sun's rays, the glow across the Eastern horizon gets brighter-and-brighter with each passing minute. Watching shadows turn into trees as they slowly emerge from a retreating fog bank, stars once bright in the morning sky eventually fade-away into obscurity. Before long, hundreds of small animals can be seen scurrying across the forest floor in search of food; a few inevitably becoming sustenance themselves, to creatures higher on the food chain.

With my left leg starting to go numb from sitting in one-spot for too long, I initiate movement that gradually evolves into a slow, extended stretch. Nearly falling out of my tree-stand from the ensuing rush of blood to my brain, I find myself invigorated with a renewed sense of awareness, and a much-deeper respect for gravity.

Eventually getting settled into my stand, I start scanning the Valley below for the buck that has literally shredded dozens of trees in my established 'Capture Zone.' Mentally preparing to engage my target at any time, I know a moment's notice may be all I'm given to spring the trap, when my quarry will be most vulnerable.

The goal for me on this hunting trip has always been to one-up my father, by bringing the buck he nicknamed "Hiney" back-home 'Alive.' I've been lucky to capture the buck several-times on trail cameras; and if I were to say, "he has a 'BIG' rack," it would certainly be a gross-understatement! The monarch buck sports a double drop-tine rack of immense symmetrical-proportion; the perfect genetic-traits I'm looking to add into my breeding-stock program.

With multiple other reasons for wanting to capture the prized buck, I continuously scan new areas of the Valley floor slowly emerging from behind retreating shadows.

Watching mesmerized; I witness a dense-fog stealthing steadily up the Valley, engulfing tree-after-tree in its seemingly relentless invasion. Approaching to within fifty-feet of overrunning my position, a sudden-onslaught of a light Westerly breeze has the shroud of white in full-retreat. The embattled mist slowly recedes back down into the Valley; gradually dissipating in volume, until becoming merely a faded memory.

Saturated leaves, formerly held captive by the departed fog, continuously shed drops of dew onto their fallen comrades littering the forest floor. Before long, dozens of deer can be seen scurrying about in search of corn, and other mast crops to fatten themselves up for winter.

A giant eagle being harassed by a squirrel high-up in a distant Ash tree leaves its perch, silently swooping away through the trees in search of food. Without so much as a flap of its wings, the eagle picks up a small feral hog from the forest floor. As the magnificent bird carries away its dinner in silence, the remaining piglets continue foraging about like nothing has happened.

Gradually coming to the realization I've misjudged distances; I

145

can see the piglets are actually mature hogs slowly making their way towards me. With the wind in the right direction, to where I won't have to worry about them catching scent of me, I begin pondering my hunting alternatives.

In fifteen short minutes, I've committed myself to initiating a push towards my father; regardless the situation I find myself in, with hogs heading in my direction. Given the current speed of the pigs, I calculate the mob will eventually reach my position, moments before I'm committed to executing my father's strategic push towards him.

Not wanting to alert every deer in the area to my presence by firing a gun, the thought of having fresh hog meat on the spit tonight is certainly tempting. Suddenly remembering one of Grandpa B's most plagiarized "Quotes," I begin contemplating 'How to make Lemonade' out of the 'Lemons' about to present themselves to me.

Still hoping to ritualistically feast tonight on the perfectly prepared tenderloins of a fresh-killed whitetail, I decide to try and compliment my meal with a wild-boar appetizer. Watching the fat round 'Lemons' making their way towards me, I envision turning one of the porkers into the sweetest, melt-in-your-mouth, BBQ bites ever to be consumed over an open fire!

Slowly reaching for the twelve-foot, javelin-like long pole leaned up against my tree earlier for added protection, I grasp the shaft just below the sharpened tip. Raising the pole in a slow, deliberate hand-over-hand motion, it takes what seems like an eternity to get the wooden spear horizontally in-place over my right shoulder.

Offering praise to Odin for letting me get the pole into position without blowing my cover, I ready to strike a killing blow.

As a reward, punishment; or, simply for his own entertainment, Odin suddenly sends 'THE Buck of a Lifetime' in my direction.

Previously seen only on film, the Granddaddy of all bucks is now heading directly towards my awaiting capture net.

Quickly calculating options on how to switch back to capturing the massive animal, I somehow must drop the weapon and spring my trap, completing the whole process before the spear hits the ground. A scary thought enters my brain. If the javelin gets caught up in the net during the drop, it could cause a catastrophic-failure during the capture process.

One thing is certain; I'll only have one opportunity to complete whatever action I decide to take. A broad grin forms across my face, the moment I decide to deprive myself of 'Fresh Lemonade,' in exchange for immortal glory.

With the opportunity to make a storybook kill suddenly presenting itself to me, I willfully abandon my original plan of capturing 'Hiney' for breeding stock purposes. The stories I'll be able to tell my progeny, on how I literally went 'Rambo' to harvest the buck will be legendary; but first, my spear must be unwaveringly-true to its target. As the massive beast presents its vitals to me at twenty yards, I let my sharpened spear fly with perfect accuracy.

Within a split second, I hear the tell-tale 'Thwack' of my spear striking its target squarely in the chest. Instantly whirling around to flee with my spear planted in its vitals, the long-pole strikes tree after tree during the animal's extended death-run. Not knowing how far the deer will run before inevitably collapsing, I listen intently for any clue that might help in tracking my trophy to its final resting place.

Giving praise to Odin, I crack the seal on my flask and celebrate, by taking several gulps of sweet nectar. Off in search of a blood trail, I head deliberately towards the last visual landmark I'd seen the buck pass nearby.

147

After walking a hundred-yards to where I'd last seen my wounded quarry disappear into a thick patch of locust trees, I spot a large pool of blood. Smatterings of red across the sides of several trees, make it easy to follow the buck's blood trail.

Soon coming across the shed spear covered in bright-red blood, I can tell my long-pole has inflicted a soon-to-be fatal lung shot. The question to be answered is: "How far will I have to track the magnificent beast, before being able to spot its white-bellied corpse?"

My pulse quickens, causing my brow to sweat profusely, as I begin to sense something is seriously wrong. With each passing yard, the once easy-to-follow blood trail begins diminishing in volume, until eventually drying up completely.

Stopping to survey the massive cow-sized tracks left in the soil, I can tell my quarry is thankfully heading in the same direction I'm currently expected to be making a push towards. Pausing to decipher a new sound emanating loudly throughout the forest, I instantly bust a gut laughing; upon recognizing the origin of what sounds like 'Ralphie's curse-laden Rant,' in the iconic movie 'A Christmas Story.'

Listening to my father rapidly spewing out profanities in multiple languages, I can tell he's found my buck about a hundred and fifty yards directly ahead. Soon breaking into one of Dad's shooting lanes, I'm provided a clear view all the way down to Lake Odin. Seeing him standing over the buck, repeatedly flailing both hands high in the air in a fit of confused-rage, he literally appears to be losing it.

Laughing profusely, I similarly begin waving my arms to get his attention. Incessantly mimicking his arm movements, as I quicken my pace towards him, he finally catches view of my mockery.

Immediately coming to the realization that it was I who killed the buck, and not some great-horned wild beast, my father's non-stop

148

cursing abruptly turns to complete silence.

Standing motionless with his arms hanging like dead weight from his sides, my father looks at me with an epic facial expression. Eventually coming to his senses, he begins shouting out a string of one-word questions in seemingly-painful succession: "How?....Where?....Why?"

With each new syllable, his facial features continuously morph into an even-more hysterical contortion than the last. Wishing I had a camera to capture the moment on film, I begin looking around for a nearby surveillance station.

When I get home, I'll undoubtedly be documenting the moment in our family Journal; as-well-as, going through every strand of video surveillance taken in the area, during the last few-minutes. Hopefully, a hidden security camera will have picked up one of Dad's 'Priceless' expressions.

Now that our Eastern Quadrant quota has been filled, my father and I will be heading back home much-earlier than expected. With nearly two-weeks of freed-up time before our next guests are scheduled to arrive, I can finally put our newly installed State-of-the-Art security system to the ultimate test.

Chapter 14

~Putting SHEILA to the Test~

Even though I've only been hunting the Eastern quadrant a little-less than twenty-four hours; the stress of dealing with my father, while being on constant 'High-Alert,' has certainly been taxing. Upon returning home, I make a beeline for the bedroom; intending to rejuvenate my body with several-hours of much needed shut-eye. The moment my head hits the pillow, thoughts begin racing through my mind like a runaway freight train.

Expecting to quickly nod-off into dreamland, like I normally do; I instead, find myself repeatedly using the back of my eyelids as a chalkboard, trying to analyze the obvious 'Anomaly' in one of the thirteen-sequences of numbers.

Comprised of only eight-numbers, instead of the normal twelve-numbers found in each of the dozen other sequences, I'm intrigued as to what the numbers "04201222" might possibly give reference too; especially, given its prominent 'Noon' positioning around the looking glass.

A theory suddenly pops into my brain about the last-four numbers of the sequence. With the importance of the Winter Solstice being on December 22nd each year, I find myself considering the possibility, that the anomaly might give reference to a ship having been successfully raided upon the Winter Solstice. Could Grandpa B have intentionally omitted; or simply forgotten, the actual "Year" of his conquest? If the numbers '1222' do actually represent the Winter Solstice, what might the first four numbers '0420' be giving reference too?"

Mesmerized by millions of stars shimmering through my bedroom ceiling's portal-window, the Sandman eventually pays me a visit. Once asleep, dreams begin flowing through my mind like class-five rapids; allowing several-hours to pass by in what feels like mere-minutes.

Waking to the sound of chimes from the grandfather clock downstairs, I find my body completely relaxed, lying sprawled-out across our King-sized bed. Initiating a prolonged stretch, I take-in the sweet smell of Anne's perfume, which continues to linger provocatively upon our sheets.

Shedding the warm comforter with a single flick of my wrist, the crisp morning air rushes-in like a tidal wave. Swimming across silken sheets, I eventually reach the edge of the mattress, and immediately plant my bare feet onto the unexpectedly cold hardwood floor. Abruptly coming to my senses, I enthusiastically turn my attention to discovering where a vast-horde of treasure might be found.

"One ship's treasure is all I'll need to validate my theory," I think to myself; instantly becoming motivated to prove there are more than just bells, and meerschaum pipes waiting to be discovered.

Wondering how Anne's reunion is going with Mona and her girlfriends, I decide to send her a quick email, before becoming fully-immersed in research. As I begin typing, an incoming Skype message flashes across my wall of monitors, synced to provide a single HD-quality picture of my wife lying in bed waving 'Hello.'

Anne and I engage in provocative conversation for several minutes, before Mona's sorority sisters all start gathering around her. As they begin giggling, and smothering the camera lens with silken scarves, our transmission is eventually terminated.

Knowing my wife is safe and having a good time, I begin researching my latest theory. Instructing our new voice activated computer to "Please provide all information known to exist pertaining to ships having fallen to Piracy upon the Winter Solstice, as well as the following dates in history," I summarily read the last eight-numbers of each twelve-digit clue written down on my now heavily tattered piece of paper; the last clue being "11181720."

'SHEILA' quickly projects it will take at least thirty-five minutes to search all databases, asking: "Would you like me to report my findings after each World Library has been analyzed, starting with the Library of Congress?"

I immediately respond, "Negative! I request only a finalized report. Please inform me the moment you have it ready. I'll be downstairs making myself breakfast."

Forced to do my own cooking with Chef J still on vacation, I decide to make myself a quick omelet. Having all the ingredients thoughtfully prepared by Chef J waiting in the fridge, it only takes a few-minutes before I'm sliding a delectable morel-mushroom, and cheesy three-egg omelet onto my plate.

Wolfing down the delicious concoction like a starving dog, it doesn't take long before I'm using a fork to scrape the last-tidbits of egg into my mouth. With hunger pains temporarily subsided, I engage the hot water 'On Demand' feature of the kitchen sink, and quickly wash-up my dirty dishes.

Chef J has taught me well, to always leave her kitchen 'Exactly' the way I found it. Having once returned home to find her kitchen 'Out of Order;' let's just say, I never wish to experience a repeat performance of the way she laid into me.

Washing the last few pieces of silverware, I finish up my

spotless cleaning by drying off the dishes, and systematically placing everything back in its proper place. Moments later, SHEILA announces over the intercom, "The summary report you requested is now ready."

Quickly making my way upstairs to evaluate the findings, I ask SHEILA: "Could the last eight-numbers of each numerical sequence I provided, possibly give reference to dates in history; where a Captain Bartholomew is reported to have captured and ransacked a treasure ship. In addition, could a thirteenth-sequence of numbers, believed to represent December 22nd, possibly give reference to a ship captured by him, upon the Winter Solstice?"

SHEILA responds immediately, stating: "No… and…No." As my heart starts to sink into my throat, SHEILA goes on to say; "However, eleven of the dates you provided are a positive match, with ships having been plundered by a Captain Bartholomew. The 12th date of inquiry, being November 18, 1720, mentions nothing of a Captain Bartholomew. Lastly, no treasure ship in recorded history has ever been reported 'Lost' to hurricanes, or acts of Piracy on December 22nd."

Momentarily stopping to ponder the significance of the anomaly, I respond by asking, "What significance does the date November 18, 1720 have in history?"

SHEILA responds, "On November 18, 1720, the only archival record found on that date mentions a notorious pirate by the name of 'Calico Jack' having been hung for his crimes."

Contemplating for a moment upon reaching the captain's chair, I ask SHEILA: "Please give me all you have on Calico Jack; specifically, anything that might be relevant as to why Grandpa B may have considered the date important enough, to document it alongside his other dates of conquest."

Before I can relax into the captain's chair, SHEILA reports: "There are no confirmed connections between Calico Jack and Captain Bartholomew, other than rumors of them once having engaged in a knife fight. Legends by local Bahamians report Calico Jack accused Bartholomew of having an affair with his wife Anne Bonnie, a notorious female Pirate of the era. Unconfirmed reports state that during the knife fight, Calico Jack was knocked out cold by a beer stein wielding, female Pirate by the name of 'Mary Read.' Neither Captain is reported to have sustained any serious injury."

SHEILA goes on to say, "While history reports Calico Jack was later captured and hung on November 18, 1720, his widow Anne Bonnie and her 'Partner in Piracy' Mary Read were both imprisoned together. While Mary Read is reported to have died during childbirth, Anne Bonnie is believed to have returned to a life of Piracy after somehow managing to escape prison. Legend perpetuates Ms Bonnie was able to slip past her guards, while they were watching Mary Read's funeral procession. Additional 'Classified' documents found buried deep in the Bahamian National archives report rumors of a bribe being made by Anne Bonnie's family; allowing both Anne, and her friend Mary to be smuggled out 'alive' using Mary's coffin."

"Alright, enough about Calico Jack's personal life"; I interject, attempting to refocus my thoughts. Quickly considering the facts just divulged, I respond to SHEILA, "Please provide me all you have on the disposition of Calico Jack's treasure." Speculating Grandpa B may have somehow inherited the bulk of Calico Jack's 'Good Fortune' upon his death, it would certainly explain the correlation between Calico Jack's death, and the mysterious sequence of numbers!

SHEILA responds, "The Bahamian National archives document Calico Jack as having made several conquests in the West Indies, before initially being granted a pardon. He eventually returned to a life

154

of Piracy, where he was soon captured and summarily hung for his crimes. There are no records in any archive, foreign or domestic, as to the disposition of treasure taken from two heavily-laden treasure galleons he is reported to have captured off Bermuda, during his brief return to Piracy."

With all the pieces of the puzzle coming together, there is one last task I have for SHEILA, which will undoubtedly put her new programming to the 'Ultimate' test. If my test is successful, her calculations will save me months of painstakingly waiting to prove my theories.

Without delay, I ask SHEILA: "Please calculate exactly where down in the Valley the shadow from Sasquatch Mountain will be pointing too, using the first four-numbers in each 12-digit sequence to represent "Minutes and Seconds" past noon; while using the last eight-numbers in each sequence, to represent a specific date. Will you be able to calculate points of position? If yes, with what percent accuracy for each location?"

It takes only a few seconds for SHEILA to respond, "Dependent upon cloud conditions, which could cause delays; it will take a minimum of five-days. to provide the information you've requested. I will need to plot points of shadow each day, to establish a baseline for performing my calculations. Percent accuracy of results will be 99.9%; or, within five-feet of the targeted location."

I respond by letting out a celebratory, "Whoo Hooo;" going on to instruct SHEILA, "Initiate your search using the data provided! Please inform me the moment results are available."

Calculating how much time I'll have for treasure hunting once SHEILA provides her findings, I figure I'll be able to enjoy a little over three-days of digging, before our next visitors are scheduled to grace us with their presence. This being the last group of guests visiting prior to the arrival of our Winter Solstice delegation, it will undoubtedly be my last chance to treasure hunt for quite some time.

I still have five-days remaining, before SHEILA is expected to provide me with specific locations, on where I should dig. Since my schedule has already been cleared, for what was expected to be a prolonged hunt in the Eastern quadrant, I decide to assist my father in his quest to harvest Bullwinkle.

Dad was so pissed off after depriving him of his Eastern quadrant trophy; that, as soon as we returned home, he bolted-off into the Valley without saying a single-word to anyone. Already packed and supplied for several-days of primitive survival in the wild, he headed straight for the location Bullwinkle was last seen.

Heading out on my ATV, I try radioing my father to let him know I've got the 'Dog Collar' on, and am initiating a push towards him. Before proceeding more than a hundred-yards, Dad is already sending me a text, saying: "Tracks heading into the Corral…he's mine! No help needed…will radio you when I have him!" Quickly gearing down, I stop to re-evaluate my hunting options.

Suddenly remembering having the perfect stand to hunt from with winds currently out of the West, I decide to alter my direction and head for Whitetail Hollow. With deer currently in full-rut, I'm hoping the buck shredding trees in my home-made clearing is still leaving his calling card; because if he is, there stands a high-probability of catching the normally-nocturnal buck out chasing does during daylight hours.

Making my way slowly through the grassland, I count forty-two deer crossing the pathway ahead. Eventually breaking into the clearing, fresh rubs can be seen on literally every tree; including several completely girdled around at their base since my last visit. Anticipation grows exponentially, upon realizing the buck is still in the area claiming his rightful domain.

Shutting off the ATV, I quietly coast to a stop. With the wind in my face, I'm confident my scent will not be dispersed over my intended hunting area; providing me an excellent chance of getting into position undetected.

Before beginning the hundred-yard trek to my tree stand, I must first ditch my ride, without alarming a pair of does currently feeding at the far-edge of the clearing. As I attempt to quietly slide off the ATV, both does bound-off with flared-tails high in the air.

Not sure what caused the does to take-off so abruptly, I look around and witness two coyotes trotting across the middle of the open field. Ever since my favorite beagle 'Snoopy' was nearly killed years ago by a coyote, I've had an insatiable hatred for these despicable creatures.

Without a second thought of my actions alerting every deer in the area to my presence, I reach for my rifle and take aim. Focusing my crosshairs on the front shoulder of the largest coyote, I squeeze off a round; immediately dropping the bastard in his tracks. As the second coyote turns to run away with its tail tucked between its legs, I fire a second round; immediately seeing the ground blow up directly beneath the fleeing animal.

Looking through the scope for any possible pathways the coyote might try using as an escape route, my crosshairs focus in on a funnel area directly ahead of the fleeing carnivore. Before the animal can reach safety, a perfectly-placed hundred-yard head shot ends its life.

Electing not to immediately run over and claim my two kills, I remain motionless; waiting and watching to see how wildlife will react

157

to my fading rifle reports echoing throughout the Valley.

As if running out to wave 'Goodbye' to their fallen enemies, the pair of does I'd seen earlier suddenly re-emerge from the far-edge of the clearing; prancing about with their tails flickering back-and-forth, high in the air.

Quietly finishing my journey to reach the deer stand, it becomes apparent the does have actually been teasing a pair of bucks getting ready to square-off. Just before the rut-crazed bucks go to lock horns, they suddenly bolt away in opposite directions. Knowing there's no way they could've caught my scent, I look feverishly about to determine what has spooked them.

A pair of trumpeter swans flying overhead provides a seemingly royal fanfare, as the King of the woods suddenly steps into the clearing to declare his divine breeding right. Being no contenders are sticking around to dispute his claim, the majestic buck struts slowly towards the does; unfortunately, before I'm able to raise my rifle, he similarly bolts away and quickly disappears into a nearby patch of elephant grass.

Shaking profusely from a rare case of Buck Fever, the reality of having missed out on an amazing opportunity starts to sink in. As my nerves eventually begin to calm, the leaves of the tree I'm sitting in quiet down proportionally; enlightening me as to why the majestic buck departed so quickly.

With the location of my deer stand divulged to every animal in the area, I decide to climb out of the tree and go on a tracking mission. Slowly trailing my departed quarry, I watch and listen for any sounds, or tell-tale movements of other animals reacting to his hasty departure.

Working the track, it quickly becomes apparent the buck is making a beeline in the direction of my Father. Expecting the buck to eventually bed down and wait motionless for me to walk past him undetected, I slow my progress to test the animal's nerves. My theory holds true as the buck suddenly breaks from cover, heading at high-speed into the labyrinth opening leading all-the-way back to the Corral.

It's anyone's guess as to what Dad's reaction will be; when he finds himself with not just one, but two monster bucks together in the same field before him. It doesn't take long to find out, as a shot rings out, followed by another; and then, yet another.

Hearing a bullet wiz overhead through the treetops, I know at least one of my father's shots has missed. The question is, "Did one of the other two-shots fired hit its mark?"

Moments later, my cell phone begins buzzing with an incoming text message. Checking the message, it reads, "Missed …gate closed… he's mine!"

Texting him back, I respond, "How long has gate been closed?"

Dad quickly responds back, "Why?"

I answer, "Just chased Bullwinkle's Father into area leading back to the Corral…keep an eye out for him!"

After several-seconds, I finally get a response, "Gate's been closed for over an hour...no way he's in with me...good luck!!"

I suddenly realize Bullwinkle's Father has eluded me for now; but I've got him trapped inside the labyrinth! Thinking to myself: "If the buck wasn't able to get through the Corral gate before my father closed it, he has nowhere else to run, but back towards me!" Crouching down, I anxiously wait for the buck to return in my direction.

Holding off on answering my cell phone, which is buzzing uncontrollably at my feet with text-after-text from Father, I dare not answer the call; fearing Bullwinkle's Dad might try slipping past me, while being momentarily distracted. Several-minutes pass, before finally reaching down to secure my phone. Without reading any of the incoming texts, I send Pop the message: "We appear to have Bullwinkle's Father trapped between the Corral gate and the Western entrance into the labyrinth, provided he doesn't somehow elude us!"

After twenty-minutes of remaining motionless, I begin to wonder if the buck might have actually used Dad's 'Cloak of Invisibility' to slip by me, like Bullwinkle has supposedly done numerous times to my Father. Suddenly catching a glimpse of movement ahead through the trees, I raise my rifle. Searching through the scope, I look around for a patch of fur, glint off an antler, or anything that might confirm my target. Just when I think I'm hallucinating, Dad steps out into the middle of the pathway ahead, waving both hands to ensure I'm aware of his presence.

Never so glad to always confirm my target before pulling the trigger, all I can think is: "If Dad has made it through the Gauntlet this far without bumping Bullwinkle's Father; then, where in the hell did the buck disappear too?" Just as I finish my thought, the clump of brush between me and my father begins shaking and moving directly towards me. In a mixture of dismay and panic, I'm barely able to execute a dive to my right, before the monstrous buck nearly runs me through in its flight to freedom.

Dad contemplates taking a shot; but, with the elusive animal having perfectly positioned himself in-line with me and escape to the North, Pop quickly reverts to 'Plan B.' Hoping to catch a shot at the buck before it disappears out of sight, my father comes running at me with rifle raised.

Expecting a bullet to soon be whizzing over my head, I flatten myself out onto the forest floor as best as possible. Moments later, my father's lifting me up with his free hand, cursing and swearing until

160

seemingly out of breath. "Are you alright?" he finally asks; bringing me back to my senses with a vigorous slap across my back, that momentarily knocks the air from my lungs.

Regaining my composure, I ask Dad: "Can you believe how well Bullwinkle's Father kept himself hidden, until the very last moment? Why didn't you take a shot?"

Dad grabs me firmly by the chin, like he always does when demanding my undivided attention, saying with conviction: "I would never risk your life to gain glory. It simply isn't worth it!"

Realizing the depth of what he is saying to me, I respond, "Thanks!"

Without missing a beat, Dad responds: "Don't worry, I'll never let you forget it... Let's go get some ale! Tomorrow, I'm heading back to the corral area to harvest Bullwinkle. He's not going anywhere with the Coral gate closed, unless he somehow suddenly learns how to climb a Tree!"

Chapter 15

~Last Chance to Relax~

Awaking to the sound of a chopper taking off, I squint painfully out my bedroom window through shades of red. With a double-take, turning into a much longer stare, I eventually realize it's Fast Eddie giving Dad a lift down-into the Valley.

Foggy memories begin to clear from last night, as I suddenly remember my father saying, Fast Eddie was supposed to take him down to the Corral come morning. Pop certainly exuded confidence in his hunting abilities; boasting several times throughout the evening, he'd have Bullwinkle 'Beneath his Boot' before next sunset.

What I remember most about our conversation last night, was the hilarious look on my father's face, after I jokingly responded back to him: "You'll have to find Bullwinkle in your crosshairs to put a boot on him; unless your plan is to simply kick him in the ass, when he runs past you."

Straining to remember more of what took place last night becomes mentally exhausting, prompting me to lie back down. As the thumping in my brain from the chopper's exodus eventually subsides, my alcohol induced headache immediately gets upgraded to a raging migraine. Groping desperately to silence the back-up alarm clock before my eardrums start to hemorrhage, I fumble repeatedly with the obnoxious timepiece; eventually giving-in to the primal urge of beating it into submission.

Refusing to let extreme-nausea and dizziness interfere with the day's agenda, my body somehow musters up enough strength to sit upright in bed. Like a prizefighter shaking off a punch, I shake my head from side-to-side, trying to remove the cobwebs from my brain. Once the ensuing double-vision clears, I find myself gazing-out in wonder at the scenic canvas currently being painted outside my bedroom window.

With the Eastern horizon ablaze in shades of crimson and gray from the approach of dawn, Mother Nature begins changing her color palette to include ever softening shades of blues and yellows. Watching the earth, stars, and sky perfectly blend together into a breathtaking masterpiece, I continue to gaze-out in awe for what seems like an eternity. Once the glimmer of Mars has slowly faded away into obscurity, my stomach starts to rumble.

Gathering up enough energy to initiate movement, I trudge wearily towards the kitchen. Picking up speed and momentum with each step forward, I think to myself, "This could be the day!" With my thoughts in the clouds, it doesn't take long before I'm seemingly walking on air! After reaching a literal trot, I call out to SHEILA, "Good Morning SHEILA! Please give me an update on your search results."

SHEILA immediately responds, "Good Morning to you as well. The results of my report are still inconclusive at this point, as I've only been able to successfully compile one-day's data. By your elevated pulse, might I recommend taking a few-days to relax, and go Crappie fishing! Crappie Cove is about to reach optimum spawning cycle for the year, and Lunar charts are predicting off-the-chart major peaks throughout the entire afternoon, for both today and tomorrow."

With the impatience of a four-year old waiting to go trick-or-treating on Halloween, I temporarily dismiss her recommendation. Exploring possible ways to advance my treasure hunting timeline, I ask

SHEILA: "In your current task, what degree of accuracy will you be able to provide me on where to begin digging, with three and/or four-days data respectfully?"

SHEILA responds, "Once three-days of data has been accumulated, I can place you within forty-feet of your target, with rate of accuracy being seventy-five percent. Four-days data will put you within eight-feet of your target, with a ninety-percent rate of accuracy."

As SHEILA finishes her report on the accuracy of her statistics, I find myself doing a jig. Her calculations on 'Four Days' data will actually put me within comfortable range of where to begin digging; providing me an additional full day of treasure hunting, before my next two special guests are set to arrive.

Expecting to be in relentless torment for the next three-days waiting on SHEILA to provide the data results, I decide to take her advice and go fishing. Not wanting to waste a moment, I grab two spinning reels and my favorite fly rod on the way to the compost bin. Soon having my worm bucket filled with plump and juicy night-crawlers wriggling everywhere, I'm hoping it'll be enough bait to last the entire trip.

You might think taking a thousand worms on a fishing trip is a bit excessive; but I like to keep my hook baited at all times with a single, whole night crawler. This means, I sometimes go through a ton of worms; especially when running into schools of fish thoroughly educated on how to strip a hook clean, without getting caught.

Once everything needed to go fishing is loaded and ready, I hop onto the ATV and quickly head-out towards my favorite fishing hole. Within minutes of leaving the house, I'm already slipping my canoe into Crappie Cove's thermal infused waters.

With certain hot-spot areas maintaining perfect water

temperatures for spawning crappies, fish get put into prime spawning mode months earlier than in other parts of the country. This reminds me about the time I was once being eavesdropped upon a few-years back, while out gathering supplies with my father during one of our 'Early' spawning seasons.

After stopping at a big city tavern to grab some liquid refreshment, a local 'Barfly' overheard my private conversation about a mess of spawning crappies I'd just caught. He actually had the nerve to interrupt our conversation; proceeding to question my integrity, by sarcastically asking where I'd been able to catch 'Spawning' crappies this early in the year?

The look I received from him, by my calculated response was hilarious. Thinking fast, I exchanged a warm handshake; eventually responding, "I was sworn not to tell anyone about this, but I actually got caught sneaking into a nuclear power station's cooling lake this morning. Expecting to catch a few catfish, I ended up catching a bunch of spawning crappies!"

Casually turning to my father, I then stated: "Can you believe it! After catching over a hundred of them slimy suckers, I got escorted off the lake by a security detail decked out in bio-hazard suits. They said there'd been some sort of 'Mass-radiation' leak, and that my fish were all highly radioactive!"

Turning and coughing in the direction of the panic-stricken man, who was obviously regretting having earlier accepted my 'Contaminated' handshake, I said to him: "I was wondering why all them sirens were going off." It was absolutely hilarious how fast he was able to vacate the building.

Reminiscing has me laughing, as I slowly paddle my way through swirling patches of low-lying fog to reach my favorite fishing cove. Soon evicting a pair of whooping cranes reluctant to leave the area, I make my first cast; just as a lone-snowflake forebodingly lands on the bridge of my nose.

The exact moment my worm hits the water, a swirl engulfs the bait, sending six-pound monofilament line stripping from my reel. Immediately setting the hook, the vibration emanating from my pole tells me I've set the hook into a monster. Regretfully, I'll never know the species, or weight of the fish, as my line suddenly snaps before getting a chance to see it.

I end-up not getting a single, new strike for the rest of the morning. With a cold front having unexpectedly moved in, all the fish seem to have developed a major case of lockjaw. Retreating to a tent I've pitched along the river's edge, I initiate Plan B; proceeding to cozy-up next to a raging campfire, while warming my eyelids awhile.

Quickly falling asleep, I slip seamlessly into dreamland. My dreams are short-lived however, when a lone-shot rings-out down in the Valley. Wondering if I've just lost my bet with Dad, on who gets 'First Taste' of ale at this year's Solstice event, my thoughts soon turn to not yet having any fish for the frying pan. Realizing I've slept longer than anticipated, with sundown quickly approaching, I rush to get back out and catch some fish. I certainly don't want to be forced to break-out the emergency can of Spam for dinner tonight!

Having fully recovered from their case of lockjaw, I catch ten crappies over the next ten casts from my fly rod; more than enough fillets for a good hearty meal. Returning to camp, I stoke the fire and anxiously begin frying up mounds of bacon. "There's nothing better than fresh fish fried up in bacon grease over an open fire," I think to myself; as my mouth begins salivating, in anticipation of the hearty meal I'm about to enjoy.

After devouring every-last crispy-golden fillet, I once again find my eyelids becoming weighted-down by gravity. Assuming the position, I mentally prepare myself to spend what I hope will be a peaceful night-out in the wild.

Throughout the evening, my dreams are as vivid as the celestial stars streaking across the heavens. Wrapped snugly in my thermal sleeping bag, I have no idea nearly two inches of snow has fallen overnight.

The next morning, after stepping outside the tent in my bare feet to relieve my bladder, I suddenly find myself performing an awakening dance befitting of a tribal shaman.

Hurriedly spreading out the heaping mound of red-hot coals from last night's fire, I begin thawing out my nearly frost-bitten toes. Once every-last piggy is toasty and warm, the griddle gets put to use in preparing a hearty breakfast of bacon and eggs. By the time I'm finished eating, most of the snow covering the ground has melted; and, with temperatures already in the mid 50's, it looks to be a perfect-day for fishing.

Baiting up both casting rods, I never get the opportunity to use the second pole, for fish are biting seemingly faster than I can get my hook back in the water. Tossing fish after fish into the canoe, waves soon begin lapping at the gunwales.

Heading back to shore with my heavily laden canoe, I mentally prepare myself for a fish cleaning marathon. While I could've thrown back many of the smaller fish, I'm a firm believer in Grandpa B's favorite adage of: 'Waste not…Want more;' especially, when the smaller crappies are averaging nearly two-pounds each!

Once I've honed my knife to a razor-sharp edge, I glean the first fillet from the massive number of fish caught. Nearly two-hours later,

I'm tossing the last filleted carcass into the slop bucket for the hogs. After scrubbing the encrusted fish scales from my hands, I load up the ATV, and head for home.

Still having a full day to relax, before SHEILA is to provide me the data on exactly where to dig; and knowing I'll be totally consumed with treasure hunting, until the very moment my next guests arrive, I decide to return home to make sure everything is ready for their visit. The moment I enter the front door, Dad greets me with a giant bear hug, saying: "I got him! Bullwinkle is mine!!"

Congratulating him on his triumph, I gracefully concede his winning 'First Taste' of ale during this year's Winter Solstice event. My humbling posture puts Dad 'On top of the World' in his jubilation.

Hoping my Father's good spirits will make him say "Yes" without questioning my motive, I try to nonchalantly ask him for a favor, by saying: "Just in case I'm late getting back from working down in the Valley, would you mind being 'on-call' to greet our next guests when they arrive?"

With a look of premonition, my father asks: "Why? You've already filled the walk-in freezer with plenty of venison and pork; and now, you've got enough crappie fillets to last for several-months." Pausing for a moment to look deep into my eyes, he goes on to say, "You're going treasure hunting again, aren't you?!"

Not wanting to divulge my true agenda, I say to him: "I've got a ton of projects to do, and I could really use your help. Would you please just help me out, without asking anymore questions?"

I can tell Dad knows by the sweat beading on my brow, that I've just tried side-stepping his question. Offering a subtle hint that he might be right, I respond: "If I find myself needing help with my project, would you be available to come help me on a moment's

168

notice?"

Dad sits back laughing, taking a long draw from one of the Meerschaum pipes recently found, saying: "Sure, if you cut me in on a fair share of the treasure!" Getting a chance to return a personal jab, he goes on to say with a broad grin across his face: "I know you don't want to risk another royal embarrassment by chasing your delusional theories, but I can always tell when you're about to embark on your next treasure hunting quest! One of these days, you might just find something more valuable, than this awesome pipe I'm using to celebrate the life-and-death of Bullwinkle with."

Not wanting to divulge the clues I'm planning to act upon, I change the focus of our conversion by confronting Dad about smoking from the meerschaum pipe. After telling him, "You were supposed to wait until the Winter Solstice event to break that pipe in," I patiently wait for an apology.

Sitting back hallowed by a ring of exhaled smoke, Dad responds, "You really can't fault me for celebrating the Life and Death of Bullwinkle."

Responding back quickly, I chastise him by saying: "No; but you know you're not supposed to be using the herbs from Odin's Garden for 'Recreational' use."

While we're allowed to harvest enough herbs to properly enlighten our guests during the Winter Solstice Ritual, Grandpa B set stern restrictions on 'Personal' consumption; because, as he put it: "The increased brain function Odin's herb bestows upon mortal men can be very dangerous, if not consumed in moderation."

For centuries we've honored Grandpa B's strict decree, as stated in his journal: "Harvest only what is needed for the Solstice Toast. If there be any leftover herbs, ye may use them for medicinal purposes, as

169

the 'Tree of Life' cures many illnesses that modern-day medicine merely masks the symptoms of. A stern warning...never let Odin return to an over-harvested garden; lest ye risk invoking Odin's vengeful wrath."

Deeply concentrating on how to deliver a proper rebuttal, Dad finally replies: "I was merely sampling the quality of herbs from Odin's Garden, to see how much we need to harvest for this year's celebration. By the many thoughts racing through my mind right now, I can tell our guests are going to be exceptionally enlightened this year. I'd venture to say this year's crop is one of the most potent crops grown, since the year Albert Einstein first visited our Valley!"

My quick response is harsh, chastising Pop by saying, "Your Dad had no right betting all our medicinal herbs for that year on a single hand of poker!" After Albert ended up winning, his subsequent enlightenment upon returning home brought undesirable media attention; nearly divulging to the World, the existence of our secret Valley.

Trying to justify his father's actions, Dad responds: "He was desperate to win back his favorite pipe. Being dealt a natural Straight Flush, he took it as a sign from Odin to make the bet. Whoever would've guessed Albert would draw three cards to win the hand with a Royal Flush!?"

To change the subject, I ask Dad: "Now that you've had a chance to conduct our annual sampling, how many plants do you think we should harvest this year?"

Pop immediately responds, "I think a half-dozen plants should be more than sufficient; but, if I were you, I wouldn't waste any time getting them hung up in the cellar to dry!"

Taking his recommendation very seriously, I'm soon making a

beeline for Odin's Garden. Since it takes time to properly cure the herbs once picked, I need to fill my father's recommended quota for Ritual right away.

Harvesting several plants resembling large Christmas trees, my ATV is soon loaded down with all I can safely transport home. Smelling as if I've just been sprayed by a skunk, I slowly navigate my way back through the labyrinth.

Pulling into the garage, I hurriedly hang each plant upside-down in the root cellar to begin the drying process. Closing the door to seal in the pungent aromas; I grab a beer from the fridge, and head straight for the bedroom to catch-up on some much-needed shut-eye.

Chapter 16

~Treasure Awaits~

Checking off the last task, on a once-long list of things needing completed before guests come to visit us next week; I now have everything ready for their arrival. This means, I'm getting to enjoy three-full-days of uninterrupted treasure hunting; while waiting on SHEILA to provide me the calculated-coordinates, on where to begin digging.

Since Grandpa B was accredited with having successfully pillaged over four-hundred ships during his seafaring career, I'm hoping to spend the rest of the weekend digging up massive amounts of treasure. If all goes as anticipated, I could literally be wading through heaping mounds of gold and jewels very soon.

Needing to recharge my batteries before embarking on the monumental task ahead of me, I wearily climb into bed. Slowly nestling my head into a goose-down pillow, the day's stresses quickly drift away on a gentle breeze emanating from a nearby fan.

Vivid dreams soon have me swimming freestyle through the clouds. Stretching out with each stroke, I grasp at silver linings that swirl tauntingly just beyond my reach. After completing several virtual laps around the Valley, my adventure ends with my body settling peacefully back into bed.

As the morning sun's rays begin tickling my eyelids with their warmth, my head slowly lifts from the pillow. Enjoying a long-drawn-out stretch, I begin mentally preparing myself for a day full of uncovering riches beyond mortal comprehension.

A rumble in my gut reminds me, that I should eat a hearty breakfast before heading out; for once SHEILA provides her findings, I probably won't get another chance to chow-down on anything that excites my taste buds, for quite some time.

Bacon and eggs have always been a breakfast that rejuvenates my soul; giving me limitless energy while out in the field. Cooking up a full two pounds of Applewood smoked bacon, I wolf down several pieces while preparing three 'Over-easy' eggs. After gliding my butter knife across four slices of golden-brown toast, it doesn't take long before I'm soaking up the yolks, and quickly devouring my breakfast like a starving dog.

Bagging up the leftover bacon as a welcomed snack for later in the day, I begin to mentally prepare myself for the long-awaited treasure hunting marathon. As minutes quickly tick away, it doesn't take long for the much anticipated 'Moment of Truth' to arrive.

Playing a trumpet fanfare over the intercom before providing her data findings, SHEILA proceeds to announce: "Due to dense cloud-cover occurring yesterday, which caused shadows to be muddled throughout most of the afternoon, I regretfully am only able to provide you with required levels of accuracy on 'Four' of the expected 'Thirteen' locations. An additional twenty-four hours without any cloud cover will be needed to pinpoint the nine-remaining dig-site locations."

Disappointed at having incomplete data on a majority of the points of interest, my momentary bout of depression disappears the moment SHEILA goes on to announce: "However, the four plotted points I was able to accurately collect data on are now available. Using newly installed laser-enhanced technology, I have identified each location, by superimposing a visual reference point onto the Valley floor below."

Racing for the Captain's chair to gaze out over the Valley, I can't wait to see the location of the four-points I'll soon be digging from. Surprisingly, it no longer bothers me having to wait an extra day, to find out where the remaining nine-other points will be located.

Gazing out through the portal window, I stare in amazement at four laser beams pointing down to precise positions on the Valley floor below. In order to quickly locate these four locations once I'm down in the Valley, I hurriedly enter each GPS coordinate into my handheld unit.

The moment I have everything input, my feet have me running down the stairs towards the garage. Once there, I hop onto my tractor and race to the first dig site, as fast as my backhoe will travel, which at the current moment, feels much like a snail's pace.

Reaching the first set of plotted coordinates, the sniper-like laser beam shining down from above, suddenly begins moving up the hood of my tractor towards me. Letting it pass by without looking up into the light, I bring the excavator to a complete stop once the laser beam rests squarely on the patch of earth directly beneath my bucket.

In what seems like slow motion as I re-position myself in the operator seat, emotions have me realizing in just a few short minutes, my life-long dream of finding treasure is about to become Reality! Without missing a beat, I plunge my bucket deep into the earth.

Quickly removing yard-after-yard of rich, black topsoil, the discarded mound of dirt continues to grow. Eventually reaching a depth of six feet, my backhoe's hydraulics suddenly bog down the moment my bucket snags into a solid, unmovable object.

Using the bucket to scrape away the thick, clay-like mud that's

174

entombed the artifact for centuries, it takes very little time to confirm another bell has been found! Already having experience in removing two similar objects from the bosom of Mother Earth, it takes only a few minutes for me to surgically extract the bell up, and out of the pit.

Setting it down on its side, I quickly hop-off the backhoe, and begin scooping-away dirt from the bell's inner-cavity by hand. Before developing my first blister, I find myself unearthing the third meerschaum pipe of my treasure hunting career.

Meticulously excavating deeper through the rest of the mound in front of me, I uncover no additional gold or jewels. With each new dig site, the limited items I continue to find have me relentlessly pondering 'what clues the recovered artifacts are meant to provide, in helping locate Grandpa B's horde of buried treasure.'

By the end of the day, I've added three more bells and three additional meerschaum pipes, to my current collection of six-pairs of artifacts. Going to bed shortly after sundown, I'm both physically, and mentally exhausted.

The next morning, my sore muscles file an unfair labor dispute, the moment I put them to work lifting my aching body out of bed. Motivation quickly dulls the pain, knowing SHEILA will soon be providing the nine remaining plotted points in which to dig. Without a doubt in my mind, I know one of them must be the 'Honey Hole' referenced in Grandpa B's journal.

Anxiously motivated and ready to resume treasure hunting, I energetically head-out the front door. Taking only a few steps, I suddenly realize it's still very early in the morning, hours before SHEILA is expected to provide me with the new dig-site coordinates.

Retreating to the kitchen, I attempt to drown my self-embarrassment by devouring a pair of pop-tarts in record time. Quickly washing them down with an ice-cold glass of milk, I head back to the captain's chair to relax and wait for SHEILA to divulge her findings. The moment I lie back in the chair, the sandman pays me an unexpected visit.

Feeling like only moments have slipped away since closing my eyes, SHEILA awakens me by announcing: "Data on the remaining nine-clues is now ready." With high-expectations, I gaze excitedly out at the newly-plotted points on the earth below.

As anticipated, two of the nine pinpointed locations are areas I've already excavated a bell and pipe from. With odds in finding Grandpa B's treasure now greatly improved, the seven-remaining hotspots hold immense promise.

Inputting each of the new coordinates, I'm off in a flash; heading at top speed to reach the first excavation site. Reaching my destination, I begin digging the moment the laser beam from above is once again positioned directly beneath the bucket of my backhoe.

After eventually finding yet another bell and meerschaum pipe, I feverishly continue digging deeper into the pit. Spending nearly a full hour of precious digging time, and not finding a single ounce of additional treasure, a sickening sense of 'De ja Vu' envelops my soul.

With the 'Anomaly' clue holding the most promise in finding actual treasure, my gut tells me I should immediately relocate to that location. Proving to be a glutton for punishment; or, simply wanting to save the potential 'Glory Hole' for last, I go against my gut by continuing to follow the originally planned dig-site order.

Finding nothing more than a bell and a lone-meerschaum pipe at each subsequent location, I continue putting shovel to earth; eventually accumulating a total of twelve-pairs of artifacts.

With my last hope of finding treasure resting firmly on the anomaly clue proving to be the location of Grandpa B's depository, the sunlight from above is quickly fading into darkness. Rather than continuing to dig in the dark, where I might miss or destroy something of major importance, I decide to call it a night and start afresh in the morning.

The next day starts out way before the break of dawn, with my heart racing, and palms itching for treasure. Heading out the door, I grab a flask of raspberry ale; intending to refrain from enjoying its intoxicating flavor, until finding sufficient reason to celebrate.

I'm hoping it won't take long to find Grandpa B's treasure; for, the sooner I unearth his treasure trove, the more time I'll have to celebrate. With expectations at an all-time high, I'm looking forward to having literally millions of reasons to celebrate at tonight's 'Welcome to the Valley' festivities.

The morning sun illuminates my surroundings, as I reach the spot where Sheila's laser beam sits pinpointing the last dig sight location. Saying a prayer to Odin, I stabilize my machine before enthusiastically planting my bucket deep into the earth.

After removing several cubic-yards of dirt, the bucket suddenly bogs down upon striking a mixture of hard-packed clay, and gravel. My heart sinks into my shoes, upon considering I may have simply uncovered yet-another clue to lose sleep over.

Instead of scooping out more of the dense material, I decide to redirect my search efforts, by sifting through the pile of loose soil already removed from the hole. After nearly an hour of meticulously picking through each shovel full of dirt, my spade finally hits something solid in the remaining mound of topsoil.

Falling to my knees, I begin scraping away layer-after-layer of dirt and sand by hand. A glint of gold, and flash of red suddenly catches my eye. Moments later, I'm unearthing what appears to be a jewel-encrusted knife and scabbard.

Reaching for my water bucket, I attempt to clean the object by thrusting and swirling it around in the water. Every hair on my arm stands erect, as I slowly remove the artifact from the muddy water.

With my right-hand firmly grasping the jewel-encrusted golden scabbard glowing brightly in the afternoon sunshine, I extract the sheathed-knife for closer inspection. It appears to be a razor-sharp sacrificial dagger, with a curved-sloping blade of sizable mass, and a diamond-tipped handle of nearly eighty-carats.

Cradling my hand around the knife's handle, the perfectly balanced twelve-inch blade exhibits several etchings, that appear to be Aztec in origin. Thoughts run wild, as I contemplate the provenance of the piece; suspecting it may have once been wielded by Montezuma himself.

Suddenly remembering the remaining four-hundred shiploads of treasure awaiting my shovel, I quickly insert the knife back into its sheath, before tucking it under my belt for safe-keeping. Grabbing my spade, I repeatedly plunge it into the ground; expecting to discover additional treasure, with each new shovel-full of earth.

Working up a considerable sweat after removing several-yards of dirt and gravel, I find no additional treasure. Soon worrying I might not find any additional artifacts; I think to myself, "The knife can't be the only piece of treasure Grandpa B brought with him to the Valley." With Leland and his clansmen claiming their Captain had departed with all their bounty, the question is: "Where could the final resting place of Grandpa B's remaining retirement fund be located?"

Refusing to believe I've found the only treasure there is to be

178

discovered, I sit back for a minute to review the situation. In each area excavated, I've dug down until reaching the water table; and in three of these areas, I've continued my search by digging well-over four feet below the surface of the water.

A 'Revelation' suddenly comes over me, as I begin contemplating the possibility of having prematurely stopped digging at each site location. With a shiver running up my spine, I think to myself: "Could the treasure be lying just a few feet-further below the waterline, in each pit already excavated?"

Grandpa B referenced several-times in his journal, "Having buried many friends six-foot under." What if Grandpa B actually buried the treasure 'Six feet Under' the water table in each location; or, possibly even deeper than that? Who knows how deep I'll need to dig at each site? With my guest's arrival time quickly approaching, I have very-little time remaining to prove my new hypothesis.

Hopping into the operator's seat of the backhoe, I begin working the controls to position the excavator over what has just become my new 'Ground Zero.' Plunging the bucket into the hole, I dig deeper-and-deeper into the saturated soil. As my discarded mound of mud continues to grow, I keep a close-eye out for any tell-tale glint of gold.

Reaching the 'Six-feet Under' mark, I expect my bucket to begin bogging down at any moment; however, after proceeding to dig down to a depth of nearly eight-feet, I've still yet to unearth a single piece of additional gold. As the minutes tick away, I eventually concede my latest treasure hunting theory has been debunked.

Lifting the stabilizer arms after securing my bucket in the travel position, I pack up my tools and head for home. With guests scheduled to arrive in fifteen short-minutes, my treasure hunting pursuits will have to be put on 'Hold' for the foreseeable near future.

Chapter 17

~Approach of the Winter Solstice~

Days leading up to the Winter Solstice are always a logistical nightmare. With responsibility resting squarely on my shoulders to ensure everything goes exactly as planned throughout the duration of the festivities, I won't be able to relax until everything is in place, and ready for the arrival of our next guests.

This year has proven to be exceptionally challenging! With less than two-weeks before the start of our Winter Solstice celebration, World Peace is being threatened by two Superpower leaders embattled in a 'Political Stalemate.' While we normally don't send out invitations for guests to visit during this critical timeframe, I felt it necessary to break protocol by arranging an emergency guest 'Summit.'

Putting into action an old strategy once used to help successfully resolve hardline political differences between two World leaders, I've invited the rival Presidents to come enjoy a few relaxing days of fishing. Crappie spawning season will still be in full swing during their visit; and, I'm hoping what worked with Ronnie and Mikhail decades ago, will once again help in developing trustworthy relations between these two Superpower leaders.

Regrettably, a highly disturbing situation has developed since my plan was put into action. The incident occurred after each President returned their signed visitation contracts.

Within minutes of receiving their emailed documents, SHEILA issued a 'Warning' that someone had attempted to upload a Trojan virus into her system. The attempted hack was made through a back-door program, only accessible by those having recently signed one of our visitation contracts. The highly sophisticated worm she found was a sleeper program, designed to effectively shut down power grids, and wreak havoc on the once considered 'Protected' financial reserves of the recipient.

If it hadn't been for our Valley being totally 'Off the Grid;' and, the fact we're not tied to any 'currency-based' financial system, SHEILA informed me the sophisticated virus would've inflicted catastrophic financial damage before being discovered.

SHEILA first reported noticing something was wrong, when a series of small credits were being requested; credits that would've automatically been paid without raising an eyebrow, had we been reliant upon a currency-based accounting system.

Having instructed SHEILA to go ahead and pay the initial insignificant amounts, I wanted whoever sent the virus to think their hack had been successful. Had we denied the first requested funds, the culprit would've automatically known his worm had been discovered within our system.

Once the person responsible proceeded to accept our initial wire transfer, SHEILA was instructed to delay payment on any future withdrawal requests. Much larger, reoccurring credits have since been requested, which would've easily bankrupted another Country's treasury reserves virtually overnight.

Tracking the initial payment made back to an offshore bank, SHEILA was then able to access the managing broker's databases. We now know which Country planted the malicious virus; and believe me when I say: "The person, or persons, behind this unconscionable breach of contract will certainly suffer Odin's wrath in due time."

Reaching the helipad at the very moment Fast Eddie touches down, I hurricdly remove my gloves to shake the hand of my first guest readying to exit the chopper. Intending to get him indoors before the arrival of my next guest, I offer President KJ a lift back to the house on my ATV. Cranking up the song 'Wipe-out' as we take off, we're soon pulling into the garage, where I quickly escort Kim upstairs to the banquet hall.

With an extravagant buffet laid out for him to enjoy, the President resembles a young child released to run uninhibited through a candy store. Once KJ begins filling his plate with mounds of seafood and his requested Beluga caviar, I promptly excuse myself.

Heading hastily back down the stairs, I once again hop onto my ATV and tear off towards the helipad; where Dad has already landed the second-chopper, and is currently escorting our last guest down to meet me at the lower landing.

My ATV comes to a sideways-skidding halt, stopping directly-alongside my next passenger; who stands frozen in a rather contorted posture, readying to receive copious amounts of mud splatter. Tossing the unscathed-President a helmet, I motion for 'B' to come aboard.

Instructing him to "Hold on tight," we quickly tear off towards the house with dirt and gravel flying everywhere. It's all I can do to keep from laughing my ass off, hearing President O screaming and praying repeatedly, "Oh God, Allah save me…!"   .

Skidding to a halt within inches of slamming into the already heavily damaged "Packers Fan Parking Only" sign, our journey comes to an abrupt end.

Glancing back at President O, his face is literally 'White as a sheet.' The color quickly returns to his cheeks as he steps off the ATV, humbly thanking me for my "Anticipated discretion in keeping recent events Confidential."

Assuring the President whatever happens in Odin's Valley remains in Odin's Valley, I escort him into the house and up the stairs. On the way to the banquet hall, I inform him; "President KJ is in the room you are about to enter, and I expect you to treat the President respectfully at all times."

I go on to give President O the same speech recently conveyed to President KJ, saying; "In Odin's Valley, all men are truly created equal in the eyes of Odin; or whatever God you may, or may not believe in. The All-Seeing-Eye is blind to the affairs you'll soon be discussing, during the truce which exists while you're here enjoying our hospitality. Whatever agreements are made during your visit, you are contractually bound by your word; for Odin's wrath will fall heavily upon you and your constituents, should you ever fail to uphold your Honor."

Before entering the room, President O stops to prepare for the introduction. Tucking in his shirt and straightening his tie, he opens the door and proudly swaggers into the banquet hall.

There stands KJ stuffing his mouth with oysters and shrimp, motioning energetically for President O to come over and join him in the feast. As President KJ prepares to take a drink from his mug of raspberry ale, he offers up a toast to Odin in his native tongue, with obvious expectations of President O reciprocating.

Minimally acknowledging the toast, President O reaches for a plate before sampling the many oysters on a half-shell. As fate would have it, President O suddenly reacts violently to the spoiled flesh of an oyster. Hastily spewing the shellfish back out onto the platter in front of him, he lashes out by saying: "How could you serve this crap? Are you trying to kill me?"

184

I respond back quickly, "I assure you; Chef J would never have served such a foul Hors D Oeuvres. You obviously disrespected Odin, by not paying him proper homage during President KJ's toast. Let this be a lesson to show you there are greater powers in the World, than the governments which run this small planet we live on."

Without missing a beat, President KJ raises his mug and offers up another toast in badly broken English, saying: "No matter how much perceived power each of us have over our governments, we are but pawns in the celestial game of chess being played. Praise Odin for providing us the opportunity to become humble servants to fate."

President O humbly raises his own mug; paying befitting homage to Odin this time, as he quickly washes away the foul taste in his mouth. After downing every-last drop of sweet nectar in his mug, President O catches his breath momentarily before responding in a jokingly manner; "I thought Reagan was just bullshitting in the Presidential Ledger, when he claimed the Democratic Party wasn't the most powerful force in the Universe to contend with."

President KJ quickly responds in a somewhat cocky manner, "There are many forces in the World, that you and your government should show greater respect toward."

In order to salvage whatever cordiality I can between the two leaders, I try changing the subject by announcing, "The boats are all gassed-up to go fishing in the morning! Who's ready to catch some giant slab crappies?!" By the narrowest of margins KJ raises his hand first, with both men nearly pulling a shoulder muscle trying to raise their hand the highest.

Offering President KJ 'Choice' of two new Ranger boats custom-made for the occasion, I add a bit of competition by announcing: "I will be fishing from the other boat currently moored at

185

the dock. Both of you will fish together; and, if you succeed in catching more crappies by combined weight than I do this weekend, you'll each get to take home your own Ranger boat! There is only one stipulation; which is, I don't want to see either of you showing disrespect to one another *ever* again! Deal?"

In unison, both leaders extend a handshake to each other, saying, "Deal!"

As if a 'Second Round' dinner bell has just rung, both Presidents turn in unison to feast like Kings on the massive spread laid out before them. Each man impressively keeps up with the other, pretty much mouthful-for-mouthful until the desert round. Once dessert is served, they both slow down to enjoy the splendid flavors beginning to fill the last voids in their now bulging, 'Buda-like' stomachs.

With each man putting on several-pounds before literally bellying up to the bar, spirits are high for the upcoming event. Both men begin establishing a sense of camaraderie, that would've never been developed publicly. Toasting each other, their mugs suddenly shatter upon clacking them together a little too aggressively. In the back of my mind, I begin hoping this is not an 'Omen' of what to expect during their visit.

During the first day of fishing competition is fierce, with both Presidents weighing in twenty-two pounds more fish, than the massive amount I'm able to land. Throughout the day, I can tell they're struggling to remain civil towards each other, as political pride occasionally shows prejudice in each other's razzing; but once back on land, conversations remain highly respectful. After jubilantly celebrating their commanding lead in the day's weigh-in, both men eventually retire for the night.

The second and last day of their visit, the morning starts off with both Presidents arriving slightly hung over from last night's bonding. The "Toast" I enjoyed most during their celebrating was the one where they both agreed to work together in the future, vowing to maintain open communications with each other, "No matter how distant the media perceives each other's posture to be."

As the second day of fishing progresses, the two men become buried in giant crappies flopping everywhere. Their teamwork in helping to release each other's catch far exceeds my ability to keep up with them fish-for-fish. We end up calling it an early day, after fearing they might start to sink from the added weight of fish, which now fills their gunwales from bow to stern.

Conceding my fleet of fishing boats will soon be two vessels fewer in number, the two Presidents enjoy one-last night of camaraderie, before heading back to the 'All Seeing Eye' of their governments.

The next morning, I see the two Presidents off to their respective choppers, confident my efforts have been successful in getting each man to respect and trust each other more. After watching my two departing guests become small specks on the horizon, I head longingly towards the captain's chair; hoping to enjoy a bit of rest and relaxation, before the arrival of this-year's Winter Solstice delegation.

With twelve guests invited to our 'Extra Special' Winter Solstice Event, Dad keeps saying he expects this year to be the most enlightening year on record; even more so, than the year Al had to fill in for President C at the last moment, after Ms Hillary refused to let him visit without her.

When Al and another guest by the name of Mr. G brainstormed during their enlightenment, the duo came-up with a highly-efficient way to exchange information across our planet. Who knows what

187

wonderful discoveries and future inventions await, during this year's 'Melding of the Minds?'

Reaching the bump-out window, I relax back in the captain's chair expecting to fall asleep in short-order. Instead of quickly nodding off into dreamland, I find myself relentlessly pondering what other clues might be out there, to help in finding Grandpa B's treasure. Unable to keep my eyes closed after a 'Revelation' suddenly pops into my head, I find myself staring curiously at our family Bible sitting on the fireplace shelf.

The Bible's front cover once provided invaluable clues to finding Grandpa B's treasure; clues that would've remained undiscovered, had the binding not split open to expose the hidden letter. Continuing to gaze at the Bible, I think to myself: "Could the back-cover be holding additional hidden clues under its binding? Might these clues; if actually found there, be even more enlightening than those discovered under the front cover?"

Reaching over to seek immediate answers, my nimble fingers begin picking feverously at the back-cover's binding. After meticulously pulling each stitch free one-by-one, I'm eventually able to slip my thumb, and index finger under the edge of the binding.

Probing for a clue, I soon find myself nearly jumping for joy! Barely able to grasp hold of a piece of paper found under the back-cover's binding, I slowly expose the letter to light for the first time in well over two-centuries.

Carefully viewing the fragile piece of parchment, I begin deciphering the many words scribed upon it in fine, flowing calligraphy. The letter translates, "By reading this, it means you are one-step closer to locating the treasures of Odin's Valley. Twelve bells I have buried, which Mother Nature will one-day point too from clues

188

prominently placed before you. A mystic pipe carved by Odin himself lay safely protected beneath each bell. Be forewarned! Ye must possess all twelve pipes during ritual, in order to expose the resting place of Odin's treasure horde concealed deep within the bosom of Mother Nature. Deception by monks will guide you to each pipe; but make no mistake, shun their deception when using the clues to locate me own treasure. Be true to Tempest when engaging in ritual, for at precisely four-minutes and twenty-seconds past Non on the Winter Solstice, all twelve involved in ritual must partake in celebration using Herbs harvested from Odin's Garden. On that day, the resting place of a celestial dowry exceeding mortal man's wildest imagination will be revealed."

Attempting to relax back in the captain's chair with limited success, I find myself staring out the looking glass pondering the significance of each word Grandpa B meticulously scribed.

With two full-hours before Winter Solstice guests are scheduled to begin arriving, my excitement in realizing I've already acquired the twelve-pipes noted in the letter, has my mind racing with anticipation.

Chapter 18

~A Problem Exists~

Relaxing back in the captain's chair, thinking everything is set and ready for the arrival of our Winter Solstice guests, I suddenly remember one highly important task yet to be completed.

The two 'Special Reserve' barrels I have saved for use during this year's ritualistic Toast, are still sitting in the cellar beneath Grandpa B's original homestead; left there for the past three-years to properly age. While the barrels could've been stored in our home's massive wine cellar, I decided to ensure Dad wouldn't accidentally tap into either one of them, by tucking both kegs safely away at this remote location.

To have any chance at retrieving the specially aged barrels; and get back in time before guests start arriving, I'll need to leave right away. My itinerary has me on a strict time schedule, leaving less-than an hour before our first guest is scheduled to land. Flying out the door, I hop on my ATV and take-off for the old homestead at full-throttle.

Eventually pulling up to the ancient stone-outcropping, once used as Grandpa B's front porch, you'd never know a cabin had previously been attached to it. Searching under a brush pile strategically placed to conceal the nearby root cellar's entrance, I eventually find the heavy iron handle I'm looking for.

Grabbing hold of the door, I give it my best shot; but it doesn't budge. Using a nearby log as leverage to turn the heavily rusted handle, it eventually gives way; allowing me access to the sanctuary once used by Grandpa B, to avoid being scalped by Indians.

Cool air from the subterranean-space slaps me in the face, as I slowly make my way down the moss-covered steps. With sunbeams streaming into the root cellar, my eyes strain to see the two-barrels of sweet nectar propped up against the far-back wall. Without wasting a moment of time, I head with conviction into the cobweb-filled cellar to retrieve my precious cargo.

It doesn't take me long to figure out something is seriously wrong, when my boots instantly begin sticking to the floor. Staring down in horror at my feet, the red-stained limestone surface looks as if someone has massively bled out across it. Cautiously lifting the first barrel of raspberry ale off the floor, I face the harsh reality of finding it completely empty!

Realizing termites have compromised the integrity of the first keg, I forebodingly reach for the second and last barrel. Upon attempting to lift the critically important keg from the floor of the cellar, its fragile shell literally crumbles in my hands. Termites have completely-destroyed both barrels! Reality kicks me in the crotch, upon facing the fact; that not-one drop of 'Vintage' ale remains available for use, in performing the upcoming Solstice Toast.

With Ritual scheduled to begin in just a little over twenty-four hours, my thoughts focus on the entry found in Grandpa B's journal; where he mentions the past consequences, of not giving "Proper Toast" to Odin during the Winter Solstice event! My entire body suddenly feels like I've just endured several-rounds of a bare-knuckle fight, with Muhammad Ali.

Desperately picking up the phone, I try calling Dad to see if he might've stashed away a specially-aged barrel for his own 'personal' consumption, in another location. With my call going straight to voice mail, I immediately call him back several-times in quick succession. On my fifth attempt, he finally answers his phone sounding rather annoyed.

"Where are you? Guests are about to begin arriving!" My Father's stern words speak volumes. Hearing no immediate response, Dad asks with a foreboding uneasiness in his voice, "What's wrong?"

Without beating around the bush, I respond, "The ritualistic ale has been lost, with not one-drop remaining to give proper Toast! I will explain 'How' and 'Why' later; but I must ask, "You wouldn't happen to have a spare keg of vintage ale lying around anywhere; would you?"

Dad immediately shouts; "Dammit!! I knew you still had two barrels stashed away for the Toast; so, I replenished my stash of medicinal herbs, by trading my last special-reserve barrel to Leland a few-days ago. Let's hope he still has some of it left, or we're going to be in a 'World of Hurt' around here!" Without waiting for a response, my father states: "I suggest you get back home to welcome your guests. I'm already in the chopper heading East to pay Leland a visit...Henry out!"

Hearing Dad hang up, I follow his instructions by beating a hasty retreat in the direction of home. Reaching the front door, I can already hear the approach of our first incoming leer jet; its high-pitched turbines echoing throughout the Valley.

With the sudden approach of a severe weather system posing a danger for travel, all twelve guests originally set to arrive over a two-day period are now scheduled to arrive within a very short, five-hour window. As the grandfather clock strikes Noon, our first guest lands at the airport.

Once chauffeured through the Valley, each guest is let out at the lower entrance of the house: where I quickly escort them upstairs to the

192

banquet hall. One-by-one, guests continue to land in regular half-hour intervals, with the exception of one.

Having lost communication with the pilot, when he predictably disappeared from radar upon final approach through the mountains, our 12th dignitary is now exceptionally late; so late, I fear something terrible may have happened.

While guests are celebrating in the banquet hall, I frantically scour my wine cellar for a possible lone barrel of vintage ale; one that might've somehow been improperly rotated. Unfortunately, with having an overly-anal method of storing the massive number of kegs, my search turns into yet another 'Lesson in Futility.'

Returning to the banquet hall, I put my 'Game Face' on like nothing is wrong, even though my gut is twisting and turning inside like nobody's business. Luckily for me, everyone in attendance appears to be thoroughly enjoying themselves, with celebration continuing well into the evening.

Not yet having heard a word from my father; and, with the disposition of our missing twelfth-guest still unknown, I eventually head to my room for the night. Feeling as if the Sandman has been issued a restraining order, I place the radio next to my ear; praying to Odin for good news to come-in over the radio, from one of our several search teams. Lying motionless in bed, while gazing out my portal window, I find myself utterly mesmerized by the abnormally high number of shooting-stars streaking across the heavens.

Fast Eddie finally radios-in, moments after three o'clock in the morning; stating, "Have spotted the wreckage of our missing guest's plane." A search party is immediately dispatched to the location; but, with the extremely-rugged terrain found there, it is highly doubtful any survivors will be found. Despite the odds, everyone remains highly optimistic.

An excruciating number of minutes later, I receive an incoming transmission from Fast Eddie, announcing he's found a parachute with an attached body dangling from a tree. As the search team closes in on the coordinates, I pray the rescue mission is successful in producing a surviving dignitary.

"Whoo Hooooo...Thank You Odin! Thank you very much!!," comes over the radio, as the first-rescuer goes on to report after arriving at the scene; "He's still alive but needs immediate medical attention! Assisting him into Ed's chopper as I speak," the rescuer announces.

Listening intently to the radio, I soon hear Fast Eddie transmit: "I'm in route to the nearest hospital. JB was able to get him to take a drink from his canteen, and vital signs are now stable. He's going to make it!" After a short-pause in his transmission, Eddie comes back, by asking: "Won't this leave you one-dignitary short for the Toast?"

"I've got everything covered with my back-up plan. Will inform you if the situation changes," I quickly respond. Sitting back pondering my last statement, I begin reviewing my back-up plan on getting Anne back in time for Ritual.

Racing for the phone in my study, providing a direct line to where Anne's been staying, I pray for the call to be answered. I'm not sure what I'll say if it ends up going to voice mail; but, if it does, the wait for Anne's reply will be agonizing.

My prayers are quickly answered on the second ring, but it's not Anne who answers the call. Mona informs me Anne and Aunt Mary actually departed nearly six-hours ago, and should be arriving home shortly with 'Extremely Important' news!

Questioning her as to what the Important 'News' is that she's referring to, Mona informs me: "I'm not quite sure!? Anne was getting her morning yoga lesson from a Coptic monk, when she suddenly bolted out of the room screaming: "Non…. oh my God! Non…that's it!!"

Bewildered and wondering what Anne might've meant from her last departing words, I terminate the call upon hearing the faint pulse of chopper blades far-off in the distance. With each passing second, the thumping sounds get louder and louder.

Security cameras engage, posting visual confirmation across the big screen of Anne's helicopter arriving at top-speed. As Aunt Mary lands the chopper at the airport, Anne hastily departs the cockpit running as fast as she can towards an awaiting Hummer. For a moment, I wonder why she didn't just land on the tarmac below the house, but quickly remember it now being within the critical 'Twelve-hour' period prior to the Solstice Ritual. Any flight approaching the house during this timeframe would be considered a 'Terrorist threat,' and be instantly eliminated by our automated security system.

Attempting to radio Anne three-times, and getting no response, I suddenly realize the volume control of my radio has been turned down to its lowest setting. Cranking up the volume, I hear Anne frantically trying to answer me with the sound of her Hummer racing at high-speed in the background.

"I've got great news! Will be there in three-minutes. Please make sure security protocols are disengaged before I get there!! …copy?!" Anne says, with a highly excitable tone in her voice.

Finally able to respond, I answer, "Copy! What important news do you have for me?"

Anne responds, "I'll tell you when I get there… Shut off the security system NOW; or, you'll never get to find out what I have to

195

tell you! Anne out!"

Immediately instructing SHEILA to disengage all security protocols leading up to the house, I race downstairs to greet my wife. "As fast as Anne drives, three-minutes really means more like two;" I think to myself.

Opening the lower-level door exactly two-minutes later, my expectations are confirmed watching Anne skidding sideways to a complete stop; but not-before, first taking out Dad's now heavily damaged 'Parking' sign.

Running up to welcome her home, I ready myself for a big hug. As she falls into my arms, our embrace melds us together as one; a short-moment later, Anne excitedly pulls away to inform me she's discovered the "True meaning of NON."

"What do you mean by NON?" I ask with a perplexed look across my face.

Anne shouts out enthusiastically, "NON means THREE O'clock! We've been misinterpreting Grandpa B's words our whole lives, thinking he was misspelling NOON!!" She goes on to tell me about how the church back in the twelfth century changed the traditional 3:00 pm. 'NON' to 'NOON'; proclaiming NOON to forever represent 'Twelve O'clock,' in accordance with the sun being straight up in the sky.

Standing dumbfounded, Anne's words cut deep into my soul as I find myself pondering the full-magnitude of the revelation. Before Anne can begin questioning me on my thoughts, I proceed to enlighten her about the hidden document recently discovered under the front-cover of the family bible.

Her jubilation is brief, as I immediately dampen the mood, by stating: "I hate to tell you this; but we have major problems taking place, that you're not yet aware of. There's been a plane crash, and one of our dignitaries is on-the-way to the hospital, fighting for his life. I'm going to need you to fill in as the twelfth-dignitary, during this year's Solstice Ritual; and hopefully, Dad will be able to secure from Leland, the specially-aged ale needed for the Toast."

Before I can inform her dad is late from returning, Anne yells: "What do you mean, 'IF' he's able to secure the ale we need? What happened to the two vintage kegs of ale you had stashed away in the cellar of the old homestead? Don't tell me your father went on another drinking binge!"

"Hold on sweetheart," I say to her.

Before I can say another word, Anne responds back angrily: "Don't you 'sweetheart' me! You do realize what could happen, if we fail to have properly aged ale on-hand for the Toast...don't you?!"

Confirming my clear understanding of the 'Highly undesirable Ramifications' of not having properly aged ale in-hand to conduct the Solstice Toast, I respond: "It gets worse! Dad has yet to return, and I still haven't heard a word from him since he left; on top of that, he's not sure if Leland still has any of the Special Reserve Ale remaining."

"What in the hell was your father doing, giving Leland all our Special Reserve Ale?!!," Anne yells out. Highly confused at this point, her temper is quickly approaching critical mass.

Suddenly realizing I've yet to inform Anne about the termites having destroyed both Special Reserve barrels, I tell my wife: "Hold on. Before we continue this 'Laurel and Hardy' skit, let me explain everything. You and I can then figure out the best course of action to take!"

Once I've enlightened her on our current predicament, Anne and I go through every-possible scenario we could possibly face during the upcoming Ritual; including, but not limited to, what will happen if Dad fails to return in-time for the Toast?

Chapter 19

~Winter Solstice Ritual~

Nearly twenty-four hours ago, my father left to retrieve the last 'vintage barrel' of raspberry ale known to exist, from Leland, who he regretfully traded it to a few-days ago. Knowing how important it is to return in time for the Solstice Toast, with whatever amount of ale he can retrieve, I find it extremely disturbing we haven't heard a word from him, since his last transmission several-hours ago.

Silence is generally 'Golden' with my father; but, with a strong frontal system moving through the mountains, I'm beginning to worry he may have experienced similar flight trouble, as that of our recently hospitalized dignitary.

The moment Fast Eddie returns from his trip to the hospital, I rush to inform him of Dad's 'Missing in Action' status. Without hesitation, Fast Eddie immediately lifts-off on another Search-n-Rescue mission, to find his lifelong friend.

Under any other circumstance, I'd be joining in on the search party; but, with the critically-important hour of Ritual fast approaching, my only option is to continue preparing for the Solstice event, as Pop instructed me to do before leaving.

Shortly after the grandfather clock finishes striking the hour of Eleven, SHEILA lets me know guests have begun to assemble in the banquet hall. Deciding to proceed with the normal Noon Ritual, as we've done each year without fail, I pray Dad arrives back in time with enough vintage ale to give 'Proper Toast.'

With everyone in the banquet hall waiting patiently for my arrival, I enter the room carrying a keg of ale over each shoulder. A resounding cheer goes up: "Hip Hip-Hooray! Hip Hip-Hooray!" Before the enthusiastic guests can issue up a third round of cheer, I'm already dispensing my own 'First Round' of cheer from a newly-tapped keg. Circling around me like a flock of vultures; I make everyone wait to indulge, until each person has received their own fist-full of ale.

My intention is to offer multiple toasts to Odin, before beginning the countdown to our Winter Solstice Ritual. Should we have no other choice; but to offer 'improperly aged' ale during the Annual Toast at Noon, I want everyone to be so involved in celebration, that no-one realizes something is wrong.

Celebrating the passing of each-minute in our countdown to the ritual Toast, the first keg of raspberry ale is quickly drained. Tapping into the second keg, I remain hopefully optimistic, in Dad showing up at the last-minute to save the day.

As the first strike of Noon begins chiming on the grandfather clock, I'm forced to begin the Annual Ritual. With each guest holding a mugful of ale, I instruct everyone to lift their steins high in the air. All twelve of us repeat the "Toast" together, exactly as it's been given each-year for over two-centuries. Finishing Grandpa B's ritualistic 'Words' at the precise moment the clock chimes for the twelfth-time, all participants begin downing their mugs of ale. Without coming up for air until the entire contents are consumed, everyone finishes up by slamming down their empty mugs in near unison.

Allowing everyone a few moments to savor the ale's intoxicating flavor, guests are soon instructed to begin preparing for the final part of Ritual. Using the ebony pipes Grandpa B hand-carved over two-centuries ago, we proceed to perform the Annual Ritual of smoking herbs harvested from Odin's Garden; doing so at precisely four-minutes and twenty-seconds past the hour of Noon.

I'd originally planned to smoke from the newly discovered 'Twelve Pipes of Odin' as part of the Noon Ritual, but decided it'd be best to wait until the newly discovered 'True Hour of Non' to introduce them.

Throughout the Valley, the sound of fish thrashing about in ever-diminishing pools of water grows exponentially louder by the minute. Having witnessed waters in past-years resume normal flow rates immediately after the Annual Toast, even my most enlightened guests begin questioning if a problem exists.

Putting on a ruse without promoting a lie, I downplay the current phenomenon taking place, by playing it off as being an 'Expected Event.' Putting forth another Toast, I thank my guests for being here on this special occasion, going on to say: "I am proud to announce, we will be repeating Ritual upon the newly-recognized hour of 'Non,' taking place at precisely Three O'clock." Once everyone has emptied their mugs once again, I instruct my guests to relax and enjoy the luncheon prepared for them.

On cue, Chef J starts bringing out full platters of shrimp and oysters, along with several entre' selections she's prepared. As guests begin chowing down like ravenous dogs, I slip upstairs to get an update on the status of Fast Eddie's rescue mission.

Attempting to reach him by radio, Fast Eddie finally answers my near-frantic calls on the third attempt, stating abruptly: "Eds to Base…have packages on board and heading home.... Be advised… encountering heavy turbulence… ETA one hour… Eddie out!" As the radio transmission is terminated, the ensuing silence leaves me longing for more information.

I try calling him back right away to confirm the ale needed is in transport; but my call goes unanswered. Figuring he's busy fighting to keep his chopper in the air, I respond one last time: "Copy your message…Will have transport waiting for you at the airport…stay safe!"

Looking down at my watch, I calculate their arrival time will be dangerously close to the 'Three O'clock' deadline. As long as they don't run into trouble getting back, the Ritual at 'Non' should go off without a hitch; provided there's still enough vintage ale remaining in Leland's keg to give a proper Toast.

Returning to greet my guests, I invite everyone up to the bay window for a final gaze out across the Valley. Allowing everyone a few-short minutes in the captain's chair, each guest gets an opportunity to experience their own personal vision through the looking glass.

Side-stepping questions about the many excavated areas being seen throughout the Valley, guests soon begin seeking a more targeted explanation as to why the artesian springs have yet to resume their normal flow-rates. Before I can offer a plausible explanation, SHEILA announces Fast Eddie and my father to be in final approach of the airport.

Wasting no time, I ask SHEILA: "Please determine if my father is in possession of the package he went to retrieve!?"

SHEILA reports, "Your Father has successfully procured ale needed for the Toast!

No longer having to worry about creating a panic situation, I introduce everyone to the recently discovered meerschaum pipes 'Hand-carved' by Odin himself. Explaining the protocol for repeating the Solstice Ritual, I go on to tell them: "Upon the third chime from the grandfather clock, we will raise our mugs and repeat the 'Toast' made at Noon. After quenching your thirst, everyone will proceed to smoke from their own meerschaum pipe at exactly four-minutes, and twenty-seconds past the newly-recognized 'Hour of Non.' I expect a mind-blowing revelation to occur at this time; an event for which, you are bound by oath never to divulge what you have witnessed."

Excusing herself for interrupting, SHEILA provides me with an important fact, stating: "Since the hour of Noon has long-since passed, security protocols will now allow flights to safely approach the house, without fear of being blown-out of the sky."

Immediately relaying the information to Eddie; he confirms the transmission, and quickly changes his flight plan to save valuable time. As everyone watches Fast Eddie's chopper approaching through the giant bay window, expectations grow exponentially with each "Tick" emanating from the grandfather clock.

Once the finely crafted timepiece begins chiming 'Quarter-till the Hour,' I instruct everyone to head directly for the banquet hall, in preparation for our inaugural 'Toast' at Non. While everyone begins filing into the elevator, I quickly head down the stairwell to help my father finish delivering the critically-important 'Special Reserve' barrel.

Running up to the chopper, I fight through the turbulence of the blades, as the door to the helicopter abruptly slides open. Dad steps out of the cabin to greet me, bellowing-out loudly over the noise of the winding-down engine: "Don't get mad...I can explain!"

I respond back, by yelling: "Don't worry about being late. You're here with the ale, that's all that matters!" Quickly stepping past Dad to retrieve the keg from the chopper, I'm taken back to the point of being speechless upon looking to my right.

There before me sits Leland in the co-pilot seat, smiling like the proverbial 'Cat that's just swallowed the canary.' Turning towards Eds in the pilot's seat with an extremely dumbfounded look on my face, I painfully ask, "Why?!" Wasting no time for an explanation, I hurriedly snatch the keg out of the chopper, and make a beeline for the house.

Not taking any chance on the elevator suddenly freezing up, as it unexplainably does from time-to-time, I manually carry the near-empty keg up the stairs. Flinging open the door to the banquet hall, I head deliberately towards guests holding out their mugs to be filled.

With less than two gallons of unconsumed ale remaining in the keg, I dispense a pint of sweet nectar into each awaiting mug. Normally we'd toast with a full-mug of ale; but no actual "Requirement" to do so is ever mentioned in Grandpa B's journal. I just hope the insignificant amount I'm pouring into each mug will be enough to pay respectful homage to Odin.

Finishing off the last of the keg into Anne's receptive stein, each participant begins uttering the Solstice "Toast" in unison. The moment our clock finishes its trilogy of chimes, everyone gulps down the contents of their mug. Like flicking on a light switch, every artesian spring in the Valley immediately begins flowing at normal volume levels. Celebration erupts, having narrowly avoided a catastrophic event of epic proportion.

Quickly preparing for what is to be the most important part of Ritual, I begin scraping together the last remaining cured herbs from Odin's Garden. Filling each mystical pipe, I hurriedly pass them around the table, until each guest has one firmly in their grasp.

With my watch in sync to the World clock, all twelve dignitaries begin smoking upon my announcement of it being four-minutes and twenty-seconds past the hour of Non. As each participant in Ritual exhales the rapidly-expanding smoke from their lungs, the rising cloud it creates, quickly starts to swirl-and-mix together over each person's head; eventually morphing into a whirlwind-like tornado, that continues to grow and elongate exponentially.

Growing into what can only be described as a 'Black Hole of Space' existing within the confines of the Valley, the newly formed vortex quickly extends all-the-way down to Lake Odin. As the whirlwind dips its finger into the water, the once mirror-like surface of the lake begins swirling like a toilet being flushed. Within a matter of minutes, Lake Odin lies completely drained of water.

Looking around at my guests all huddled together, trying to keep from being swept away by the vortex, I attempt to calm their fears by saying: "There's no need to worry! You're about to behold an amazing revelation! Stand fast and give praise to Odin!!" Seconds after finishing my words, the vortex dissipates, and winds immediately subside.

With the sun beginning to set behind Sasquatch Mountain, the far-end of the Valley exhibits an awe-inspiring golden glow. The retreating sun's rays appear to be refracting in all directions off the newly exposed lake bottom.

Seeing all my guests staring around dumbfounded at each other, I let out a celebratory yell; immediately bringing everyone back to their senses. Instructing the Winter Solstice dignitaries to "Stand Fast," I rush out to investigate the source of the glow.

Within minutes, I'm running across the tarmac to where Fast Eddie already has the Huey warmed up, and ready for take-off. Hopping into the aircraft, I give Fast Eddie a 'Thumbs Up;' directing him to get us to Lake Odin's shoreline as quickly as possible.

Yelling over the turbulence of the blades to "Hold on tight," we immediately take-off at near breakneck speed for the far-end of the Valley. Looking back towards the house upon departure, I can see the golden glow reflecting off my guests' faces, as they gaze in awe out the giant bay window.

With a foreboding sense of soon regretting the answer to the question I'm about to ask, I yell out to Eddie: "So…Do you happen to know, where Leland and my father took off too?!"

Fast Eddie gives me the 'Are you kidding me?' look, that I was expecting; saying, "After you took the keg inside, I overheard your father ask Leland if he wanted to take a little 'Road Trip.' They loaded-up their ATV with a couple of kegs and took-off in the direction of Odin's Garden."

Rolling my eyes, I respond nervously: "This is the last thing we need! If Pop's not careful, he's going to end-up pissing off Odin!"

During our journey, it becomes readily apparent that the glow emanating from the bottom of Lake Odin is quickly beginning to dim. With very little time for exploration before darkness fully-engulfs the Valley, we arrive at the original shoreline of the lake.

Setting down on the beach, Eddie and I exit the chopper like it's on fire. Running excitedly across the black sand of the recently exposed lake bottom, I'm the first to reach the edge, where it drops-off abruptly into the deepest part of the lake. Staring down into the ever-darkening abyss, Fast Eddie shines his high-beam, portable spotlight around to illuminate areas of the lake bottom below.

To our astonishment, we both stand staring in awe at countless golden structures shimmering in the light. Stretching for as far as our spotlight allows us to see into the seemingly endless cavern, the vast amount of gold is simply breathtaking.

Fast Eddie turns to me with eyes as wide as saucers, saying: "Do you know what this looks like? We may have just found the mythical 'City of Gold!' This is Awesome!!"

With the sun sinking into oblivion, I hear what sounds like an enormous bear in the not-too-far-off distance. Quickly realizing we're not in a 'Safe Zone,' I respond, "You may be right about it being 'El Dorado;' but for now, let's get the hell out of here!"

Intending to return in the morning with the proper gear needed to rappel down into the cavern, we hastily make our way back to the chopper as fast as our legs will carry us. Once safely back in the air, we hover over the area using the chopper's 'Nightsun' search light. Taking in one-last look at the amazing treasures, that literally cover the entire lake bottom; the sight is truly breathtaking!

Dominating the conversation for a majority of our short flight home, Fast Eddie and I discuss what we'll do tomorrow if the lake suddenly starts to rapidly-refill itself; while we're down on the bottom, heavily laden with treasure. We certainly don't want to be forced to swim for it; especially, since I once made a pact years-ago with an old friend, to never attempt swimming in the lake ever again.

The last time I went swimming in Lake Odin was decades ago, when my friend and I both almost drowned while scuba diving. On our first and befittingly last dive, we'd found ourselves caught-up in an extremely powerful undertow. Jacque had never encountered swifter currents in all his Worldly travels.

Given the extremely hazardous diving conditions existing within the first few-feet of the surface, one thing is certain…It will be impossible to retrieve any treasure, once Lake Odin returns to full-pool.

On our way back to the house, we buzz over Odin's Garden; soon seeing the headlights of Leland and my Father, making their way back through the labyrinth. Circling them once before resuming our flight plan, it looks as if they're bringing home a Christmas tree to be decorated; but something in my gut tells me, I won't need to break-out any ornaments.

Arriving back at the house, guests rush out to greet us; eager to confirm the origin of the 'Golden Glow' they'd witnessed. Giving limited explanation, I inform everyone about the massive horde of golden treasure found on the lake bottom.

With everyone scheduled to depart at first light, I make the following promise: "If I'm able to safely retrieve the treasure in the morning; like I hope to do, each of you will soon be receiving, an anonymous special-delivery of your weight in gold."

After cheers temporarily subside, I proceed to blow their minds by announcing: "In accordance with prophecies handed down by many cultures claiming its existence, for which many races have been exterminated by those seeking its possession, we may have just discovered the mythical 'City of Gold;' better known as 'El Dorado!' Planning to retrieve as much gold as I can before Lake Odin refills itself, I will be anonymously donating a majority of the treasures recovered to charities of your choosing."

Silence consumes everyone for what seems like an eternity, until the King lets out a tremendous cheer that reverberates throughout the hall like thunder. Reawakening everyone to reality, the resounding cheers that ensue literally shake the windows.

The amount of ale consumed throughout the night unsurprisingly nears record proportion. In the wee hours of the morning, I bid "Goodnight" to the last of my guests; watching them all slowly retire back to their respective rooms.

Not yet having an opportunity to speak to my father, on why he decided to bring Leland to our Valley; as well as, why he considered it 'Acceptable Behavior' to conduct a raid on Odin's Garden last night, I certainly intend to have a scathing conversation with him in the morning. Heading up to my bedroom for the night, it doesn't take long before I'm checking the back of my eyelids for holes once again.

Chapter 20

~Revelation~

With the Eastern horizon glowing a beautiful shade of crimson-orange from the approach of daybreak, a rogue rooster perched outside my bedroom window begins exercising its vocal cords. Proving himself worthy of 'Sainthood,' Roscoe chases the obnoxious bird away; moments before I'm about to put my double-barreled shotgun to good use.

As the first rays of sunlight begin knocking at my eyelids, I defiantly cover my face with a pillow, hoping to enjoy a few-extra minutes of peace and quiet; but before my body can completely relax, a sense of forgetting something 'Important' abruptly awakens me. Suddenly remembering guests will soon be gathering for departure, I spring upright in bed.

Flinging off the bedspread with a flick of my wrist, the cool morning air rushes in. As silken-sheets cascade from my mattress like a waterfall, I hurriedly slide out of bed; planting my bare feet onto the freezing-cold hardwood floor. Instantly re-energized at the thought of what the day will bring, I throw on some clothes, and quickly make my way downstairs to the banquet hall.

In route, I proceed to ask SHEILA three quick questions, including: "How long do I have before guests begin assembling? What's the weather report today? And can you please provide me the projected timeline, for Lake Odin returning to 'Full Pool' status?"

Responding immediately, SHEILA announces: "Your guests are

already assembled in the banquet hall, chowing down on Chef J's Annual 'Departure-Day' Feast. I expect it to be partly cloudy today, with a thirty-percent chance of rain this afternoon; a high near fifty, with low around forty-two this evening. To answer your last question, Lake Odin does not appear to be retaining water at this time; however, should the basin start to retain 100% of the water-volume currently flowing in, the lake will be able to completely refill itself within approximately ten-minutes time."

"Ten-minutes is not a lot of time to get out" I think to myself, as I quicken my pace towards the banquet hall, where guests have been patiently awaiting my arrival. In route to greet them, thoughts race through my mind, while seeking a simple answer to a troubling question; one that's been bugging me, since first seeing Leland in the chopper. The question being: "Why would Pop risk everything, by exposing an outsider like Leland to the secrets of our Valley?"

Whatever his delusional reasoning, on why he felt it acceptable to conduct a midnight-mission into Odin's garden last night, I'm sure my father's excuse will be a good one. I just pray Dad's raid last night doesn't cause us any future sufferance; should Odin become upset and seek retribution.

Making my way energetically downstairs to the banquet hall, my olfactory senses begin savoring delectable aromas emanating from our kitchen. Quietly slipping into the banquet room, I'm pleased to see everyone enjoying the farewell festivities. My presence initially goes unnoticed until leaning-up against the bar; at which point, I'm immediately flocked around by everyone in attendance.

Like a pack of reporters going after a hot storyline, guests begin throwing out questions about the treasures found at the bottom of the Lake. Holding up my hands to make an 'Official' statement, I announce: "I will be going down to the bottom of Lake Odin later

211

today, in-order to properly catalog all the artifacts found there. We do not want to disturb any of the treasure, until a complete security sweep of the area has been conducted; this unfortunately means, you'll not have the honor of being here to witness its recovery. As I told you last night; each of you will soon be receiving a special delivery of your weight-in-gold, to show my appreciation for you being here to assist in the discovery."

Letting guests know it's time for departure, I go on to say: "I wish you all a safe and memorable journey home. May Odin shower down on you continued good health and success throughout the upcoming year. Your chauffeurs will now take you to the airport in limousines waiting outside!"

Handshakes and hugs are exchanged as everyone departs the room; except for Dad and Leland, who are still chowing-down on the breakfast buffet like it's their last meal.

Clearing my throat loudly to get their attention, Dad and Leland suddenly realize they're the only other people left in the room. Pausing in his feasting, Dad senses from my folded-arms posture, that I'm still highly upset over his total disregard of our visitation protocols.

Declaring he wishes to explain his 'Reasoning' for bringing Leland to our Valley, Dad raises his mug of ale; boldly offering up the following toast, "May Odin bless this family, and keep us all together as one from this day forward." Seeing by my expression, that I'm completely baffled by what he just said in his rather prophetic toast, Dad goes on to say: "There is much to be explained. You will need to keep an open mind about the truths I'm about to divulge! Can you do that?"

"What are you talking about?" I say with growing frustration.

With a Cheshire cat-like grin on his face, my father relaxes back

212

in his chair, slowly proceeding to explain: "This is going to take a while! I suggest you grab your pipe, fill your mug with nectar, and plant your ass in the seat you're in; while your 'Grandson' over there explains everything!"

Being I have no offspring of my own, I find myself even more confused at this point. With my father continuing to point directly at Leland, after calling him my "Grandson," all I can do is stare at Dad in bewilderment.

Leland slides off his barstool, grasping my shoulder with a firm-but-gentle squeeze to secure my undivided attention. Expecting to hear him speak in his normal back-woods dialect, Leland surprises me by responding in perfect English, saying: "I have always wanted to tell you this, but a promise made years ago to Aunt Mary has kept me from doing so. Please forgive me for having deceived you all these years. Now that you've discovered and interpreted the Code you once left yourself, I am finally able to give proper introduction."

Feeling my knees starting to shake a bit, I decide to sit down and seriously reduce the amount of nectar remaining in my mug. Coming up for air, I nervously nod and say: "I don't know what the hell you're talking about, but go ahead, … I'm listening!?"

Leland replies, "Let us first smoke, so you can more easily understand the truth in what I'm about to tell you!" Sensing anxiety, Leland tries to calm my fears by saying: "Don't worry! I know herbs from Odin's Garden are only supposed to be smoked during Ritual, unless being used for medicinal purposes. This may be hard for you to believe; but yesterday while in the garden, a freakish lightning bolt came out of nowhere. The mega-watt discharge created a vortex, where Odin was able to come down and pay us a visit. The 'Big Guy' himself actually sat down and partied with us! I don't know if Odin was overly parched from his journey, but he can really put away the ale!"

Leland goes on to say, with a bit of envy: "He proceeded to down an entire keg, without coming up for air once! By the way...Odin wanted me to convey his 'Gratitude' for having tended his garden so-well, all these years. To show his appreciation, he instructed me to jog your memory about your 'True' past."

"What about my 'True' past?" I ask, sounding rather perplexed at this point.

Leland responds back quickly, "Smoke first; then, I'll be happy to explain everything."

By the time our pipe has been passed around three-times, my mind has been enlightened enough to keep my 'Perceived Reality' from casting even the slightest doubt, on what Leland is about to divulge. As Leland takes a firm hold on my chin, like my father always does when demanding my undivided attention, I ready myself to get hit with a bombshell!

In a stern voice, Leland begins by saying: "I'm going to start out by telling you; Odin's Valley happens to be the very-Valley, in which the mythical 'Fountain of Youth' is located. The waterfall gushing from the rock fissure below your house, is what has; in fact, sustained your body and mind, at the same age you were upon first coming to the Valley as Grandpa B, nearly three-hundred years ago."

While open-minded to the possibility; what Leland is saying could be true, I find myself blurting out: "Then why don't I remember ever being known as Grandpa B?" As I'm saying the words, it suddenly dawns on me I have absolutely no-recollection of my youth! In fact, the only memories I have of my past, start-out in the days following an extremely-bad car accident; which Anne and I were nearly killed in many-years ago.

Before I can question if I've been lied to all this time about my

214

'accident' decades ago, Leland interjects by saying: "Why don't you let me explain everything first; then, you can ask any questions you may still have?" Before continuing with his explanation, Leland instructs me to first go and bring back Anne.

Not wanting to wait any longer than I must to hear the rest of Leland's outlandish, but somehow believable explanation, I rush to find my wife. Within minutes, I'm practically dragging Anne back towards the banquet hall; offering only minimal explanation as to the urgency in needing to follow me. The only thing I say to her is: "It may be hard to believe what you're about to hear, but please keep an open mind. I promise you will soon be enlightened to something truly amazing!"

As we burst into the banquet hall, my father continues to sit perched on the same barstool he was using when I left him earlier. Reaching for his pipe, Dad offers it to Anne; saying jubilantly: "Let us smoke to open your mind, to the unfathomable truths you're about to hear; while at the same time, pay homage to Odin for bringing our family back-together, after all these years."

Anne initially refrains from smoking the pipe being offered; but after telling her about Odin's recent visit, and his instructions to indulge for purposes of our enlightenment, she smokes with mixed reservation. Once Anne has inhaled the mystical smoke several-times, she similarly becomes completely open-minded to what Leland is about to tell her.

Leland returns to divulging what he has waited decades to get off his chest. Choking back tears before continuing his explanation, Leland goes on to tell his 'Grandmother' about our Valley containing the mythical 'Fountain of Youth.'

While Anne listens intently to what Leland is telling her, she soon poses the question: "How could I possibly be your grandmother, when you are obviously so much older?"

215

Leland passes the pipe to Anne, going on to explain: "Water from the Fountain of Youth stops the aging process, in the first-generation of mortals who consume it. First-generation consumers feel euphoric and rejuvenated after drinking from the fountain; but each succeeding generation exponentially suffers the reverse effects of anti-aging, due to a 'Curse' placed on the fountain. With you being the first-generation of your bloodline to drink from the fountain, consuming its water every-day for one-full year, you slowly started regressing back to a younger state of mind, and body. This continuous consumption is what caused you to eventually forget your past."

Questioning a flaw in Leland's superfluous story, I state: "Anne and I have consumed water from the Valley almost every day, for as long as we can remember since our 'Accident' years ago. If your story is correct, how would we be able to remember everything that has happened to us for so many years?"

Leland responds, "Smoke first to clear your mind; I will then continue my explanation in complete detail! Please do not interrupt me again until I am done explaining, and all your questions will be answered in due time!"

After passing the pipe around once again for everyone to take a draw from, Leland continues: "When Mary first came to the Valley with you and your husband, she experienced an allergic reaction and nearly died. Fearing she was allergic to the Valley's water, Aunt Mary would secretly venture out of the Valley to bring back her own personal water supply, from natural springs found high-up in the mountains.

The very first full-year living in the Valley, upon the stroke of Mid-Night on New Year's Eve, Mary witnessed what subsequently became your 'Annual' re-occurrence of amnesia. After decades of dealing with your Annual affliction, she found your amnesia easier to explain and much easier for you to believe, by claiming both of you

216

had been in a 'Terrible Accident.' Using your Journal to remind you about your past lives, she essentially 'Reset the Stage' for you each year.

Before the first bout of amnesia left you ignorant of where your treasure was hidden, you'd luckily informed Mary about your journal holding clues to help locate your amassed fortune, should anything bad ever happen to you.

Mary knew if she ever hoped to see her share of the treasure, she'd have to wait for you to one-day figure out the 'Clues' you left behind in the journal.

After twenty-years of watching you both retain your youth, while she continued to age normally, Mary one-day accidentally drank from Anne's glass of water drawn from the fountain. Instantly realizing the 'Mistake,' she expected to become violently ill as in the past; but instead, Mary ended up feeling rejuvenated for the first time in many years. Discovering she was no longer allergic to water from the fountain, Mary was finally able to benefit from the anti-aging effects of the water.

While you and Anne continued to drink water from the fountain on a daily basis, Mary still preferred her artesian bottled water. Drinking only occasionally from the fountain, she would feel rejuvenated each time she drank. Not suffering the Annual New Year's Eve memory loss that each of you would experience, Mary began to develop a theory.

Getting ready to 'Reset the Stage' for you on your next yearly bout of amnesia, Mary planned to pull a harmless 'Ruse' to prove her hypothesis. By simply inserting a letter into Grandpa B's journal, Mary made you believe Grandpa B had decreed: "Everyone must pay homage to Odin, by drinking only raspberry ale during the last two-days of the Winter Solstice Event." If her ruse proved successful in keeping you from lapsing into another bout of amnesia, it conceptually would be the last time she'd ever need to re-set the stage for you.

By the time Mary conducted her experiment, I had already rapidly aged to very-near Mary's own age. Being a third-generation consumer of the fountain's water, I was suffering horribly from the fountain's curse, and aging exponentially faster than my father.

Attempting to make our age differences seem less confusing, when resetting your memories of the past for hopefully one-last time, Mary decided to portray my father, as being your 'Dad.' To make the ruse more believable, I was supposed to play the part of being your Grandfather; but for my own continued health, I decided it best to not take-on the role.

Rapidly aging into a decrepit old man from the fountain's 'Progeny' curse, I was desperate to find something that might slow down my affliction. It was at that time, I decided to leave the Valley; in-order to pursue a theory of my own. Taking on the role of 'Leland,' Mary and I both thought it best to keep you unaware, of me being your actual Grandson.

Seeing a perplexed look starting to form on my face, Leland responds: "Let us smoke once again. I will then continue to explain everything. There are many secrets about the Valley, that Odin instructed me to jog your memory about. It is imperative you refrain from interrupting me with any more questions, until I am done providing explanation. Be aware, conversations I had with Odin during my recent enlightenment will be forever forgotten, once the effect of Odin's herb has faded-away for the last time."

After consuming the last ration of herbs provided by Odin for our enlightenment, Leland continues his explanation, by saying: "For many years, I thought I was suffering from a very-rare, advanced aging affliction called 'Progeria;' but, through Aunt Mary's detective work, we discovered a progressive 'Aging' curse had been cast upon subsequent generations of those drinking water from the Fountain."

Mary found the relevant passage in your journal, where you as Grandpa B stated: "Be aware, the tribal Shaman setting me house ablaze could be heard placing a 'Curse' on the fountain; loosely translated, I believe it to be a rapid-aging curse with a dreadful 'multiplier effect' cast upon future generations consuming its waters. Should me progeny ever experience suffrage from this Curse, Odin hath promised an herbal cure may be grown, using waters outside of our Valley."

Looking for anything that would make bearable the excruciating pain caused by my advanced aging, I decided to search for the promised cure. Following Grandpa B's advice, I began growing my own crop of medicinal herbs in a remote location, outside the confines of Odin's Valley.

Leaving home to live with the ancestors of your original shipmates, I harmlessly appropriated a small-quantity of seed stock from Odin's Garden, to begin propagating my own medicinal-strain. The herbs I ended up growing, not only provided relief from the pains of my rapid aging; but as promised by Odin, they thankfully provided a 'Temporary' antidote to the rapid-aging curse.

The first-year's crop grown outside of Odin's Valley quickly proved to have many substantial medicinal benefits. One of the most surprising benefits I discovered, was when several members of the McCallister clan found relief from the excruciating pain of their terminal cancers; using a concentrated-extract made from these medicinal herbs. Amazingly, everyone's cancers steadily began to improve; and today, no-one has suffered from that ugly affliction in many years.

Providing my father; or technically, your 'Perceived Father' with plenty of herbal antidote, he was finally able to enjoy the benefits of anti-aging from the fountain's water. This is why your biological son regularly partakes of the herbs I've grown; doing so to remain healthy and provide immunity from the dreaded curse.

Your son would then reciprocate, by regularly providing me with water from the fountain; allowing both of us to finally enjoy the reality of no longer aging.

Even though herbs grown outside the Valley provide many medicinal benefits, they do not provide the awareness properties one experiences when smoking herbs harvested from Odin's Garden.

World leaders invited to the Winter Solstice find their IQ's exponentially increased, after smoking the mind-blowing herbs from Odin's Garden. They experience an increase in cognitive thinking for months after leaving the Valley; helping them maintain a higher approval rating with their constituents, while becoming better leaders in the process. It is also the reason many governments have fought so hard to keep their constituents from having access to the herb; fearful the general public might experience their own increase in cognitive thinking, and theoretically undermine political power.

This leads into the last statement made by Odin, before he departed back up into the sky; via a bolt of lightning, that nearly knocked us both off our feet. You're probably not going to like this; but, before he left, Odin decreed: "Be forewarned… My city is open for your pleasure till the sun sets on the next-day; but do not succumb to greed, by removing more than one's weight in gold each year. Consider it a gratuity for having perpetuated my strain of herb so well."

In a somewhat state of shock over Odin having complimented

me so grandly on my gardening skills, I soon find myself trying to grasp the limitation he placed on the amount of treasure I'm able to remove. Unable to hold my tongue any further, I end up blurting out: "Might I be able to extract the combined weight of my guests who participated in Ritual?"

With a look of frustration, Leland frowns at me saying: "You had to ask a question; didn't you!? Just couldn't keep your mouth shut for one more minute; could you?! If you would've just shut up a few moments longer... (shaking his head slowly) ...Sorry..., I no longer can remember anything else Odin told me now!"

With Odin's decree limiting the amount of treasure that can be removed each year to two-hundred and fifty pounds, I'm afraid there are going to be some very disappointed guests.

Chapter 21

~Conclusion~

Instantly bringing everyone back to their senses, Leland bellows out: "What in the hell are you waiting for?! We only have until sundown before Lake Odin refills itself!" Pausing momentarily before bolting through the door, Leland issues a personal challenge; saying with a broad smile across his face, "You know what they say about being the last one there!"

With the door starting to close behind him, Dad and I instantly scramble to see who can make it through the exit next. We soon find out the hard way; the indisputable fact, that two large men cannot fit through a standard-sized doorway together at the same time.

Finding ourselves wedged together, so tightly within the framework of the door that both of us can barely breathe, we end up declaring the first part of our sprint a 'Draw.' Quickly prying ourselves free of the doorway, we race to catch-up with Leland.

With the Huey already warmed-up and waiting to take us down to the lake, Leland readies for lift-off. As Dad and I approach the chopper, Leland bellows out over the noise of the accelerating prop: "We won't have much time to get treasure out... Jump in and be quick about it!"

Diving simultaneously into the open cargo door of the chopper, we end up declaring the second leg of our race a 'Draw' once again. Taking what seems like only a few-short minutes to reach our destination, Leland is already setting the Huey down on Lake Odin's original shoreline.

We dare not attempt landing the aircraft directly on the lake bottom; for fear of losing the chopper to rising water, should the lake begin filling back up too quickly. Forced to repel down into the depths of the cavern, the real challenge will be getting back-up the lifeline heavy-laden with treasure, before the sun sets.

With late-afternoon quickly approaching, I figure we'll only have enough time to complete one mission into the cavern. Thoughts race through my mind upon exiting the chopper, as to what types of treasure might be most desirable to procure, with having to climb back-up the rope; especially, if rising water forces a hasty departure.

Having had quite a bit of experience dangling from a rope lately, I'm the first to plant my feet into the massive horde of golden doubloons blanketing the lake bottom. Walking about mesmerized by the colossal amount of treasure within easy reach, the magnitude of the horde is beyond my wildest expectations.

The combined wealth of countless extinct civilizations lies strewn everywhere, with beheaded-statues of forgotten rulers, who once foolishly tried immortalizing themselves in gold, littering the landscape. Rolling hills of golden doubloons stretch farther than the eye can see into the subterranean cavern. Atop the tallest mound sits a Golden Palace; prominently exhibiting nine-massive pillars, made of interwoven elephant ivory.

Making our way towards the Parthenon-style structure, we marvel at a jewel-laden river of gold coins, seemingly flowing like a moat around both-sides of the palace. Arriving inside, we sit down to rest; while enjoying the bowl of herbs that Odin has rewarded us with, for our continued enlightenment.

As the smoke begins opening my mind to countless memories

long-since forgotten, my long-term bout with amnesia abruptly ends. Remembering the first few-days spent in the Valley like it was yesterday, I clearly recall sitting around a raging campfire with Odin himself, while killing-off several kegs of his raspberry ale.

Downing mug for mug while negotiating the original lease on the Valley, Odin enlightened me to several important tasks he needed performed. In exchange, he would allow us to live here 'Rent-free, in Perpetuity.' Being a mere mortal, I humbly agreed to the strict 'Terms' of his long-term lease on the Valley.

The first task he instructed me to carry out was the meticulous planting of the labyrinth, which he called his resurrected "Yggdrasil." Since planting the thousands of Ash trees used to create Odin's labyrinth, Yggdrasil has conjoined together into a massive living entity, that continues to grow taller and thicker at the base each year.

One of the most indenturing stipulations in Odin's lease, was the Annual task of tending his garden. In return for being its curator, Odin has been highly-gratuitous in providing me with everything I could possibly need in life.

It has indeed been a labor of love for me; providing Odin and his extended family with the best medicinal-grade herbs found anywhere in the universe. As a plethora of memories begins flowing through my mind, I sit processing my long-forgotten thoughts with a feeling of euphoria.

Looking up out of the cavern, the glowing redness of a sinking sun instantly brings me back to reality. Within seconds, I'm dragging Leland and Pop towards the drop lines; instinctively knowing we must quickly climb back-out of the cavern, before the lake refills itself.

Having spent far too much time staring mesmerized at the massive amount of treasure, I find myself regretfully being forced to leave near empty handed. As water quickly begins rising all around us, we unanimously decline Davy Jones's invitation to dine with him tonight, at Odin's golden banquet table.

Barely keeping ahead of the rising water, all three of us hastily climb back up the lifelines. Eventually making our way out of the depths of the cavern, we head swiftly towards the original shoreline of Lake Odin.

Leland and I are lucky enough to make it back to dry land just ahead of the rising water, but Dad ends up being forced to swim the last few-yards back to shore. Truly a sight to behold, my father is sitting along the shallow shoreline acting like a baby, splashing water everywhere with the golden scepter he managed to bring back tucked under his belt.

Dad might've retrieved a golden scepter, but I was able to snag hold of a diamond and ruby encrusted golden spear. As I stand admiring the weapon, Leland begins laughing uncontrollably. Starting to choke on whatever it is that's blocking his windpipe, Leland suddenly coughs up a diamond the size of a golf ball into the outstretched palm of his hand.

While each of us has removed a single object of immense value, it is far from being our combined weight in gold; even so, no one is disappointed in what we we've been able to retrieve.

The evening brings immense celebration throughout the house, with every resident of the Valley invited to our Annual Christmas party. Breaking the seal on over a dozen barrels of raspberry ale, everyone's having a great time watching the band lay down some truly amazing blues. After gifts are exchanged and the band finishes up their last set, it doesn't take long for the banquet hall to clear out.

As Anne and I support each other down the hallway to our

bedroom, SHEILA politely informs us temperatures in the morning are expected to be unseasonably warm. Before reaching the door of our room, we take SHEILA's advice, and make plans to get up early in the morning; hoping to spend some quality-time relaxing together on the 'Meditation Stone.'

Getting very little sleep, morning arrives way too early. With the Meditation Stone beckoning our presence, I awaken Anne with a gentle kiss on the cheek; then quickly make my way downstairs, to prepare us both a hearty breakfast. As I'm sprinkling the final ingredients of salt-and-pepper onto our sizzling-hot, morel mushroom and cheese omelets, Anne finally enters the kitchen.

With her nose being pulled along by the scent trail that's evicted her from a warm cozy bed, Anne deliberately makes her way toward the table, and sits down. Coming out of her coma-like trance, Anne suddenly realizes her dream to be reality. Grabbing a nearby fork, she begins wolfing down the breakfast I've placed in-front of her.

Finishing our feast near-simultaneously, we both sit back for a moment to aid in our digestion. Anne soon nestles up alongside me and begins to gently caress my inner-thigh. Showing her appreciation for the perfect start, of what she expects will be a perfect day, Anne proceeds to lay a quick kiss on my cheek.

Suddenly jumping to her feet, Anne races over and pulls two large beach towels from a nearby drawer. Throwing one at me, she exclaims: "We'd better get going if we're going to get any sun today!"

It doesn't take long before we're stretched out on the Meditation Stone in our birthday suits, enjoying the warm sunshine. With the sun quickly warming up the massive slab of limestone, a bead of sweat starts to form on my brow. As the first drop of perspiration slowly trickles down my forehead, it becomes readily apparent we are no longer alone.

"Mandy must have figured out how to open the door again," I think to myself, as the aging hound begins making her way up the outcropping of rock towards us. Surprising my wife by licking her in the face, Anne momentarily fights Mandy off; until unconditionally surrendering to her beloved old pet, with a loving hug.

"You know what's really bothering me?" I say to Anne with a concerned look on my face.

"And what would that be?" Anne replies, finally letting Mandy refill her lungs, after a lengthy bear hug.

"The fact that my guests will be disappointed, in my not being able to provide them the reward I'd promised them," is my reply.

"Who says you won't be able to give them the reward? Have you forgotten your own treasure still lies buried out there, waiting to be unearthed? All you need to do is have SHEILA re-plot the twelve-points of shadow; this time, corresponding with 'Minutes and Seconds' past Non," Anne states. Leaning over, she gives me a reassuring kiss on the cheek.

"You're right!," I respond. With all the events taking place, I completely put out-of-mind; the fact, that there is still literally tons of my own treasure waiting to be recovered. Rejuvenated by the thought of being able to fulfill my guest's expectations, I excitedly sit-up and give Mandy an energetic scratch behind her ears.

As Mandy begins enjoying an orgasmic state of perpetual bliss from my scratching, I lean over and say in her ear, "That's right girl, we're going digging again!"

Thinking I was speaking to her, Anne asks, "What did you

227

say?"

Feeling the need to offer explanation, I respond by saying: "The last time I was up on the Meditation Stone, I ended up having a dream, which included Mandy in the plot. She disappeared into a hole over there;" pointing to the exact spot where the raccoon had disappeared into, during my dream.

I continue by saying: "After chasing a raccoon into the hole, her bays became increasingly less audible. Thinking Mandy was lost; and might not be able to find her way out, I went-in after her. My rescue mission ended-up taking me deep within the earth. After awakening from my dream, I found myself sprawled out over there, all battered and bruised;" pointing to where I'd landed, after falling off the Meditation Stone.

"All the way down there?" Anne asks, pointing to the Valley floor below.

"Yes! At least I was able to get away from all the burning bodies hurling fireballs at me," I say; while remembering the vivid dream, like it had just happened.

"What in the hell are you talking about?!" Anne replies. "What bodies; and, what about fireballs?" Slowly lifting her right eyebrow, Anne gives me a look that appears to question my sanity, over recent statements made. As if blowing-off my dream as insignificant, she announces our sunbathing session to be over, and quickly gathers-up her clothes.

Soon heading back-down the rock outcropping, I ask Anne: "Didn't I ever tell you about the dream I'd experienced?" Thinking I'd told her everything about the dream, I truly expect Anne to suddenly remember every aspect of my story.

228

As if expecting to be 'Entertained' by my awaited response, Anne replies rather skeptically: "No…Tell me all about your dream."

Realizing I'm now committed to explaining my dream to her, I proceed to rehash events that took place in my 'Nightmare.' Obviously holding back her laughter, while trying desperately to compose herself, Anne sarcastically says to me: "Now…where 'Exactly' did you say this hole was located?"

Attempting to show her, I jump high into the air; landing directly on the spot where Mandy had disappeared into the hole, found there in my dream. It doesn't take long for the ground beneath my feet to give-way; and I quickly find myself standing neck-deep, in a newly-exposed cave entrance.

Staring up at Anne from within the sink-hole, I validate my sanity; saying, "See…I told you!" As I look back into the hole, a faint glow emanates momentarily from deep within the underground passageway. Shaking my head to clear the cobwebs from my brain, the source of light is no longer visible.

Flying out of the depression, I grab Anne and take off for home as fast as our legs will carry us. Upon reaching the house, I head straight for the garage; where I immediately fire up the backhoe. Not wanting to take any chance of my premonition being real, I race back to seal-up the newly opened cave; intending to permanently sequester deep underground, any-and-all evil entities that might one-day try to escape their underground confines.

One I've securely placed a large boulder over the entrance to the underworld, I immediately exhale a huge sigh of relief; then, slowly relax-back in the operator's seat to collect my thoughts. Watching memorized as a giant-eagle soars effortlessly high above, I'm soon giving humble thanks to Odin for the privilege of enjoying yet-another wonderful day in Paradise.

THE END

Made in the USA
Monee, IL
13 August 2023

40949589R00128